Mirror Man

Jay Sauls

Mirror Man

Dedication:

This book is dedicated to my wonderful wife, who had to sit through hours of edits, rewrites followed by yet more edits and rewrites.

Huge thanks to the East Atlanta Literary Guild. Stephanie Hickey, Susan Spain and Sandy Lyle. You ladies were there when Jonesy took his first creative steps. There's a heart-shaped derriere award out there waiting for you!

Additional thanks to the members of the Chapin Chapter of the SC Writers Association for helping Jonesy leap from the digital pages into the published world!

And most to all, to my family and friends who have put up with all my requests to read the early copies of Mirror Man. All you guys ROCK!!

Chapter One

I crouch in a ditch just off the highway and watch the black sedan circle past for the third time. Instinct cautions me to stay invisible, to ignore the icy rain. Hiding in the brush and debris lining the road, I follow the scarlet taillights as they grow smaller in the distance. The lights flash twice before swerving out of sight.

I have the overwhelming urge to get moving, to run. Scrambling up the bank, I glance quickly to the left and right, then sprint across the blacktop and into the trees on the other side. I pause behind a century's-old water oak, its spidery limbs brushing the ground and swaying in the heavy wind. I realize I'm clutching a wide-brimmed hat and put it on, bending the front over my face. After pulling up the collar of my coat, I walk away from the road and toward the dark cityscape.

My nerves are tingling, electric. The sensation of time running out is becoming tangible. I stuff my hands deep into the pockets of this unfamiliar leather coat and move with haste toward the silent buildings. Lightning crashes close enough to feel the vibration, bathing the town square for a nanosecond in silver light. Thunder echoes off the buildings. Leaning into the storm, I walk faster, my breath releasing in white clouds.

Long, icy fingers of fear tickle the nape of my neck.

"Screw it," I mutter and start running—hard. Increasing my pace, I angle down a dark alley toward a covered loading dock illuminated by a weak security light. I splash through the rain and dodge a pair of rats the size of raccoons. The platform is a few inches higher than my belt. I take the steps two at a time and vault to the top. Rain soaks the first few feet of the dock, but I find it almost dry when I move to the rear and deep into the shadows. The tattered, faded, moldy awning offers protection from the storm.

I bend over, my hands on my knees, my breathing ragged and harsh. A five-gallon bucket offers me a place to sit. I catch my breath and relax for the first time since I don't know when.

Reaching into an interior pocket of the coat, I pull out a crumpled pack of Camel cigarettes. But it's not empty. I find a Zippo lighter in an adjacent pocket and thumb the wheel in a quick grinding flick. The brass torch flares to life, allowing me to stare into the cigarette pack. My body spasms, threatening to spill the contents of my stomach.

I stumble across the bucket and trip over several large garbage bags, tearing them open and spilling the contents. I glimpse a dark form as I stumble back into the driving rain. My lighter sizzles and dies.

Shaking uncontrollably, I struggle to flip the lighter's top open. I nervously thumb the wheel once, twice, three times before the amber glow bursts from my trembling hand. Before my eyes can adjust to the sudden yellow illumination, I know that the severed finger in the pack of Camels will perfectly match the body lying at my feet.

I regain my composure and confirm the contents of my stomach will stay put. The young blonde woman appears to be in her mid-twenties. It didn't take long for me to figure out that the severed finger didn't cause her death. The single red and black bullet hole in the middle of her forehead accomplished that.

Thunder explodes close by and I instinctively duck.

"There he is! There's the bastard!" shouts a voice from the mouth of the alley.

I see flashlight beams bouncing off the wall, scouring the ground, and weaving toward me. A second volley of thunder rumbles down the brickwork canyon. I duck as this thunder whines and sends sparks dancing off the bricks beside me.

My mind is foggy, but it doesn't take long to figure out that the "bastard" they are looking for is me and that the thunder is their guns. I jump from the loading dock as the bucket beside me splinters and shoots into the air.

I obey my body's basic instincts. When my mind screams, "Run!" and my ass takes off down the street, I don't argue. I just keep my feet pointing in the right direction and try to maintain my balance. And that is the situation I find myself in: fleeing blindly down a debris-laden alley, rain in my eyes, and wind in my face as hot rounds of lead scream past my shoulders.

A blistering whine sends sparks showering off the wall beside me, letting me know the shooters are getting their range. If I don't find some place to hide soon, wondering why a severed finger is in my pocket will be the least of my worries.

I exhaust the last of my adrenaline as my lungs burn hot inside my chest. The lead continues to fly as if I am in a western movie, where bad guys never run out of ammo and Colt six-shooters blaze like hand-held Gatling guns.

My coat snags on the rear bumper of a stripped-out Volkswagen Beetle, spinning me around and taking my feet out from under me. My head smacks the pavement with a blinding thud. Torrents of pain and a meteor shower of stars explode inside my skull. The second I lose my footing, a bullet rips through the rear of the Beetle. The car rings like a distorted church bell in a Stephen King novel. Rolling across the ground, I hear several shots crease the air over my head. The Volkswagen continues to chime its deadly requiem as additional rounds tear through it.

A door on the left side of the alley stands slightly ajar. I grab a fist-sized brick and throw it down the corridor as far as I can. It bounces and crashes against garbage bins one-hundred fifty feet downrange. The men aim their flashlights in the sound's direction. With their attention elsewhere, I lunge toward the gap in the wall, through the open door, and roll into the dark building.

I grab the remains of a dilapidated filing cabinet and push it against the entrance. It falls against the closed metal door with a heart-stopping crunch, jamming it shut. The temporary barricade won't hold forever, but it should last long enough for me to escape and put a little distance between me and my pursuers.

The room is almost pitch black; a few streaks of muted light seep through the grime-coated windows facing the alley. Keeping my back to the frames and shielding the lighter with my body, I thumb the wheel on my Zippo; it blazes forth with a burst of yellow-white light. Squinting against the fiery glare, I survey my temporary sanctuary.

It had been someone's office years or decades ago. A collapsed desk sits in one corner of the room; one of its cracked and splintered legs lies under it. Remnants of the ceiling cover most of the desktop. I push off the crumbling plaster, searching for a weapon, even a long-forgotten letter opener, anything to protect myself with until I sort out what is going on.

The only thing I find of interest is a men's magazine from 1992. Most of the pages are stuck together from years of sitting in the musty room, but one retains the image of a young woman lying on her back, stretched out seductively on a zebra skin rug. Her blue-eyed, rosy-cheeked face turned up toward the camera, a pouting kiss frozen for eternity on her face. She is clad in nothing but a pair of staples. Damn those staples.

It is time to move on, to find a place where I can make sense of what is happening. Besides, the Zippo is getting hot and running short on fuel. Maneuvering by the feeble light, I trip over something that rattles and rolls away. I set the lighter down and drop to all fours, scrambling around on the slick moldy carpet like a blind man playing a solitary game of Twister. My fingers brush across a heavy, cold pipe.

I nod my approval.

Gripping it hard in my hand makes me feel secure. I take a couple of practice swings; it carves the air nicely, the open-end singing like wind over an empty bottle. Until a better weapon presents itself, the pipe will have to do.

The lighter flickers and dies. It relights feebly on the fourth try, the flame only a half-inch high and sputtering.

Holding the flame at waist level, I make my way through the ruins of the office, searching for an exit door. I sidestep collapsed shelving units, piles of wire hangers, and bolts of rotted cloth. In the back corner of the room,

I find a heavy metal door that leads deeper into the building. I try the knob and find it frozen shut. I push against it, trying to rock it loose. The door doesn't so much as creak; the only exit remains the one to the alley and its pack of incredibly unfriendly men. Picking my way across the office floor, I detect movement from the corner of my eye. I spin to find a disheveled, animalistic face appearing ahead of me. The person blocks my path and moves to intercept me, no matter which way I step.

"Back your ass up, or I'll arrange your face in a way nature never intended!" I raise the pipe.

The silent man wordlessly mocks me as I speak.

"I'm warning you!" I tense and wait for the man to respond.

Call me chicken, call me a coward, but I have had enough of being shot at, nearly electrocuted, and mocked. I am getting the hell out of Dodge.

The face rushes me as I step toward the door. I bring the pipe down in a quick, singing slash. The face explodes and drops in a shower of glass.

"What the hell?"

Darkness blooms the second I swing my makeshift club. I thumb the lighter once more, coaxing it back to life. Despite my soggy clothes, being shot at, and running for my life, I laugh. My brass friend provides just enough light to realize that I have whipped the shit out of a freestanding full-length mirror.

Picking up a shard of glass the size of a dinner plate, I stare at the image, first in disbelief, then in shock. The face in the mirror fragment is that of a stranger.

A mind-numbing realization settles over me. I recreate my day. The last thirty minutes are easy, but everything muddles and becomes confusing. My hazy memories start when I stumble—or am thrown—from a car. Before that, nothing, nada, zip. The previous hours, days, weeks, and years are all gone.

I shuck out of my coat and rifle through the pockets, avoiding the one with the severed finger. From the right front pocket, I pull out a blue Bic pen with the cap chewed up, seventeen cents in change, a small brass key, and a pack of matches from the Center Rack pool hall. That one surprises me. I don't feel like a pool shark, so why the matches and lighter? Preparation, as in the Boy Scouts? That is one thing I am sure of. I am no Boy Scout.

All the clues to my existence lay scattered on the grimy desktop, illuminated by the failing light of the Zippo.

Knowing that my existence began a little more than half an hour ago is sobering. A stiff shot of strong liquor would help to cure that feeling.

Drawing up my courage, I force my hand back inside the coat pocket and extract the crumpled Camel cigarette pack. I dump the contents on the table. First, the finger with the bright red nail polish tumbles out, followed by a few shreds of tobacco. I reach into the pack to see if anything else is crammed inside. A small picture folded in half falls out.

When I unfold the photograph, I receive another shock. It is an image of the dead woman. She is sitting in a restaurant booth; her legs crossed, her arms folded at the waist, and her head cocked to the side. A mug of beer with the head still foaming sits at the edge of a plate of nachos. Okay, maybe not as wholesome as I thought, but definitely not deserving of having her life blasted away and dumped with the garbage.

A bolt of lightning strikes nearby. The concussion rocks the walls and causes more plaster from the ceiling to fall.

I flinch and try to get my buttocks to relax their grip on my shorts.

I fail.

The lighter blinks out and refuses to ignite.

Angry voices at the door freeze me in place. I grip the iron pipe hard enough to make my hands cramp. Someone tries the knob. When it refuses to turn, they throw themselves against it. The door shudders on its hinges but doesn't budge. Without a visible rear exit, I will have to put my faith in the rusted-out filing cabinet and wedged-shut metal door.

The sounds outside were quiet for a moment. Then another crashing explosion rocks the door. The top bends in slightly. Two more attacks, each as vicious as the one before, cannot budge it another inch. Someone cusses rather eloquently in the alley. It is something about mothers and fornicating, but I can't be sure. When the voices fade, I relax.

Their footsteps echo down the alley, growing fainter.

I sit heavily against the desk and let the pipe drop from my hand. It hits the damp carpet with a muffled thud. My heart skips a beat as I fear the men might hear the sound and return. When no one tries the door again, I manage a deep breath. I count to a hundred and back to zero before making another move. I need to think to sort out what is happening and how my world has turned

inside out. I need a place where I'm just another face in
the crowd.

Chapter Two

By my best guess, it has been a couple of hours since I climbed from my personal briar patch and slipped out of town. I walk along the tree line for several miles until I come up behind the West 82 truck stop. A dozen big rigs sit idling by the pumps, having their tanks refilled as their owners' rest in the diner, drinking coffee and swallowing caffeine pills by the handful. I stop by a coin-operated paper rack to check the date. I am in Waynesville, Alabama. A red digital clock inside the truck stop advises it is a few minutes past midnight and Sunday morning. The side door of the diner attracts my attention. There is a scattering of cars parked nearby, their operators stumbling and staggering in and out the door. A neon bar signs flickers in the tinted windows, attracting drunks like a siren's song catches sailors. Before I get within fifty feet of the door, I smell the stale odor of beer and smoke and hear loud, scratchy country music playing on a dying jukebox.

A farm boy with puke still trailing from his chin slides past me, clinging to the side of the door to keep his balance, his boots already shined by the contents of his gut. I do my best to avoid touching him and enter the bar. The joint is busy despite the late hour. I make my way through the rowdy crowd, careful not to make eye contact with anyone, and ease into a booth in the building's dark recesses. Cigarette burns scar the table, and the seat is patched to within an inch of its life.

I rest with my elbows on the table, palms against my forehead, and don't notice the waitress until she clears her voice with a rough cough. Glancing out of the corner of my eye, not wanting to turn my face, I ordered without considering what I wanted. "Bourbon, neat." Apparently, that is my drink; it came out so naturally. The girl turns without comment and disappears into the haze of smoke and people.

Quicker than I thought possible, she returns with my bourbon, drops it to the table, and slides it across to me. Once again, I react instinctively. My hand reaches for a wallet that I suddenly realize I don't have.

"Don't worry about it, Jonesy. I've got you covered, as usual. So, I don't wanna hear no song and dance about how you left your money at home. Just drink your damn drink and get the hell out of here," she growls with enough ice to turn Death Valley into a skating rink. I glance at the waitress as she glares at me before disappearing into the haze.

Jonesy? My name's Jonesy? I am still mulling it over when I discover a wad of paper hidden in my coat. My hand found something that my mind wasn't unaware of. I pray it's not wrapped around another digit. Unclenching my fist, I stare in awe at a rolled-up wad of cash. The flickering decorative candle on the table confirms my discovery. I cup the bills in my hand, spreading out a collection of dead presidents like a poker player trying not to show too much of his hand. Jesus! The roll comes close to four thousand dollars, most of the money in hundred-dollar bills, with a handful of twenties and smaller bills mixed in.

And blood. Most of the stash is sticky with someone's blood. The blondes? Mine? I don't seem to be bleeding, though anything is possible after what I have just been through. And since I hurt all over, I could be bleeding from anywhere.

The rabbit hole I have stumbled through continues to twist and turn.

I drink the bourbon in one gulp, grimacing as the whiskey burns my throat. Sitting back against the booth, I feel a full night of fatigue collapse on top of me. My eyelids droop. I catch myself in the middle of a snore and jerk upright, knowing I can't sleep here. It's imperative to put distance between Waynesville and me. With the cash in my pocket and the truckers outside, I have my way out of town. It doesn't matter which way they travel as long as it puts me hours from here. Once I'm far beyond the city limits, I'll check into a motel and sort things out.

Sliding from the table, I make my way past the waitress station and into the brightly lit lobby of the truck stop. Just as I am about to exit, I'm grabbed from behind and jerked into the women's bathroom.

"Jonesy, are you crazy? I can't believe you came back here," snaps the waitress, who could freeze the sun's surface with her frosty disposition. She shoves the door closed, locks it, turns, and glares at me with a mixture of hatred and exhaustion. Her eyes are red and glazed, her mascara smeared. She wipes her face with the back of her hand. "Carl is questioning everyone between here and Harper's Crossing. And his piece-of-shit deputy is slinking around here somewhere." She wipes tears from her eyes. "Christ, why'd you have to come back here? Why now?"

I don't answer. Instead, I pull the collar of my coat higher and cover the left side of my face with my hand. I still don't feel like a 'Jonesy,' but apparently, I am one.

I shrug.

"That's just like you!" she hisses. "Get yourself in all kinds of trouble and come running back to me. What goes on in that drunken mind of yours? *Oh, Sheila will take care of me!*" She walks over to the sink and splashes water on her tear-streaked face and tries to tuck loose hairs behind her ears. "Is that what you want me to do, Jonesy?" she asks, glancing at me in the mirror. "Take care of you, like your mama? Want me to stroke your ego when you're down and smooth the waters behind you when you've gone and really fucked up?"

At least I know her name now.

Sheila composes herself in the mirror. She rewashes her face, reapplies her mascara and lipstick, then fixes her shoulder-length ponytail. When she finishes, she spins, grabs my wrist, and pries open my hand. "Here, you need this more than me." She drops a small diamond ring into my hand. "Wait until Jimmy's Pawn on Sycamore opens. Ask for Ronny; he's an old friend of mine. Tell him I said for you to speak only to him. Tell him I said to give you full value and not to cheat you. He'll understand. That should get you enough money to hop a bus as far as Birmingham or Tuscaloosa." She sniffs back tears and checks her emotions. "And this time, stay away, don't come back. I can't keep doing this every few months."

I feel like someone has punched me in the gut. I don't know how to react and don't dare speak. The best thing to do is quietly leave while I can. I nod, unlock the door, and pull it open.

Sheila kicks the door shut. "Go out through the kitchen. There're enough trucks parked back there that you should be able to weave in and out of them without being seen. Once clear, stay in the woods until you come to the railroad tracks, then…." She waves me away. "You know the drill; you've done this enough times."

Her crying trails me out the door.

Following Sheila's directions, I cross the lot, hit the woods, and keep walking until I come upon long-abandoned tracks. Hours later, I circled the outskirts of the town and find myself in the middle of nowhere. The tracks cross Hwy 9—according to the often-shot highway sign—far enough from town that I quit jumping at shadows. I need to make one more stop, and a small convenience store is my target. The bells on the door clang off the glass, once again setting my nerves on fire. The tired, unenthused clerk doesn't acknowledge me as I pass. I quickly duck down the first aisle, grab a small stash of chips and drinks, then pay with a bill from inside the roll, one that isn't stained with blood. I stop at the icebox in front of the store, slide the bags of ice to one side and place the cigarette pack with the severed finger as far back as I can. It slips under a brace and out of view. I push the untouched bags of ice back over the empty camel pack and close the door.

The sun is now peeking above the horizon, coating the pines with orange and red streaks. It's time to get moving again. I put my back to the brightening sky, stick my thumb out, and start walking West.

Chapter Three

It feels like I have just closed my eyes when the trucker says, "Hey fella, will this one do?" I use my shirt sleeves to force my eyelids open, grimacing at the grit that feels like shreds of sandpaper lodged against my eyeballs. I squint into the morning light. We are closing on a rundown motor lodge sitting just off the highway. The towering, rusting motel sign leans toward the edge of the cracked asphalt and identifies the inn as the 'Dreamland Motel.' A sagging chain-link fence circles a rectangular concrete sidewalk, marking the resting spot of a long-abandoned pool now filled with dirt and grass. On the side, a pair of rusting step rails sink into the knee-high weeds. The building's once vibrant pink and green day-glow paint is dull and peeling. Rust stains trail down the side of the building where neglected gutters have rusted.

"Where are we?" I croak, still exhausted from my all-night run.

"Oh, we's about fifty miles from where we was, a little crossroad called 'Turners Corner'. Ain't much here but the motel, a gas station and a so-called gen'ral store. Store's got a short order grill and a post office. Used to be the county seat about a hundred years ago. In a few more years, probably won't even exist, just dry slap-up and blow away like tumbleweeds in a blizzard." The driver takes a sip from a well-traveled and battered thermos, spilling some around the corners of his mouth. He wipes away the coffee with the cuff of a sleeve.

"You should be able to catch another ride out of here fairly easy. Lots of trucker's stop here in the evening, most of 'em lookin' for a little conversation before they move on." The trucker drops a gear, moving the shifter with the ease of one who's done it thousands of times. "It's a nice little way station. Food's decent, if you don't mind a plate of grease served with more grease." He laughs at that and pats his grease-grown belly. "And sometimes the boys can get a date for the night, if you know what I mean!" He sends me a knowing wink. I try to smile but feel it comes out as more of a grimace.

I sit up straighter, scratch the remaining crud from my eyes, and run my fingers through my hair. A stab of pain pierces my right eye. The skin above my brow, as well as the area around the side of my face, is swollen and tender. I pull a cheap vanity mirror off the visor and notice the black and purple bruise stretching from my right eye to my hairline. Once again, I am clueless about how this happened.

"Looks like your ol' lady done caught you cattin' around!" the driver says with another of his fat winks and a quick laugh.

My first reaction is to say something about his mother and losing his virginity, but I hold my tongue.

"Something like that," I say as the truck engine growls in protest to the downshift.

Pointing with his thermos toward the motel, he continues. "She ain't much, but the rooms are dry, and the beds are, mostly, clean. You can hide out here for a few days or until whatever is troubling you moves on."

I want to say, "What makes you think I'm hiding?"
then think better of it. That would open me up to more
questions than I could possibly answer, questions I don't
have answers for myself. Instead, I turn my attention
back to the motel. The sign is missing many of its letters,
and the paint's peeling off the trim, but the blinking neon
'vacancy' sign is flashing—like it ever changes—and the
rate is $29.99 a day. I offer the man a twenty for his
troubles. He glances at the bill and shakes his head.
"Mister, I think you need that money more than I do. I'm
just obliged I could help." I shrug and stuff the bill back
in my top pocket.

The trucker swings his rig off the highway, stopping
it as quickly as he can, smiles, calls "see ya" out the
window, and is working the gears only seconds after I
jump from the cab. Less than thirty seconds later, he
disappears into the hazy, early morning light, diesel
smoke trailing behind him like gray contrails.

I straighten my hat, pulling it snug against my head,
and start toward a weathered 'office' sign. Twenty-odd
rooms sweep off to the left and right like cinderblock
wings. I push through the door and into a dirty office
with a water-stained ceiling. A vintage black-and-white
TV sits at the counter's far end, with tinfoil-wrapped
rabbit's ears sticking up behind it. And beneath the TV, a
small column of smoke drifts lazily toward the water-
stained ceiling. I reach the counter and ring the bell. The
smoke sputters as the attendant stands up behind the
desk. The man is in his late sixties and wearing a
threadbare T-shirt stained with a multitude of fast-food
condiments. He sets his cigarette down on the counter
and wipes his nose with the back of his hand.

"Rooms are $10 an hour, $30 a day, or one and a quarter a week. Now, if you stay a week, you only get maid service on Monday and Thursday." He coughs a ragged, hacking cough and wipes a trail of mucus from his face. "And everything's paid in advance." A new round of hacking staggers him. He grips the ledge with his bony hands and coughs into a grungy handkerchief. The old man steadies himself with one scrawny arm, curls the rag back in his fist, retrieves a poorly disguised liquor bottle from under the counter, takes a gulp, and returns the bottle. "And we don't put up with no shit. You beat her up, we call the law." Through bloodshot, yellow eyes, he looks me up and down. "And no drugs. We catch a hint of you pushing anything on the grounds, and we call the law." He slides the registration form toward me. "Steal any of the towels, and we…."

"Call the law," I add for him with an eat-shit grin. He glares at me again, this time wrinkling his entire face. His lip curls into a snarl, then flattens.

"And we deal in cash. No checks, no credit cards."

I nod and complete the registration form with the first name that comes to mind—Bruton J. Smith—then place ninety bucks in front of him and wait for my key. The old codger scoops up the cash without asking for identification or questioning my signature. I figured he'd do as much. He's seen enough illicit actions to not challenge his guests or be fazed by traces of blood on the edge of the bills.

He flings the key at me without a second thought. The clerk slaps the TV, lights another unfiltered Camel, then disappears beneath the counter. As I leave, I glance his way and see him in the convex security mirror.

Sprawled on a filthy cot, wearing nothing but his T-shirt: no pants, no socks, or underwear, is the clerk. If I'd seen this when I walked in, I wouldn't have touched the pen.

The cold, damp wind hits me square in the face when I leave the office. My room is on the far side of the East wing. Pulling my coat tight, I walk in that direction. The door to my room opens without using the key or knob being turned. It just swings wide when my hand hits it. I enter, shove the door shut, and realize the lock doesn't function. I loop the thin chain through the cheap, useless latch and cram a chair against it.

Once the door was secure, I discovered why this room was only $30. It has a sharp undertone of body odor covered with a heavy misting of Lysol and hasn't been aired out in weeks; the bed appears to have been slept in and remade.

I take my hat off and stuff it in the bottom of the wastebasket. Tomorrow, I'll dump it and my clothing miles down the road. But for now, it is time to crash. And as tired as I am, I can't convince myself to get under the covers. I strip out of my coat and shirt, leaving them scattered across the floor, and use a towel, which for some strange reason smells clean, as a cover.

Sleep tramples me into unconsciousness. I wake shivering, the towel on the floor and the door cracked open, letting in a current of frigid air.

I push the door shut, gather up my clothes, and flip on the TV. The morning weatherman predicts highs in the upper 40s for the next few days, with a gradual warming trend on Friday. The part about the next few days rattles around in my head, searching for a place to stop. Then it hits me like a slap in the face: it is Tuesday. I slept straight through Monday.

The local news report is on next. I sit on the edge of the bed, watching as the anchors play cutesy with each other before getting to the serious topics of the day. The report is out of Dothan but covers the surrounding cities and counties. Waynesville is within its broadcast area. For fifteen minutes, they talk about robberies, assaults, and problems with city services but make no mention of a murder. Could they have discussed it on Monday?

I dress quickly, wearing clothes I have worn for an unknown time. They reek as if it has been more than a few days, and I walk to the general store, where they have clothing to outfit the southern redneck.

I have several destinations on my schedule. One is for food. I am starving to the point of weakness. I have the grill fire me up a cheeseburger while I stuff a basket with every day, man-on-the-run staples: spam, crackers, beer, bread, and peanut butter. It isn't nutritious, but I won't starve.

Next, I make a trip down the aisle marked 'personal care,' scooping up deodorant, soap, a toothbrush, and razors. A quick shave would change my looks dramatically, and I'm not talking facial. If I have to hide until I figure out what in the hell is going on, my shaggy, disheveled, collar-length brown hair will have to go all the way down to the scalp.

I also need new clothes since I only have one set everything, and they are beginning to stink.

With a final thought, I stop by a news rack and scoop up several local papers. With a cheeseburger basket containing fries and slaw, I make my way to the register with my stash of food and clothing. It is time to head back to my room and thumb through the local rags. Hopefully, I'll find some clue as to whether or not I am a murderer.

I choke down the food as fast as I can tear it apart and swallow. The beer makes me feel almost whole again. Almost, except for the black hole in my brain where my memories used to live.

I shower and dress in clean, stiff clothing. Sitting on the edge of the bed, I spread out the Monday and Tuesday editions of the Beacon County Times and methodically sift through all the stories, hoping something would jump out at me.

Nothing does.

Crumpling the papers into a gray and black basketball, I toss it into the wastebasket. The paper's a bust, but on the bright side, I don't find my face pasted all over the front page as a wanted person. Living in limbo is unnerving and tiring. I have a damn hard time believing a young blonde woman could be shot dead and abandoned in an alley without being noticed.

A heavy rap on the door startles me. "Yeah, who is it?" Quietly pushing out of the seat, I glance around the room, looking for escape routes. The window out of the bathroom is too small to slip through. I grab the trashcan and clench it in both hands. With some luck, I might be able to make a cartoon move and slam it on the head of whoever pushes through the door, then beat the crap out of him with my fists. Or I could get gut-shot and die right here in this dingy room. It could go either way.

"Front desk, Mr. Smith." came the rough, hacking response through the door. He said 'Smith,' as if he believed it as much as I do. "Checkout's noon. If you're gonna be staying, I need you to come on up and pay."

I glance through the peephole. It is the old man from the office, this time with pants on. "Yeah, I'll be there in a minute."

He shuffles out of sight. I grab the stack of cash from my coat and clean more blood off the bills. Grabbing my coat, I head toward the registration desk.

I have to wait as two truckers with half-naked women sign for their rooms, each registering as Mr. and Mrs. Smith.

"Must be a damn Smith family reunion," the clerk quips out of the corner of his mouth, his cigarette dangling between clenched yellow teeth, the ash angling out across the desk.

The old man dispenses the keys, then turns to me, his eyes widening with delight. "Mr. Smith, I presume." He stands with his hands clasped across his small fat belly like a cat savoring the torture of a mouse.

"Right," I answer. "Room 22." The hair on the back of my neck prickles.

"Yes, yes," he murmurs. "Sometimes, my mind ain't too sharp. And forgive me, but all you damn 'Smiths' look alike." He winks at me—sort of. One eye was already half shut when I stepped to the counter. The other slowly closes, then opens again. I'm not sure he is conscious of its movement.

"Now, you don't resemble 'Horace Smith' or 'Johnny Smith', the two fine gentlemen who just checked in." He leans my way, as if studying my face in great detail. I curl my lip. Another instinctive reaction. The geezer smiles, slides along his side of the counter like a snake tracking its prey, and retrieves a sheet of paper from below. "But you bear a damn striking resemblance to this gentleman. If I were a gambling man, I'd bet his last name is also 'Smith.'"

A chill races down the length of my spine when he spreads a slightly smudged thermal-fax paper sketch of a man wearing a wide-brimmed hat. A paragraph above the image states that the police chief in Waynesville is searching for this person in connection with the abduction of a local woman. I stare hard at the fax, at the artist's rendering of a face, my face—a lightning flash of memory shrieks through my mind. I see a hand—whose I can't be sure could have been mine—holding a gun, the barrel still smoking.

As quickly as the memory is upon me, it is gone, leaving me momentarily speechless. I dismiss the image as a hallucination brought on by stress, but can't ignore the picture sitting on the counter. It looks like me. Not so much the eyes or hair, for a wide-brimmed hat covered them. But the shape of the mouth and set of the jaw are dead ringers for my own.

Tracing the image with my finger as if studying it, I shake my head and turn to the pervert. "Don't ring any bells with me. But you're right, if you stretch the image a bit, he does bear a passing resemblance to me." The chill has spread to my blood.

"Uh huh, sure as hell do, don't he? Let's try one other thing." With that, he retrieves a hat from under the counter. It is the same hat I threw in the trash after checking in. "If you don't mind, how about humoring me?" His eyes narrow.

Pushing the hat to the side, I force a smile. "I'm not going to put any crazy notions in your head; I just want my room for another four nights." I peel off another seven twenties. "There's an extra Jackson for your time and fresh linens."

As if forgetting the previous conversation, he scoops up the cash. "Well, that's mighty kind of you," he begins. "But we just entered our celebrity season. Every year about now our rates climb."

I peel off more bills.

"Yes, sir, about now the rates take off rather steeply."

I drop more cleaned-off twenty-dollar bills on the counter.

"With all the local media disturbing the peace of my guests, we really need to recoup some of our lost monies." He smiles at me again, his tongue licking between missing teeth. It is a smile that contains about as much humor as a bottle of cyanide.

A sizeable chunk of my original wad of cash is now on the counter.

"You do understand, don't you?" His face drops all pretense of a smile.

"Yes, yes, I do." I push the cash, nearly five hundred bucks, toward him. He scoops up the money and grins.

"Now, Mr. Smith, will you be needing any additional towels?" he yells as I slam the door shut.

Chapter Four

It is now Friday. I have scoured the papers and newscasts for the past few days, but have yet to find a single word—written or spoken—about the body. I find it hard to believe unless there is a cover-up. But a cover-up by whom, and why? Running the idea around in my head, I examine it from all angles as I stare out the window, watching the traffic fly by on the cracked and lonely highway.

A black Ford speeds past, the morning sun flashing off its windshield. I follow the car until it disappears down the highway. Something gnaws at me, badgers my mind like an off-tune, lingering melody. I pace around the room, smacking my fist into my hand and growling under my breath.

What is it about the Ford that teases me so? Throwing the door open, I march to the edge of the highway and stare down at the tarmac. The gnawing tick is still pulsing but fading.

The hell with it all. I turn back toward the warmth of my room and the television droning but take a side trip to a drink machine. I feed a handful of coins into its silver mouth-like slit, settling on an Orange Crush. Opening the can, I swallow and cough as the drink surges down the wrong pipe. I hold the can at arm's length as if it has bitten me and find my thumb tracing the title. Back and forth, my finger slides, following the letters, my mind absently freewheeling, lost in its own world while I stand freezing on the sidewalk.

A bulb flickers faintly on and off. Christ, what is it? I drain the rest of the soda, then crush the can in my palm. I watch the metal crumple and twist, the thin shell of paint cracks as my hand mangles the container.

I toss the empty can into a garbage bin near my room, annoyed to the point of fighting anyone in sight. The wind whistles down from the sky, sending a cloud of dust and candy wrappers past me.

A cog in my brain slips into place, awarding me a rare moment of clarity. The paper! Yesterday's Beacon Times had something in it, something that… hells bells, what is it? Something insignificant, something I glossed over before moving on to other items. I don't even know why it has stuck with me. It's nothing, just a blurb, a sidebar in a much larger article. I can't remember what it's about, but I know the answer will smack me in the face when I see it.

Sprinting into the room, fearing that this fragmented thought will disintegrate before I can make it through the door, I snatch the paper's front section out of the trash and brush off crumbs from last night's dinner.

I scan the first section with trembling hands, barely reading the headlines, skimming over the type with my finger. Nothing. There isn't a damn thing in it. Pissed, I crumple it up and want to rip the paper to shreds, then pause, shaking. It's here. I know it is! With my adrenaline spiking, I unravel the pages and flatten out the creases. The local section is void of information. Crap, it has to be here. I scan the area again, this time reading every article out loud, ignoring nothing. I even scrutinize the marriage announcements.

"To hell with it." I fling the paper over the bed, where it flutters down to the covers. I grab a beer and flip on the TV. A golf tournament is just beginning. This time, the flash of inspiration explodes in my head. I trip as I leap from my chair, bruising my shins on the bed frame. Grabbing the sports section, I rip it in half. And spread the paper on the small, scarred desk. I scan it again like an addict trembling over a line of coke. And there it is. Just as I thought… a small blurb sandwiched between box scores from last night's sports recap.

It is the account of a local high school football game that was rescheduled earlier in the week. No wonder I missed it. I read the story, closely digesting every word, mouthing them. "A car found burning behind the Waynesville High School stadium, along with the body inside, has just been identified. Sheriff Carl Fordham says the death is being treated as a homicide, and the investigation continues. Names are being withheld until the next of kin can be notified."

"Treated as a homicide!" I spit out, laughing. My spirits lift. Finally, something I can sink my teeth into and I'm not gonna let go of it. No-way, no-how. I have a damn good hunch that the taillights I remember seeing after being tossed out on the street will be a very close match to those of the burned-out car.

Random thoughts surge through my brain, drowning me with ideas and directions. Dumping the wastebasket on the bed, I scatter the contents, ignoring the leaking cans and stale potato chips. I grab another section of the paper, one several days old, dry the last drips from a coke can, and smooth out the creases. Thumbing through the pages, I open it to the section on local events, then pick up the phone. I dial a number from the list of local emergency numbers beside the phone, not sure what I will say until someone answers.

"Beacon County Sheriff's Department. How might I direct your call?"

"Information officer, please," I say without thinking, running on instinct again. I feel like a voyeur spying on someone else's mental processes, not knowing what the next thought or comment will be until it happens.

Muzak and infomercials on how the Beacon County Sheriff is everyone's friend ends with the sound of a receiver being lifted. "This is Deputy Styles. Is there some way I can help you?"

Her voice is friendly, youthful, and very Southern. I circle the picture the paper took of her at a recent community outreach event sponsored by the Sheriff's department. Luckily, they print every officer's photo with their full name. "Hey, is this Debbie?" I ask in my most upbeat neighborly voice.

"Sure is! Who's this?"

Her southern drawl and friendly voice are infectious. I grin without even trying. Staring down at her smiling picture in the paper, I imagine her sitting at her desk wearing pigtails and passing out candy to poor children.

I also picture her in leather and spiked heels with a whip in her hand as she leans over a chopped Harley. Dwelling on that image, I fail to realize she's waiting for an answer.

Snatching another name from the front of the paper, I continue. "Why it's Clifford Barnes with the Beacon

County Times," I say after a pause, adding as much Southern accent as I thought believable. There is silence on her end, so I continue. "We did the spread on you folks and your community outreach program." I stop talking, this time waiting for her to respond.

"Mr. Barnes?" She says, as if wracking her mind to create a picture of me.

"Oh, just call me Clifford!" I glance at the byline under the article. "I work with Jeremy Richards. He's the reporter that did the story on the Sheriff's outreach program. I'm the senior assistant editor in charge of local events and forgive me for this minor break of etiquette, if you will, but I have a question for you."

"Sure, what can I help you with, Mr. Barnes?"

"Clifford, please." I say warmly.

"Clifford," she responds with a chuckle, "what's on your mind?"

"Forgive me for this question's from way out in left field, 'cause I know that this is the last question you expect to be asked, but…." I let the 'but,' hang in the air for a moment. "If you weren't in law enforcement, I'd have to convince our ad department to seriously consider you for some modeling work. You're very photogenic." And damn if I didn't mean it.

I hear hard laughter and a snort from the other end. "Oh, puh-lease!"

"Just saying, if you ever tire of fighting evil and the injustice, call me. I'd be happy to make the introductions."

"Why thank you, Clifford!" she says with a chuckle. "Now, I know there must be an actual reason for your call, not that I haven't thoroughly enjoyed our conversation."

Now that I have baited the hook, it is time to fish.

"Indeed, there is. We're working on a story we want to run over the weekend on the Waynesville High School car fire. Kind of an update, really, and we want to run it Sunday with all the local ads. But we're still light on some details, and I hope you can, you know, fill in some blanks.

There is a pause, followed by typing on a keyboard. "Well, we really aren't in a position to release any additional information on it, what with the investigation continuing. I'm truly sorry, Clifford."

"Oh, darn!" I say with much drama. "Dang it all! We were hoping to get something out for the weekend edition." I pause and click my tongue as if I'm mulling over the article. "Guess we could run it Tuesday. But I sure was hoping we'd get the release before The Dothan Times does."

"Well, if it's going to run Tuesday, I think that'd be okay. Now you gotta promise me this won't hit the pages until Tuesday morning."

"Sweetheart, you have my greatest promise and deepest gratitude."

I hear more typing sounds, and her voice comes back slightly louder than a whisper. "According to the press schedule, we're supposed to release more information Monday afternoon. Okay, here it is. The car is an early 90s Ford Crown Vic like we drive, you know?"

"Uh, huh," I murmur, making a mental checkmark. That fits perfectly with the scant images I can recall. "Do you have anything yet on the driver?"

"Let me see," there's a pause. "Well, yes, and no. We haven't been able to I.D. the victim—poor man is burned beyond recognition. Whoever did this wanted to make it difficult for us. But we were able to get an I.D. on the vehicle. Even though the plates were missing, we have been able to run the car's I.D.. The vehicle is registered to a Bruton J. Smith from Central, Alabama."

It is when I hear her repeating, 'Mr. Barnes?' that I realize I have zoned out. I drop the phone and fall back against the bed, staring at the water-stained ceiling.

Chapter Five

The harsh buzzing of the phone returns me to the here and now. Rubbing my eyes, I drop it back on the cradle and climb to my feet. Too many facts swirl around in my head. I have leads with ends, some with beginnings, and none with both. And now this car adds another item to my already growing list of entanglements. What I thought might be a clue to end this nightmare is just another teasing, dangling thread.

I fill the sink with cold water and splash it on my face. The water clears some of the fog clouding my thinking. I close my eyes, set the washcloth on my face, and sit back on the bed. That the car is registered to a Bruton J. Smith, the same name I scribbled on the hotel registration list, doesn't escape me. It scares the hell out of me. I am just beginning to deal with the not-knowing-who-I-am thing, and now this. Each hour since I woke—for lack of a better word—I have created memories that give me a 'past.' Granted, my past is less than a week's worth of memories, but I have grown accustomed to it. It provides me with a tangible place to start each day. And fresh memories are filling the void inside my head. But now, I feel I know myself less than when I first checked into this fleabag motel. The answers I need are back in Waynesville. It is time to reverse course and head back into the ever-twisting goddamn rabbit hole.

I dress in my new clothes, laughing as I see myself in the mirror. With my John Deere tractor cap pulled tight on my head, coveralls, heavy boots, and hunting jacket, I could model for Field and Stream. I cut the lights and walked toward the general store. Truckers are stopping hourly to fill their tanks and their stomachs. I plan to stay out of view until a driver leaves, then either ask or bribe him for a ride back to town. Once in the truck, I'll let my instincts take over and see where they lead me.

Twenty minutes later, I'm riding in a rusted-out El Camino, sharing my part of the tattered and taped bench seat with Orville, an eighty-pound black lab.

"Yeah, ol' Orville ain't never met no strangers in his life," the driver says as I push the dog's snout away from my face. The mutt is practically whining to lick me. I glance at the driver and nod.

"Orvy thinks everyone's a friend. Shoot, he wouldn't hurt a fly unless it's a squirrel or a duck. Then whoo-ey! He just about goes nuts and comes out of his skin."

I scratch the dog between the ears, and that settles him. He spreads out across the seat, and his big heavy head drops into my lap with a hearty sigh.

"Nice dog," I say, meaning it.

"Yep, sure is." He pats the dog's rump, and Orville responds with a round of satisfied thumps of his tail. "So, what's your business?"

I glance at him, wondering how he can see through his thick coke-bottle glasses. The driver is twenty-something, thin, with a scraggly beard and mustache that amounts to about thirty wild hairs. "Just visiting friends." I turn my attention back to the world passing by at highway speed.

"Anybody I know?"

Still staring out the window, I answer his question. "Who do you know?" I can't imagine the fashion plate beside me getting out all that much.

"Nobody really." He sighs and slumps in his seat. "My cousin's the Sheriff and that kinda runs folks off. Unless they want a ticket fixed or somethin'." He concentrates on driving for a bit before speaking again. "He's a bit of a dickwad, thinks he's got some kind of license to harass folks. Personally, I think he's a wuss. Likes to show off his badge and gun."

Of all the damn cars to catch a ride with, it would have to be the one driven by the Sheriff's cousin. But by the thickness of his glasses and the smears that mark them both—dog licks, I'm sure—I could dress as a pink bunny in a flashing tutu, and I don't think he'd notice. "Yeah, that can make it tough. My dad worked for a bonding company. He moonlighted as a bounty hunter and private dick." The words escape my mouth before I realize I'm saying them. I do not know from what section of my damaged brain they originated.

"Your dad was a bounty hunter? No way!" The boy brightens, and all but comes off the seat, sending us swerving across the road. He snatches the wheel back before we take out a speed limit sign and swerves across the westbound lane and off the road again. As the kid fights to regain control of his truck, I clench the door handle with a death grip. Orville yawns and then sits up to lick himself. "Man, are you serious? That is so cool!" He laughs as we barely miss clipping the east end of a westbound semi and rights the vehicle, more or less, in the center of the eastbound lane.

"No shit, man," I say slowly, waiting for my heart to retreat from its frantic pumping.

"You're serious, aren't you?" He slaps the steering wheel. "Man, I would love to do that!"

"Yeah, I am." My words form gradually. I still can't believe they come out of my mouth. I glance out the window to end the Q and A and watch the pine trees fly past in a blurry, hypnotic way.

Somehow, the word 'father' has disturbed me. Of all the things I have stumbled through the last week, this is the one that floors me. If there is a dad, I can only assume that there is a mom. Does this also mean there is a brother and sister? New sensation swarms over me, settling deep in my stomach: homesickness. Not knowing who I am makes the idea of finding out where I am from that much more imperative.

I feel empty, void of everything. Sitting back against the seat, I pull my hat down over my eyes and cross my arms. Orville nudges me under my elbow. I scratch his snout, and he responds with a hot, moist lick of the back of my hand. I decided then and there that if I ever get out of this mess, I'm gonna get a dog. A big one. One with a stupid name, fathead, and uncertain parentage.

My eyes close, and I zone out for a while. The next thing I know, we are passing the city limits.

"Hey mister, we're here. Any place in particular you want me to drop you off?"

I think for a minute before answering. "Town center would be fine if it's not out of your way."

"Nope. I'm going in that basic direction."

Ten minutes later, he pulls over to the curb and throws the truck in park. "Hey, if there's anything I can do for you while you're in town, give me a shout." With that, he hands me his card.

"Robbie's Hunting and Fishing"? I ask after examining the card.

"I'm kind of a local guide." He shrugs, slightly embarrassed. "Take folks to where the fish are biting and the deer are running. Sometimes take 'em for tours of the swamp."

"Are you any good?" I ask, putting the card in my pocket.

"Good?" He plays shocked and clutches a hand to his chest as if he's mortally wounded. "Mister, if it weren't for me, deer would be running down the streets and fish would be chokin' the rivers!"

I laugh at that. The thought of this skinny, no-driving kid with an acne-covered face and glasses half an inch thick leading beer-chugging rednecks through the woods is too much. Robbie and Orville — what a pair.

"Like I said, if you need anything, give me a shout. With winter setting in, there ain't too many requests for guides. So, I've got some time on my hands."

I shake his hand, offer him a twenty for gas—which he readily takes, much to my surprise—and step from the car. He speeds away, with Orville perched beside him like a canine date. He takes the next turn and disappears.

The air is clear and crisp, the square lit by the early morning sunlight unhindered by a single cloud. The temperature has warmed into the high forties, not balmy by any means, but not the freezing drizzle I last experienced. I walk toward a gazebo, letting my mind trail along the edges of my memories the same way the fingers of a blind man slide along the walls of an unfamiliar room, guiding him and feeding him tidbits of information.

I stand in the middle of the city square and open my mind to whatever might be drifting in on the wind. Nothing jumps out at me. The windows of the buildings along the square stare back blankly, uncaring; the doors refuse to open upon my gaze and allow access to the secrets hiding behind their brick-and-mortar walls.

Shit. It is just a city square, nothing more and nothing less. I stuff my hands into my coat pockets and walk in a westerly direction. I'm not sure what my destination is, but I trust that I'll know it when I see it.

At the mouth of the alley, I linger. In the daylight, it isn't as claustrophobic. While my conscious mind dwells on the horror of that night, my subconscious delivers me to the loading dock where I had taken refuge. The lack of blood doesn't surprise me. Intelligent killers cover their tracks well. Every crime scene wiped clean and sanitized; all probable loose ends dealt with.

According to the sign on the door, the business behind me is the Center Rack Pool Hall. I stare down the alley, trying to figure out my next move. The door bangs open, and a garbage bag flies out, startling me. The man tossing the garbage glares at me as I try to compose myself.

"What the hell are you doing?" he growls, his eyes narrowing as the muscles in his python-sized arms flex.

Surprised by the door crashing open, I freeze. It feels like an eternity before the ice in my veins thaws enough to allow my instincts to flow. "Nothing much. Just out looking for my dog." The words aren't as smooth as I would like, but they are far better than the silence that hangs between us like a smothering chasm.

"Your dog, huh?" The man drops the other bag he holds and takes a step forward, his fist clenched and jaw held tight. His words come out in a growl. "Well, he ain't here." He continues to scowl at me as if I am someone he needs to punish. "So why don't you just move on? Now."

With a finger as thick as a cue stick, he pokes me in the chest, rocking me on my heels.

"No problem," I smile, then whistle twice. Cocking my head to the side, I wait for a reply that I know won't be coming. "Yeah, he ain't nowhere around here." The man doesn't respond; he stands with his fists on his hips. "You have a good one."

I jump off the loading dock, wave goodbye over my shoulder, and continue down the alley, whistling and calling 'Hea' boy!' Glancing back, I notice that the man is still on the dock glaring at me. When I reach the abandoned office, I turn around once more. The man is gone, but his presence remains entrenched in my mind. Do I know him, or does he recognize me? When I am sure I am not being followed, I slip back through a rusted metal door and into the office I previously hid in, then push the door shut behind me.

The shattered glass from the mirror crunches under my feet as I inspect the room. Nothing has changed. The room is still damp and cold. Using a table leg from the desk, I scratch paint from the window facing the alley. If there hadn't been a wire mesh on the outside, my earlier pursuers would have come through it.

The room brightens enough for me to have a closer look. The length of pipe remains by the door. My lighter, matches, and little brass key are on the floor beside the desk. In all the confusion, I had forgotten them. I pick them up and stuff them deep in my pocket. I leave the matches. They are wet from the carpet and will never light again. I fling them down on the desk and open the door. A gust of wind swirls in, blowing the matches over on their back, where they flop open. The inside cover has writing in blue ink, now smudged, and blurred by the wet carpet. I close the door and scoop up the matches. The ink is almost indecipherable, but I can make out two things: a time and date. The date is the day my nightmare began. The time is roughly two hours before the onset of this madness.

Once again, I am full of questions I can't answer. Is this my writing? The dead woman's? It is hard to tell by the smeared ink. I stuff the soggy matches in my pocket, slip out the door, and set a quick pace down the alley.

I'm running on instinct again, driven forward by a silent call connected deep in my brain. I feel like a blind homing pigeon returning to its perch. I hope my journey doesn't end with a cage door being slammed shut behind me.

Block after block passes beneath my boots. I angle toward a rundown strip mall. It doesn't bring any memories to the surface nor seem to hold any importance. But my gut instinct has yet to fail me. As I close in on the long string of attached shops, I notice that most of the stores are boarded up, and the walls tagged with gang graffiti.

The fast-morning walk, combined with the sun's glare on my eyes, tires me out. I feel as if a trance-like veil is being woven over me. I slip into what feels like a dream—images of what I call 'the night' flicker beneath my consciousness. Once again, they are almost close enough to identify and grasp before they abruptly vanish into the hidden recesses of my mind.

I give up on trying to catch the dreams and have a hard, cold memory flash that staggers me. I cover my eyes with my hand and stumble against a wall, hoping to steady myself as my legs weaken. I slide down the wall and sink to the ground.

In my vision, I see a gun leading the way, fire spitting from the barrel, smoke trailing behind it. I can't see the face of the wielder, nor can I tell anything from the hand that holds the revolver. A black leather glove grasps the weapon and is in constant motion. I can see the woman from the loading dock. She is soaking wet; the rain drenching her hair and clothing. The woman is screaming. Her screams are as silent as the reports from the gun. The blonde flees down the alley.

I jerk awake with a gasp. Somewhere deep inside, I realize I have been shouting. The only response is that of a barking dog.

Chapter Six

Coffee. That's the first thing to breach the fog swarming my head. Not just any coffee, but the smell of a potent brew. Black, undiluted by milk or sugar, the way a man should drink it.

My stomach rumbles a greeting as I pull myself up and stretch. My bones initially balk at the movement, chilled from sitting too long on the cold asphalt. I stumble onto the sidewalk and past a line of empty newspaper boxes filled with garbage.

A door three shops down opens, and a rush of voices fill the air along with the aroma of breakfast. My stomach doesn't so much growl as roar. God, I am hungry. My last actual meal was before falling down this damn amnesia-laden rabbit hole. I'd eaten a few cheeseburger plates at the motel, but nothing substantial since. The thought of something fresh—veggies, fruit, whatever—puts an extra bounce in my step. I pull my cap down low and duck out of the way of a young couple attached at the hip as they exit the diner. Sliding through the door, I aim for a table in the rear, drop into a booth, and sit facing the entrance.

The cracked and worn vinyl booth is still warm from the last patron and feels good under my tired, cold ass. The picture menu disappointments me, revealing no fruit, no veggies, but every other combination of greasy, artery-clogging, heart-stopping ways to package eggs.

"What'll it be, sugar?" asks a waitress.

I hadn't heard the woman approach over the constant babble of conversations and the clatter of dishes. The waitress is a tall, heavy-set black woman wearing a floral uniform with the name Delilia's Coffee Shoppe stitched across the chest. The nametag, in the shape of a steaming coffee pot, reads Permillia. As she stood patiently waiting for me to respond, I let her question run around. *What did I want?* Jeez, if she only knew what a loaded question that is. I can't help but grin. I want to order a nice heapin' slab of memory, served with a double order of answers. And to drink, I'll have a belly washer full of truth, but I check myself instead and ask for coffee. "Black, please. No sugar or cream."

"Can I get you anything else? Eggs?" which came out sounding more like 'aigs.'

I shake my head and slide the menu across the table.

"How 'bout the 'chef special'? It's three eggs, bacon, grits, toast and jam." She holds her pad as if expecting me to jump on the suggestion. Instead, I feel my gut curdle at the thought of grease. My body hungers for something with a bit more nutritional value.

"No thanks. But if you have anything green—beans, peas, even an apple—that'd be great."

"Somethin' green for breakfast?" she asks, her face wrinkling as if the word is offensive. "Honey, that won't stick to your ribs, no-how. You'll be hungry again before you know it!" She places a hand on my shoulder and sighs. "Someone young as you needs more in their belly than beans! At least have some toast. You're gonna make Jerry in the kitchen all upset if you don't order nothing more than coffee."

I shake my head and smile at her. The discussion is closed. She squeezes again, then let's go with a heavy sigh. "All right, I'll go see if Jerry has anything *green* and get you your coffee."

"Throw in a side of toast," I call back to the waitress as she makes her way through the crowded diner. I might as well take her advice and try not to piss off the cook. She turns back to me, looking pleased with the partial victory. "But no butter!" I shout over the low roar filling the coffee shop. The waitress is still writing on her pad as she disappears into the kitchen.

While I wait for my breakfast, I make use of the facilities. The bathroom is dim and smells of chlorine. The tile floor is slick, and the sink is rust stained. I step in front of the mirror, remove my hat, and run my hand across my head, intending to straighten my nonexistent hair. The shine of my bald head continues to startle me. I stare in the mirror, still not recognizing the face or the eyes. The bruise over my left eye is settling to a mottled brownish-yellow stain, no longer tender to the touch. In the center is a gash and abrasion that is scabbed over. Is that where the blood came from? Somehow, I can't convince myself that the wound is the source of the blood. I would have had to carry money in my hat.

"To hell with it," I mutter and leave the bathroom. The diner is as noisy as ever, but my food, including a bowl of butter beans, is now sitting on the table. I resume my position facing the front of the building and sip my coffee. Staring out across the mostly empty parking lot, I watch the wind swirl a wave of leaves and debris along the asphalt, twirling them into a mini tornado before abandoning the leaves and disappearing. Pretty much the state of my memory.

I dig into the steaming bowl of beans, surprised at how much I enjoy them. The bowl is nearly empty when a shadow drifts over the table.

"How'd you like them beans?" The waitress asks as she refreshes my coffee. "Jerry done souped them up to make them stick to your ribs a bit better."

"Pretty good," I answer, polishing off the last few bites.

"Good, glad we found something for you." She smiles, pats me on the shoulder, and says she'll check on me later. I watch as she works her tables, hugging some men around the shoulders, teasing children, and spoon-feeding a few bites to an old man who clanked his way across the diner with a battered walker. I bet she cleans up in tips.

I am still watching her in awe as I pick up my bread and spread a thin layer of grape jelly from a little square blister pack. My arm freezes with the knife frozen over the bread. I had ordered a stack of toast, but what I found under the first piece isn't listed anywhere on the menu.

Thankfully, the waitress is off performing her duties, allowing me to eat slowly and contemplate the note that was placed between the two slices of toast. I remove the top piece and avoid acknowledging the business card beneath it. As I spread a thin layer of jelly, working the glaze back and forth, I scan the restaurant for a pair of questioning eyes.

I shoot my vision to the kitchen, back to the patrons, and out the window. Maybe I watch too much television, but I'm half expecting to catch a pair of restive eyes attempting to get my attention or swinging from side to side as if to point me in a direction. Nothing. Not a soul acknowledges my existence. Whoever left the note is hiding or has left the building.

I eat the toast. I flip the card off the remaining bread and onto the table with my free hand, then brush the card off the table and onto my lap. I retrieve it, then hide it in my palm, dropping it in front of the table sign advertising the daily special. Now I can read the message without tipping off anyone that I have seen the note.

Reaching for my coffee, I wait until the cup is almost to my mouth before glancing down. The message is brief, just three words written with a red pen in block letters: 10:30, Greyhound, J19. I am still staring at the cryptic message when Permillia's shadow falls over the table. Before I know what I am doing, my arm streaks forward and scoops up the card, abandoning all pretense of trying to appear nonchalant. My elbow catches the sugar jar, knocking it over and sending my coffee cup careening off the table. Permillia, showing the quickness that belies her size and age, catches the cup before it descends toward the hard tile floor and sets it back on the table in one smooth movement.

"Sweetie, I think you've had enough coffee!" she laughs, taking a quick swipe of the table with her towel, mopping up the sugar and coffee. "You're about as jittery as a long-tailed cat in a room full of rocking chairs." the waitress adds with a chuckle.

"You startled me." A bloom of embarrassment spreads across my face as I feel heat in my cheeks. I glance up and into the waitress's large, amused brown eyes. "I was daydreaming a bit, thinking about all I have to do today," now adding one more stop to my schedule. I sit up straighter in the booth, forcing myself to relax.

"Uh, huh," she says and refills my cup with a fresh spot of hot, black brew. "Your dream must have been something exciting. It's been a long time since I've seen a young man flinch like that."

"Yeah, it was." I reach for my coffee, hoping to break the string of questions and give my jangled nerves a chance to settle. My arm trembles as I lift the cup, sending small waves of coffee lapping over the edge.

Permillia's gaze stays locked on me, her eyes staring over the top of her glasses. "Well, if your dream was as exciting as you say, I suggest you drop everything you have to do and go home." She wipes the table down again, cleaning up the fresh rings my coffee cup is leaving.

"Son, why don't you go home and make up with your wife?" With her head turned back toward the front of the diner, to the sound of the door opening, she looks at me from the corner of her eyes. "If you know what I mean, that is."

She winks, and I almost spit my coffee across the booth. First, she orders my breakfast and then suggests that I attend to something more —satisfying, for lack of a better word. Embarrassed, I feel the heat rising, forcing me to blush again. I don't enjoy exposing my emotions, especially those that show vulnerability. I push the embarrassment down and let the stronger emotion of annoyance twist my lips from a smile to something more neutral.

Drawing on my tattered restraint, I force my hand down, carefully setting the coffee cup back on the now ringless table. And as smoothly as I can, I ask, "Who said I'm married?"

Permillia smiles. "Child, I've been pushing coffee and grits here for thirty-eight years and I was married almost the same. I've seen every facial expression that God has allowed man to have. And," she pauses, staring into my eyes as if I am a wayward child she is gently having to scold, "I've heard every story from joy to sadness. And most I heard from watching, not listening." Permillia wipes down the seat across from me and drops into the booth. A grin splits my hardened expression as the couple on the other side of the booth lurches forward. My smile fades as I turn back to her.

"But like I said, I'm not married. Not even dating." The words feel honest, but I don't know how well I can trust them. In the past week, I have learned that what I think might be the truth often isn't.

"Okay, then recently divorced," Permillia asserts

I shake my head.

"Can I ask you a question?"

I shrug.

Permillia slides the sugar and other condiments to the side of the table for a more direct line of sight.

"Go ahead, ask away."

She begins to speak, but I hold up a hand, freezing her mid-word. "You can ask, but I might not answer it." I didn't tell her I might not be *able* to answer it.

"Fair enough," she says, nodding. For a moment, she sits with her lips pursed, the dishrag continuing to wipe down a table that is now polished to a shine. She reaches across the table and taps the ring finger on my left hand. "What's this?"

I glance down at the faint line that circles my finger. My jaw falls in response. I can't find any words to answer as I stare at my hand. My lips crack to speak, but the constriction in my throat makes it impossible. "Apparently, I'm…." I glance up into Permillia's warm, patient eyes, the words leaking from me, "Or was–" I stammer, "married."

I lean against the back of the booth, closing my eyes. "Like I said, I don't have an answer for you."

Chapter Seven

"Excuse me," I say, sharper than I intended, and push myself from the booth. I throw a ten on the table, knowing that my meal couldn't have been over five dollars. I'm done with the conversation; my head is spinning. I am mentally trying to swim upstream in a raging torrent of madness but feel I'm coming closer to drowning. Too damn many questions. Too damn few answers.

I rush past several truckers trying to enter the diner, shoving one against the back of the doorjamb and eliciting some crude comments about my questionable breeding. Turning from the protection of the building, I regret leaving the warmth of the dinner. I'm chilled to the core by the stiff wind swarming my face.

I pull my collar around my throat and shove my hands deep into my pockets. I walk, staring at the ground with no direction in mind, and find myself in front of the bus station. Once again, I'm operating on instinct alone.

I pull the door open and shuffle across the threshold, half expecting to see my face on wanted posters plastered on every door and window. Instead, I find a dozen bored men, women, and children sitting in scuffed plastic chairs. The hot, stuffy air assaults my sinuses with the smell of sour clothing and stale cigarette smoke. Kids attempt to entertain themselves by crawling around on the black and white tile floor, chasing toy cars, and playing with dolls.

The kid's hands and knees are as grimy as Kentucky coal miners.

With the bill of my hat pulled low, collar still upturned on my neck, I make my way around the large, square room. I grab a dog-eared, two-year-old *Sports Illustrated* off a wobbly table and merge with a small group of passengers waiting to board buses to who-knows-where.

Nothing jumps out at me as to why I have been 'requested' to be here. Regardless, my nerves are still jumping, and my heart is racing. I have visions of a gun barrel pressed against my ribs or an ice pick driven to the hilt in the base of my skull.

Neither happens. Obviously.

After allowing my sizzling nerves to settle, I move beside a rack that holds dusty fliers for local attractions and finger through them. As I do, I gaze over the lobby, studying it in greater detail.

The building is nothing more than a non-descript four-corner concrete block traveler's way station. The faded posters on the wall show luxurious vacation spots. I doubt these grungy people will ever travel to. There is a pay phone ringed with cigarette burns mounted to a support, its directory missing. A paunchy, middle-aged clerk in a rumpled and grease-stained *Greyhound* uniform sits on a stool behind the counter, appearing more bored than the passengers who wait in the over-heated building. He leans against the counter with his nose buried in the local paper, making small red circles on a page that can only be the classified ads. And to his left sits an overflowing ashtray with smoldering, half-smoked cigarettes.

I turn my attention to the people slouching in the worn-out seating. They are the typical assortment of down-on-their-luck folks who can't afford to travel any other way. The surrounding floor is littered with tattered luggage and worn coats drape over the backs of chairs. They barely react when the clerk pulls a microphone from beneath the counter and, with no excitement in his voice, announces that the 10:15 from Birmingham will arrive on time and that the 10:25 for Granger, Burlington, and Wexford will depart in 15 minutes. Without a clue what I am going to do next, I drift toward a corner, dragging a chair with me, and sit under the shadow of a broken RC Cola machine. I can see both doors from here and will be almost invisible to those entering. I pull the magazine up to eye level and wait.

Time moves slowly. A Red Baron Pizza LED clock counts down the minutes. At 10:15, a hiss of air brakes and a sudden influx of tired passengers announces that the coach from Birmingham, as the clerk has predicted, is on time. While passengers make their way through the station, I study them from the cover of my blind. There are no sparks of recognition from the travelers. Most ignore me or sweep their eyes over me with a cursory glance.

The numbers on the clock roll over to 10:28. The station empties as the last of the waiting passengers shuffle toward a bus that has just arrived. If anything happens, it will have to be in the next few minutes. I move my chair from my corner to get a better angle at the parking lot. The lone bus driver is stuffing suitcases and duffel bags under the carriage. A few stragglers meander around the bus, stretching their legs and waving goodbye.

The station is now vacant; even the man behind the counter has deserted his post, leaving me with the electronic humming of the fluorescent lights. The clock rolls over to 10:32. The person who left the message is late, and I feel increasingly vulnerable. I'm getting antsy, and my gut urges me to move on. Plus, all the coffee I drank earlier has worked through me. With a final hesitation, I slip from my blind and make my way toward the restroom. I linger only long enough to wash my hands and think about the note. This building has to be the only Greyhound station; the town is too small to have more than one. And I'm on time, that much I am sure of. But why would someone slip a note between my pieces of toast and then not show? My gut warns me to make myself invisible, to vanish like a fish diving deep in a murky pond. But I can't do that, not just yet. I must figure out why I was drawn here.

What am I missing? I flip the card over several times; it's blank on one side and has scant information on the other.

Using the toe of my boot, I push the bathroom door open, afraid to touch the knob with my now-clean hands. There is no telling what skin-eating disease lingers here. The lobby is just as empty as it was when I left, the ticket counter is still vacant, and the bus that had been loading is now rolling toward the highway.

Braving the cold, I ease out the door to the loading dock and glance up at both sides of the terminal. The place is now abandoned. Did the rapture happen and only take Greyhound passengers? Not the way I pictured getting to heaven. Stepping back inside the terminal, I glance through the windows in the double doors that lead deeper into the station. My pulse quickens—lockers! I dart through the doors and make my way to the rows of cabinets lining the wall. Most of the units stand open and unused. Some labels were peeled off ages ago. I arrive at section 'J' and count the doors. And there it is, scratched, dented, and locked. I give the door a hard tug. It rattles against its frame but doesn't budge. A quick inspection of the room confirms that there is nothing I can use to force it open.

Leaning against the wall, I put my hands in my pocket, needing the time to think. Then, almost as if a cartoonish bulb pops into existence over my head, I remember the little brass key. I practically rip it out of my pocket and stare at it. "Well, little friend, let's see what secrets you guard." I hold the key up to the lock, gauging whether it will fit, fearful that it will be another loose end, just another tease.

It slides in without effort.

The lock turns without hesitation.

I pull the door open and retrieve a tan, shoebox-sized cardboard box with *Jonesy* written in careful script. I rotate the package in my hands, turning it upright, then upside down. Besides my name, there is no other information written on the box. The box is light, maybe a couple of pounds at most. I shake it lightly, trying to get a feel for what is inside. The contents barely move. It could be anything from papers to more body parts. Opening it here is out of the question. I run my eyes around the station, trying to find a place to hide the box until I can come back for it. I decide on a place to stash the box and hope it's the correct decision.

I stroll back through the lobby, whistling and smiling, trying to look as nonchalant as possible. Just another happy traveler. The desk clerk is back at his post as I round the corner. He glances up once, his tired, bloodstained eyes rolling over me before returning to his paper. In the past fifteen minutes, the waiting room has gained a few stragglers. The ones awake ignore me. The others snore. Halfway to the door, the payphone rings. No one moves to answer it. The desk clerk's attention is still on the paper. He ignores the ringing. I slow my walk, waiting to see if the ringing will end.

After eight rings, it does.

I count to three and walk forward again. The moment I do, the phone rings. This time the clerk looks up, annoyed. He folds the paper, walks over to the phone, and yanks it off the cradle. "Bus station!" he snaps into the mouthpiece. "What? Hell, if I know! Hold on, and I'll ask." Turning in my direction, he nods, "You Jonesy?"

My surprised expression is all the answer he needs. I shrug, and he drops the phone, leaving it swinging by its cord. "You got a phone call." He barks.

Goose flesh spreads down my neck. I glance around the depot. Who in the hell knows I'm here? I take my time walking to the phone while casting my eyes across the station. Keeping my back to the payphone, and positioning myself so I can see both entrances, I speak quickly. "Somethin' I can help you with?"

"Jonesy-boy!" the voice drawled as if we're old friends. "How's things going?"

My spine turns to ice. The feeling of being watched confirmed.

"Who's this?" I ask. The voice teases on the fringes of familiarity.

"Jonesy-boy, you slay me son, you really do!" the man on the phone chuckles. "Where you been lately? Nobody, and I mean nobody, has seen you around. It was like you're hiding or somethin'. You're not hiding, are you?"

"Been around, here and there," I say, leaning against the phone with the receiver cradled against my neck. "I didn't know I'm such a curiosity."

"Oh, Jonesy-boy, you're, like, way more than a curiosity. They're folks that have been out looking for you." The laugh returns, but not as hearty as before. "And I mean, looking everywhere for you."

"Should've called my secretary. She's got my itinerary." *Who the hell is this?* The voice tickles my brain with recognition. Twisting my head as far as the chain on the receiver will allow, I scan the room, then the parking lot. "Listen, this call has made my day, but I'm afraid I've got places to be. So have your machine call my machine and we'll do lunch."

"Now, son, let's quit pussyfooting around." The frat boy tone darkens. "What'cha got in the box? Somethin' that don't belong to you, son? How 'bout you just leave the box below the phone and take a bus trip to Vegas?"

I swing my gaze around fast enough to get dizzy. "Box?" I laugh, trying to stall. "What are you talking about?" Despite the foreboding sense of danger that wells up inside me, I grin, albeit a small one. For in my head, I hear myself saying in a cheap Mexican accent, *box? I ain't got no steenkin' box!* I'm stalling again, waiting for my instincts to catch up. I still don't know why I was called to the station, but I feel the box is meant for me. I mean, *Jonesy* being scribbled across the top is a sizeable clue.

"Quit fuckin' with me, boy. I ain't got the time for it. Now wipe that damn smirk off your face before I do it for you and listen up."

Where is the sonofabitch? I snap my head back and forth, staring out the dusty windows, trying to get a glimpse of the caller. He has to be close by, maybe standing outside the building with a pair of binoculars. The warning feeling in my spine blossoms into an all-out fear. I back closer to the wall, putting my back against it and the headset on my left shoulder.

The man laughs hard. "Man, if you could just see your bald-headed ass trying to hide! Peek-a-boo, I see you!" He sang into the phone. "Can't see me, can you? Well, I can see you! Turn around to your 9:00 position. See that white van with the black windows?"

"Yeah, that you?"

"Nope!" More hearty laughter. "Turn to your twelve. See the old man talking to the tree?"

Across the parking lot, I can see several old men, one using a walker and one standing against a tree. "You look much older than you sound."

He answers with an even sarcastic laugh. "Well, got to give it to you, Jonesy, still got that damn smart-ass attitude. But no, wrong again."

"What's your point?" I growl, this time catching the attention of the people sitting nearby.

No laughter this time. "Point is… point is, my friend…."

Somehow, I don't feel I was his friend or ever have been. Call it another gut reaction.

"You've involved yourself in shit that you have no interest in. Granted, you were recruited to help—let the little head do too much talkin' for the big one and all. But you were warned, repeatedly I might add, to stay clear. But no, you had to charge in playing Billy-Badass and put your damn nose where it didn't belong. And now look at the mess we got. You have something I want, and I have answers I'm sure you want. My first inclination is to drop you where you stand, but that's more problems and more messes to clean up. Not unlike that rather untidy little mess on the loading dock, eh?"

How much did this sonofabitch know?

"Besides, I'm on a tight schedule. And as much as I hate to admit it, I'm gonna give you one more chance to back off, to make yourself scarce, as an honor to your old man. Unlike you, he knew when to step away. I'm gonna give you this one last opportunity to hit the fuckin' road."

I rub my chin as I consider his words. "All right, say I agree with this. What next? If we see each other in the future, we pass like two ships in the night?" Like, I'd know who he is. "How do I know you won't renege?"

"You don't."

"How much time do I have to think about it?"

"Oh, I'd say you have about 9 millimeters to think."

"Not much time."

"No."

Whoever this is, he holds all the cards. So, I ask myself a question: do I bluff, or do I fold? "Okay, fine. What do you want me to do?"

"Pick up that magazine you were reading…."

"Excuse me?" I say, interrupting.

"Open that fucking magazine, turn to the center."

I do as he says. A bus ticket falls out, wrapped in a copy of the registration from the motel. And stapled to it is the bill from the coffee shop. "What the hell is this? How long have you been following me? When the hell did you…."

"When, what, why doesn't matter. You're in no position to question jackshit. So shut the fuck up and listen!" He is shouting. "Leave the box in the locker where you found it. Scratch a 'J' on the key and leave it on top of the locker. Catch the 11:00am non-stop bus to Vegas. Do not get off, leave the bus terminal, or make another phone call. There's a room for you at the Bonaventure. If you haven't checked in by midnight tomorrow, people you care about are going to disappear, one digit at a time. Understand?"

Crazed fury envelops me. The bastard knows more about me than I do. I clench the phone tight enough to send cramps up my wrist, my jaw tight enough to crack teeth. "Yeah, sure." I growl. "One more question," I say, but the phone goes dead in my hand, leaving me with a mocking dial tone. Who is being threatened now? What have I unknowingly unleashed on people that I can't remember?

I let the dial tone hum in my ear for a few moments before hanging up. I step from the wall and scan the parking lot outside the bus station. The caller could have been anywhere—in the station, hiding behind a tree, or in a van. Maybe right behind me.

I don't know much about myself yet, but I know I don't like being told what to do, played like a punk-ass fool.

Sonofabitch has had me in their sights from the very beginning. They've been following me, hoping I'd lead them to whatever's in this box. Next time I see that gaunt bastard at the motel, I'm gonna wring my cash out of his neck for 'protecting' me.

Glancing up at the Red Baron Pizza clock, I realize I have only twelve minutes to devise a plan of action. I can go to Vegas, take a chance with my remaining cash, and see, as they say, what the cards hold for me. Even though I may put more lives in danger, my gut is already recoiling against that idea.

Then again, the threat could be a bluff, one I might still have to call. The door to the station opens, and my wildcard walks in.

Chapter Eight

The man is filthy and in his late twenties or early thirties. He is wearing at least a week's worth of beard, and his clothes hang off his frame, bunching up at the ankles; his hair drapes down across his shoulders in black, matted clumps. The man drags with him a tattered and stained duffle bag. He ignores everyone as he passes through the lobby.

Without turning my head, I follow his reflection on the plate-glass windows as he makes a slow trek around the station, scouting the luggage, looking for something to lift. He stops by the candy machine long enough to check the coin return before pushing on. His circle brings him past me as he checks the payphone for forgotten change.

"What's up?" I ask and nod to him with a quick tilt of my head.

His half-closed, bloodshot eyes wash over me as if sizing me up for some later nefarious action. "Nothin', man. Nothin' at fuckin' all," he replies before trudging by. He then stops, drops his gear, and turns back to me. "Yo, man, can I bum a smoke off you?" He holds out his right hand as if expecting one. His nails are nicotine-stained, his hands are filthy.

"Sorry, fresh out," I say with a smile and a shrug.

"Yeah, right." He lifts his duffel bag.

"Maybe now's the time to quit?" That always pisses them off.

He stands for a second with his head cocked and lips pursed as if trying to decide if I am truly fresh out. "Whatever," he mutters and angles for the bathroom.

My smile widens after the door shuts. Yeah, this wild card should work fine.

I wait a few moments, spin on my heels, and follow him in. He has his head buried in the sink, allowing the water from the faucet to pour down the back of his head. "I don't have a smoke, but I can help you get a carton or two. Maybe even a fifth of Jack."

He hadn't heard me enter, and startled, the drifter bangs his head on the faucet as he pulls back. A shard of anger lances across his face as he throws his head back, flinging water on the walls. He wipes his face dry with the sleeve of his ragged sweatshirt. "What the fuck are you talkin' about?" he demands with a sneer. "If you're lookin' for a blowjob, I'm tellin' you right now I don't suck dick. So, the best thing you can do is take your ass back the way you came in."

The bum actually takes a step forward. My indifference to his feigned threat and my laugh create a flicker of concern in his eyes. "So, what the fuck do you want?" He wipes drops of water from his forehead and moves toward his duffel bag, which I feel contains a weapon.

"Relax, will you? For Christ's sake, chill out a bit." He doesn't appear convinced and takes another step toward his bag. "I've got a proposition for you. How'd you like to make a cool hundred bucks? All you gotta do is shave your head and face, swap clothes with me, and catch a bus out of town."

He stares at me as if he hasn't heard me correctly. "Are you fuckin' nuts? You want me to shave my head and switch clothes with you?" He leans against the sink, dumbfounded. "Why? Why the hell would…." He favors me with a glance at my coat, and the feral gleam I noticed in his eyes returns. "Fuck, I don't care why. If you want to wear this shit, go right ahead. But if you want me to shave my head, that's gonna cost."

I nod without comment and drop a handful of twenties on the counter, along with the bus ticket. "No problem, here's a buck-fifty. Start shaving. Hope you like Vegas."

The man shrugs and slips his sweatshirt over his head, revealing a dingy, sleeveless tee shirt. He reaches down to pull it off as well.

"Whoa, slow down, hotrod. You can keep the wife-beater."

Five minutes later, he has hacked his dregs off to the skin and is now dressed in my former LL Bean togs. With my cap pulled down tight on his head, he'd pass for me from a distance. He grabs several items from his duffel bag, stuffs them in his pockets, and heads back into the terminal. I count to thirty, then exit dressed in his rancid clothes.

But I'm not finished with my disguise. I will need something on my head and face. The lobby is busy, but the ticket counter is unoccupied. I glance behind the desk, and sure enough, a box labeled 'lost and found' is tucked under one corner. Inside the box, I find a dark gray hooded sweatshirt and a pair of scratched glasses. I pull the hoodie over my borrowed sweatshirt, lift the hood over my head, and slip the glasses on. All that shows of my former self is a thin swatch of skin just below my eyes.

The scratches on the glasses are more than a little irritating, but I have completely changed my appearance. I entered the station as Ken, the GQ redneck model. I leave as a nondescript drifter and alcoholic. Pausing by a mirror in the maintenance closet, I inspect my appearance. Not bad at all. It is time to hit the road and dig up a few more answers.

I keep to the back wall of the terminal, ensuring only my back is visible in the windows and angle for the rear exit. Pausing in the door frame, I take a moment to scan the buildings and land surrounding the station. The parking lot is empty except for a faded and rusting Buick Century. Steeling my nerves and trying to appear as nonchalant as possible, I push through the door and into the bright light of late morning. The wind whips my hood back before I can stop it. I spin around on my heels and step back against the building, pulling down my hood and hoping it looks like a natural reaction. Regaining my composure, I step into the wind with my head down and hoodie pulled tight to prevent the cover from flying loose.

I cross the parking lot and move briskly toward the road. Thankfully, the traffic is nonexistent. I wait for a smoking Ford to sputter past before sliding under the comfort of the shadows lining the far sidewalk. I settle into a casual stroll, glancing into the shops, feigning interest in the contents inside. The glass reflects the road behind me, acting as a block-long rearview mirror. A pickup truck slows as it approaches and swings toward the curb. My body tenses on instinct, my legs preparing for flight as my shoulders and arms knot up for an impending confrontation. I slow my breathing and sweep the road and sidewalk with my eyes, searching for potential avenues of escape or weapons.

The truck rumbles up to within a dozen feet of me, close enough to hear the belts squeaking and the crunch of sand under its tires. I can smell the sickly sweet odor of coolant leaking from a faulty cooling system. I continue to walk, gradually picking up the pace, still searching for alternatives.

The creaking vehicle rolls behind me on the sidewalk, the mufflers echoing off the brick front of the buildings. The vehicle stops, and the driver's door opens on rusty hinges. I hear boots hit the ground and increase my pace. I catch the reflection of the parked truck in the storefront mirror. The driver is shorter than me and well-muscled. Heavy gloves cover his hands, and a camouflaged hat is pulled down low, partially covering his face. I won't get any more clues about what I am dealing with until he is on me.

I continue to slide along the windows, moving just fast enough that the man will have to jog to catch up. Hopefully, he'll be slightly winded when the shit hits the fan, if it comes to that. I count down, anticipating the moment the driver makes contact.

Reaching the end of the block, I step around the corner of the building, back up against it, and wait. A stray ray of hope flickers in me that this is all a coincidence, that this driver has business on this end of the block and I'm just getting all wigged out over nothing.

My countdown reaches two.

Then one.

No pursuer. I feel an incredible relief rush over me as I let my breath out with a loud whoosh of air and a weak laugh. I drop my hands to my knees and lean against the building, waiting for my heart to slow down. I'll need to quit jumping at shadows to figure out what is going on. After another deep cleansing breath, I rub my hands together, stuff them in the pockets of my hoodie and turn back toward the sidewalk.

"Whoa, shit!" I squawk when I turn to find the small, compact-built driver of the truck standing in my shadow. What I was in a previous life, the one before the godforsaken rabbit's hole swallowed me up; I don't know. But some instincts and traits remain despite the loss of conscious memories. In a blur of movement, my hands shoot from my pockets and grab the driver by the shoulders as my foot sweeps his legs out from under him. Falling backward, he bounces off the store's red brick wall, and I ride him to the asphalt.

With a fist cocked to remove the man from consciousness, I pause at the sound of a revving engine and the sharp squeal of brakes. I look up in time to see the black waitress from the diner leap from her car and rush over to the man on the ground. She kneels beside him.

I have an 'Oh shit' moments where my gut loses its ability to stay put and sinks to the bottom of my shoes. The black woman turns to me with her hands on her hips, brow pinched, and mouth set in a snarl. "Bruton J. Smith, what did you do to my boy?"

Chapter Nine

"Who are you?" is all I can stammer before she stomps over and spins my head around with an open-fisted slap that leaves me seeing stars and my glasses flying.

"What the hell's gotten into you, boy?" She yanks my hood off and smacks me again, this time above the ear.

I step back with my fists raised in case another of her vicious slaps comes my way.

The waitress cocks her head to one side as she stares at me. "I thought that was you in the diner, but I wasn't sure." She reaches between my fists, cups my chin between her thumb and index finger, and twists my head from side to side like a farmer checking the teeth on a free mule. "You're different now. Much different. You've changed from that little boy who used to fall asleep in my lap and cry like a baby when it was time to go home."

"What the hell are you talking about?" I ask as the stinging in my face fades to sporadic tingles. Her hands fall away as she steps back.

"Like I said, I've known you since you was a little boy."

"Really? Because I don't have the foggiest notion who you are."

The woman has a hurt, crossed expression on her face. She runs her eyes over my face and stares hard at me.

"Hmph, well, I'll be. You ain't just pulling my leg, are you? You really don't remember me."

"Mama, I told you there's something wrong with him." The man picks himself off the ground and stands beside her.

With concern in her eyes, the waitress's voice softens. "Jonesy, what's happened to you, son? What's with the hair and them…." She takes a deep breath and shudders, "… filthy clothes? You smell like a sewer! And you sure wasn't wearing them earlier."

Does everyone know my name but me? I lean against the wall and stare over the woman's shoulder.

"Son, what's going on with you?"

I feel a hand on my shoulder. "Jonesy, I know I haven't seen you since your mama's funeral, and then only for a few minutes before you was gone again, but I can tell that there's something you're not telling me." She paused, as if waiting for confirmation. Instead, I stare back toward the street.

"You've done gone and gotten yourself into something bad again, haven't you?"

Hey, hey, this one wins the big prize! But Bad? She hadn't a clue what I'd been dealing with. "Listen, I appreciate your concern, but I've got to be going." I pull my hood back up, reach down, and retrieve my glasses.

The waitress is up in my face before I can move, her brown hands holding the strings to my hoodie tight. "Son, listen to me and listen good. I don't care if you remember me or E-Lee or not. But I took care of you from the time you were in diapers until you were in high school. And I made a promise to your mama as the cancer was eaten' her up that I'd watch out for you, even if you thought you were too big for your ol' aunt

Permillia. That's why I sent my boy after you. Call it a mama's instinct."

"Mama," it's her son again, "I think we need to get going ourselves. At least take him home with us. Then he can figure out what he wants to do."

The woman whose name I now know is Permillia, points toward a dented and faded, late-seventies Chevrolet Caprice. "Son, I've been up since 4:30 this morning and I'm cold. So, get in the car and we'll finish this when we get back home. You can take a nice hot shower and get all cleaned up. That might make you feel a bit better. We'll talk some more after you've freshened up."

Call it a man's instinct, but I knew she wouldn't give it up. I nodded toward her car. "Lead the way." I climb into the passenger side and close my eyes. After a couple of deep breaths, I begin to relax and yawn. The next thing I know, the car stops beside a small white clapboard house on a lonely dirt road. The truck glides in beside us.

I sit up, rub my eyes, and stretch. The town has given way to pastures and farmland. We travel down a dirt road lined with barbwire fences and cedar trees.

Permillia smiles at me, unbuckles her seat belt, and opens the driver's door. "C'mon, let's see if we can do something about that memory of yours."

I nod noncommittally, remove my seatbelt, and open the door to the old Chevrolet. I stand and glance over the top of the car. Neither the house nor the surrounding land spark anything inside me. I shut the door and follow her up the cracked sidewalk to the wooden steps that ascend to her home.

"Jonesy, c'mon son! It's cold out there and I know that head of yours is full of questions for me." Permillia stands framed inside the door to the house, looking down at me.

I rest my hand on the cold steel pipe that serves as a railing and slowly climb toward the small porch, listening to the old, weathered boards creak and groan under my feet. "I'm getting there," I call back, indecision making me more irritable than I should be. Permilla smiles, not noticing my ill mood, and disappears into the shadows beyond the door.

As promised, Permillia waits just inside a small, simply furnished living room; the couch and television are vintage 70s, the walls cluttered with dusty family photos. Through the den, I see a small, simple kitchen. The old, white laminate countertops are sparkling clean; the vintage gas stove in the middle of the kitchen is the same. A wooden table with ladder-back chairs occupy one corner. A crack appears in the armor as a vaporous memory slides past, whispering *home*. Under her right arm, she holds a pair of worn, faded jeans and a plaid flannel shirt that has been washed to the point of being one mottled collage of red and orange fabric.

"I was going to give these to Goodwill, but you look needy enough, so I guess you'll do. Now, I couldn't find you no under-drawers to wear. I asked E-Lee if he had a pair you could borrow, but he said it wouldn't do no good if he did. You'd probably rather do without." She grins at me, enjoying the quick, short-lived reddening of my cheeks.

I take the clothes she hands me with an appreciative nod.

"Now you get yourself all cleaned up and we'll sit for a while and chat." Permillia leads me by the elbow like a child, her grip strong enough to let me know that the Q&A will continue after I am clean. "Shower's down the hall on the right. You'll find soap and shampoo, though with that scalp job you got going on, don't think you'll need all that much!" She cackles, slaps me on the back, and points toward the hallway. "You'll find clean towels in the bathroom closet."

"Thanks," I mutter, annoyed at being treated like a kid, and make my way toward the bathroom. I look over my shoulder to make sure she isn't following. I step into the cramped room and flick the yellowed light switch with my elbow. The room is bathed in the oily brilliance of a weak bulb that barely pushes its way through the aged fixture. I set the clothes on the countertop by a rust-stained sink and start the shower flowing with the turn of a balky valve. Within minutes steam creeps around the edge of the shower curtain, signaling that the temperature is just about right.

The pulsing hot water erases the day's irritation and burns deep into my tired bones, leaving my skin as red as the underside of the sun. But it feels good, damn near antiseptic. I am just starting to relax and enjoy the stinging pain of the hot water when I hear knocking on the door.

"What?" I bellow and step out of the shower, raising my voice above the drumming of the spray against the tub. The good feelings vanished.

"Just wanted to see if there was anything you needed. I had E-Lee put a new razor in there for you. I thought you might want it."

She has been outside the bathroom the entire time. I glare at the door, trying to deliver a psychic shove to back her up. The thought of her lingering outside the door while I stand naked and dripping is unnerving. I feel… violated. I mumble my appreciation and return to the once steaming shower, only to discover that it is now flowing with glacial temperatures. Maybe she should take some of her tips and buy a new water heater. Shivering, I turn off the water and dry myself with a towel hanging on a hook. I dress and almost whole again. With the damp towel draped over my shoulder, I return to the cramped living room, ready to answer questions and nab a few answers.

"Okay, let's talk," I say, feeling better than I have in days. "I've been getting nowhere on my own."

"Jonesy," a woman interrupts from the corner of the room, her soft voice and southern drawl piquing my interest.

I stop and face the voice. The woman stands in the dim light with her back to me. A pair of long, smooth, slender legs stretch up and into a tight, snug skirt that perfectly accents her heart-shaped derriere. So, the day is improving! I suck in my gut, puff up my chest, rest my thumbs in the front jean pockets and take a couple of steps in her direction, essentially putting my best pectoral muscle forward. "Well, hello there," I smoothly say as I brush a hand through my nonexistent hair.

She does not turn but remains in the poor lighting, facing the bookshelf with all the old family pictures. "I didn't think I'd ever see you again," she says while replacing a picture she'd been holding. "Especially here. I thought you'd moved on," her voice still as silky as the skirt hugging her ass, now carries an edge to it, "and found someplace to hide until all your *shit* blew over. Again."

The silkiness evaporates.

She steps into the light, and I stumble, dropping my towel to the ground as my gut falls, my pectoral muscle slackens, and all the cool I possess dissolves like cotton candy in a thunderstorm.

"You're the chick from the bar, the waitress," I stammer as the godforsaken rabbit's hole widens, sucking me ever deeper. "What the hell are you doing here?"

"*You're the waitress from the bar.*" She says, repeating my words, mocking me. "Is that all you've got to say?" She stands across the room from me, her eyes burning with gargoyle-like hatred, then storms over to me, stopping bare inches away, green eyes large and teary. "You bastard," she spits.

"What were you expecting?" I ask, dumbfounded. "Hey, bitch, how 'bout a beer?" The room spins in a sick, wobbling circle as the walls flare blood red, and my vision glazes over. I feel my face swelling.

"You jerk!" she cries before punching me in the stomach. I deflect most of the next blow, but enough gets through to send a shard of lightning rolling up my abdomen. I block the next punch, grab her by the wrist, and spin her away from me.

"What the hell's wrong with you?" I growl, digging my fingers into her wrist, trying to avoid the urge to snap the thin bones in her arm, forcing her down.

The woman glares at me, her lips struggling to form words. She is almost to the floor when Permillia steps into the room and throws a shoe at me, hitting me where

Sheila just slapped me. I flash my eyes at her, anger coursing through me.

"Jonesy, what in the world is up with you? Let go of Sheila right this moment before you hurt her!"

I focus on Permillia, my blood boiling. "She hit me first!" I shout, refusing to let go and realizing how juvenile my answer sounds.

A second shoe bounces off my head as I wrestle with the waitress. This time it's a hard-soled shoe and not an old worn-out sneaker. Once again, stars explode behind my eyes, and the room blurs red.

"Have you both drank the same poisoned Kool-Aid and lost your collective minds?" I shout and rub my forehead with my free arm, almost expecting to bring back a bloody forearm..

"Son, let her go right now before I bash your brains in!" Permillia demands as she charges across the room with a broom held high, her eyes narrow and fiery, her jaw set somewhere between a lioness protecting her cub and a cottonmouth about to sink its fangs into a soon-to-be-dead sewer rat. Above her head, she twirls the broom, spinning it as if she is a possessed Ninja-Maid assassin. Releasing my grip on the waitress, I give her a none-too-gentle shove, putting her between Ninja-Mama and me. Permillia catches the woman with one hand, sweeps her toward the kitchen in one fluid move, then swings the broom at me, barely missing my nose.

"All right already!" I yell, raising my hands in what I think would be the best way to protect myself from being battered by a worn-down floor cleaner. "I let her go! Now, will someone please tell me what in the hell is going on?"

Permillia jabs at me with the broom handle, the fire in her eyes fading like a cooling ember. I dance out of the way of the first attempt, almost shouting 'Ole!' in the process—not that I found her half-hearted attempt to impale me with the narrow end of a broomstick funny—but the smart-ass in me has yet to take a break. I grab the broom on the second and wrench it free.

"Damn it, woman!" I snap and throw the broom down. "Knock it off!"

Permillia retreats to the kitchen, puts an arm around the woman, and pulls her in close.

"I only came here because you *insisted* I do, that you could help me. Not to be ambushed and bloodied." My head is pounding and I'm seething.

Permillia guides the woman to the kitchen table and stands behind it, using the table to keep us apart. She then lowers herself onto a chair with the grace of one sitting down for a Sunday dinner. Permillia clenches her hands together as if praying, resting her chin on her laced fingers. "Jonesy, if you've calmed down enough to have an *adult* conversation, maybe we can start over." She pushes a chair out with her foot. "Have a seat."

"Why? You want to get me close enough to brain me with a skillet?"

Permillia smiles, showing a mouthful of white, misaligned crooked teeth, a conniving shark's grin if ever I saw one. "Son," she begins, all sweet and friendly, "what makes you think that I'd hurt a hair on that now-bald head of yours?" She tilts her head and smiles.

"Because you hit me in the head with a goddamn clod-hopper of a shoe!" I fire back, still standing with my back to the front door, not giving up on the idea of hitting the street and escaping this macabre carnival madhouse.

Permillia rises from her seat, eyes narrowed, jaw tight. "Now, Jonesy, you know how I feel about using the Lord's name in vain!" She shakes her finger at me. "Do it again, and I will smack you upside your head with a mop, and I might not take it out of the bucket first." She pauses, closes her eyes, takes a deep relaxing breath, then runs a hand down the front of her waitress uniform. "Now sit. Me, you, and Sheila have a lot to talk about."

Taking a deep breath, I let it out slowly, nod and lean the broom against the wall. Trudging over to the table, I feel my animosity wane. "Sure, what the hell," I mutter. "How many shoes can you have left to throw?"

I sit across from Permillia and Sheila, the former smiling broadly, her white teeth gleaming. The latter scowling, sucking as much life from me as her bitter eyes can accommodate. I lean back, glance from one woman to the other, and crack my knuckles over my chest. "So…." I say.

"You two seem to be getting along well!" Permillia says with a wry grin and a wink. "Just like old times, hm?"

"Oh yeah, very funny. Ha ha," I growl and flash a mildly obscene gesture with my hand. Permillia's smile doesn't change, but something sharp smashes into my kneecap, threatening to leave me a begging cripple for the rest of my life. I bite back against the pain, trying not to show any sign that I noticed the sub-table assault. Then the true force of her words hit me like a bag of hammers. "What do you mean by 'old times'? Until last week, I'd never even seen her before." Permillia's smile dips and then returns to full wattage. The change in the woman beside her is more profound. Her face goes flat, the anger-driven tension holding it firm before evaporating.

Sheila drops her head in her hands. "Eat shit and die, but this time don't come back." She mutters.

"What is this?" I demand, wishing I had hair on my head so I could yank it out. I massage my temples with the heels of my hands, rubbing in circles, trying to drown out the pounding inside my skull. "Is this about that ring you gave me? I've still got it, for Christ's sake. Figured I'd give it back to you the first chance I got, still don't know why you gave it to me. But…." I stop when I see the tears flowing down her face.

Permillia sighs, stares at the ceiling, then slides a manila folder across the table.

"What do you want me to do with this?"

"Just open it. I think it should be self-explanatory." Permillia turns to the woman beside her, dabs the lady's tears with a Kleenex, then slips an arm around her, giving her a brief hug.

The first thing to slide from the folder is a small beige envelope embossed with gold lettering. I move for it, then stop.

"Go ahead, it's okay." Permillia encourages.

"I don't want to," I answer quickly.

"Why?"

"Don't know… I think I'm afraid to." I know my fear is irrational, but it's also genuine.

"Jonesy, what are you afraid of?"

I look up at Permillia, her eyes losing their intensity. They are now slightly closed, her hands drawn close to her chest.

"I'm afraid of what might be in that envelope."

Permillia doesn't respond. She continues to stare at me with half-closed lids.

"Maybe ignorance is bliss, y'know? And not having a clue who I am or what's going on is for the better." I stretch out my hand and twirl the envelope with one finger, watching the embossed lettering melt into rings of spinning gold.

"This is bullshit." Sheila says and slams her hands on the table. "Just Jonesy playing more of his sick, twisted games." She snatches the envelope from under my fingers and throws it at me. "Open the goddamn envelope!"

"Maybe later," I say, attempting to stall.

"You chicken-shit weasel," she snarls, jerks the envelope off the table, rips it open and tosses a wedding announcement in front of me.

Chapter Ten

"Married? Us?" I stammer. I suck in a deep breath, holding it until I think my lungs will seize, then let it out slowly. "I don't even *know* you."

Sheila places the wedding announcement back in the torn sheath. She caresses the ripped side of the envelope, running a tear-moistened finger over the jagged breach. She almost let a smile slip through. "This week would have been our two-year anniversary." Permillia sets a hand on her shoulder, but Sheila brushes it off, her chest heaving as tears escape.

Sheila dabs her cheeks with a napkin and drops her gaze to the invitation.

"I guess I shouldn't have been all that surprised when you didn't show up at the church; you've a history of disappearing." She lifts her head and stares at me with red-streaked eyes. "And when you would show up, you always had perfume on you—*her perfume*—all over you, like she was teasing me, showing me she could still play you like a fool when she wanted to."

I close my eyes and press my fists against my temples, rubbing hard circles against the side of my head, hoping the pain will snap me out of this week-long nightmare. "Who… who in the hell are you talking about?"

"Your ex," Sheila growls. "She only wanted you when she got bored with her other boy-toys. And you were too willing to be her flavor of the week." She drops her eyes and lets the smoldering hate fade to a dull glow. "You're so weak and pathetic."

My mind is twirling counterclockwise, the fog thickening. I face the women. "Please tell me that this is some kinda sick joke."

Permillia shakes her head; Sheila remains motionless, eyes distant. "Then who… when?" I ask after taking a few seconds to digest this unpalatable serving of madness.

Permillia takes over the Q&A.

"You met a girl from Lake Sebastian about ten years ago, dated for a few months, then ran off to Vegas and got married. Her family was furious. What with you being—shall we say—less than affluent and her being an heiress to the Parson-Brice cookie fortune. They thought you were after her money, tried to buy you off."

"Not too fond of me, then?" I ask, leaning back and staring at the ceiling, counting the dark water stains and trying to connect small brown spots to form a picture.

"Despised is too soft of a word for how they felt about you from the get-go. Her parents even tried to get the marriage annulled. But you two were so in love—at least in the beginning—that you just flat-out thumbed your nose at them." Permillia smiles and laughs, but the humor is short-lived.

"Eventually the constant fighting with her family was too much and y'all started bickering and you started staying out late, drinking all night. This led to some awful blow-ups and at least one case of her knocking you out with a wine bottle." A wry grin crosses Permillia's face.

"How do you know this?"

"Because after she kicked you out, canceled all your credit cards and burned your Porsche…."

I quit staring at the ceiling and returned my attention to Permillia. "I had a Porsche?" This revelation is almost as shocking as discovering that I had once been married. "And she burned it?"

"… you moved in with me and E-Lee—again."

"You're saying I had a Porsche, and she burned it?"

"That's exactly what I'm saying. That little car was parked right out front. She pulled up beside it, poured a can of gas in through the window, lit a match, and that was it. She drove off without so much as looking back. By the time the fire department got here, it was just a smokin' heap of metal."

"Where was I during all this?"

"You was hungover and sleepin' in the den — like you were on most Saturday mornings. When you saw what she had done, you cried like a baby. Not that I blame you or anything. All your clothes—well, all that you could fit in that little bitty thing — burned up with it."

I take a deep breath, stare at the wall, and let this new tidbit of information sink in. Shaking my head, I glance back at Permillia. "She must have been a real bitch."

Permillia lifts her hand to warn me about cursing, then lowers it. "Maybe so, but living with you ain't no picnic either. Trust me, I've been there too."

Somehow, I knew that already.

"Tell me about it," Sheila says, breaking her silence. "That's the only redeeming thing about your ex. She didn't put up with your shit." Her eyes are clearing, the glassy red dissipating. She places her elbows on the table and leans forward, staring straight at me. She is getting her strength back, ready to jump back into the fight. I like how her breasts sway back and forth under her shirt when she moves, providing a sweet view of her cleavage. Nice ass, nice tits. And fiery to boot. No wonder we were a couple.

"So, did she tire of you again?" Sheila said. "Is that why you're here? Wanted to 'test the waters', see if I'd take you back, hide you while your shit blew over?" She notices my leer, closes the front of her shirt.

"Well, let me tell you something, mister. We are *sooo* over. So don't even think about trying to talk your way back into my life, not now, not ever again."

Her mouth says 'over,' but her eyes keep returning to me, washing over my face as if searching for something. I keep finding my gaze drawn to Sheila, watching her chest heave with emotion and her long fingers drum on the table.

"I'll tell you why I'm here, or still here, to be accurate," I begin. "Permillia offered me a chance to clear my head and get a hot shower. So, there you go." I cross my arms and lean back from the table. "But why are you here, in this house, now?"

Sheila shifts in her chair, brushes her hair behind her ear, bites on her bottom lip, then nods toward Permillia. "Because she said I *needed* to be, but wouldn't tell me why. And as far as I'm concerned, this has been a complete waste of time. A *painful* waste of time as well." She delivers the last of her statement at Permillia, who doesn't react. I know then that Permillia is holding more cards than she's showing.

Sitting up straighter in my chair, I rest my forearms on the table and clasp my hands together. I fix Permillia with a hard expression. "What the hell's going on? This isn't some stupid-ass attempt to get us together, is it?"

"No, I would never do that!" She says with a chuckle. "When you two split, you made it perfectly clear that you wanted no more to do with each other. I just thought that she might be able to jar that memory of yours, help you clear your head and figure out what you're running from."

Sheila turns toward Permillia, her eyes darting back and forth between the dark-skinned woman and me. "Oh, this is too much," she brays like a donkey. "As many times as he's lied to me, you and everyone he knows, don't tell me you actually *believe* him?" Sheila barks a quick, shrill laugh. "Oh, please, this is too much!" She wipes away a tear that leaks past the corner of her eye. "Well, I needed that little laugh."

I lean over the table, drawing myself as close as possible to Sheila. "You know, I don't give a rats-ass whether you believe me or not. The fact is, I *don't know you*, and I *don't know her* either," I point toward Permillia, "and I sure as hell don't know why I'm wasting my time here." I shove back from the table, almost tipping my chair over. "I think we're done. All I've gotten out of all this crap is a somewhat hot shower, a worn set of clothes and a forty-five-minute bitch session."

"Wait!" Sheila shouts, as I kick my chair out of my way and turn toward the door.

"What the hell for? What could you want now?"

"Just one more second, please." Sheila's voice has lost all its hatred, its anger. She runs to the back of the house and returns with a shoebox. "I'm not saying I believe you, but… humor me." She offers a quick, fleeting smile.

I stare back at her, twirling my finger in a 'let's get this over with' movement, making an obvious move to check my nonexistent watch.

"Who is this?" She opens a box filled with faded photographs, both color and black and white. She hands me a picture of a middle-aged white couple.

I take the picture, hold it by a corner and stare at it. "I have no idea."

"Look closer. Please."

"Your parents?"

"No. But never mind, you haven't seen them in quite a while. How about this one?"

It is a picture of me and Sheila with another couple standing behind us on a set of church steps, their hands on our shoulders. "This one has to be your parents."

"Yes, they are." She takes the picture and places it back in an envelope. Then she pulls out one more, her arms trembling as her lips quiver. "And this one?"

I hold the second picture, flip it over, and feel my heart go stone-cold; my throat latches tight. The past week's nightmares explode inside my mind as I stagger backward against the wall, my lungs dry and hot. "Who… what is this? Where in the hell did you get this?" I croak.

"You don't know?"

"Who the hell is it?" I reply in a small voice.

"It's your ex," whispers Sheila, now standing behind Permillia.

"Jonesy, what's wrong?" Permillia asks.

"I have only seen this woman once before." My voice is shaky, my breath coming in cold, raspy snatches.

I focus on the picture. When the photograph was taken, the blond was very much alive. She sits on the hood of what had apparently been my Porsche with me standing beside her, one arm around her waist. "This is… my ex?"

Permillia walks over and pulls the picture from my hand.

"Jonesy, talk to me. Has something happened to Claire? E-Lee told me she was on an assignment."

I cup my face in my hands and lean against the wall. The light in the room grays.

Chapter Eleven

"Son, have you seen her?"

I nod without looking up.

"Where?"

I tell her of the storm, the platform, and the body.

"Oh, son, I am so sorry," Permillia says as she places a hand on my shoulder.

I let gravity pull me to the floor of Permillia's small, clean living room. Permillia drops to her knees, then sits beside me. She stares at the ceiling, shaking her head. Sheila settles into a kitchen chair with her elbows on her knees, her face in her hands. No one speaks. The only sound is the ticking of an old round wall clock hanging above the stove.

"Dear God, son, what have you gotten mixed up with now?" Permillia asks with a sigh, breaking the painful silence.

"Who the hell knows," I mumble. "Right after finding the body, some men came charging down the alley, shooting at me. I hid in an old building and waited for them to pass. I later stumbled across Sheila's bar and make my way out to the Dreamland Motel. I've been staying there for the past week, trying to figure out what the hell is going on."

"And what did you figure out?" Permillia asks, still staring up at the ceiling.

"Nothing. There hasn't been jack in the papers, on the news or radio. It's like it never happened." I turn to Permillia. "Tell me something, if this woman—my ex, as you say—was so wealthy and connected, how come there hasn't been so much as a blip on the media? That doesn't make a bit of sense."

"Maybe no one knows she's missing," offers Sheila.

"How the hell can that be?" I blurt out. "If she's as prominent as what you suggest, there'd be folks asking questions everywhere. The law would crawl all over this town, diggin' in every dumpster, checking out every abandoned house."

"Could be that she hasn't been *reported* missing," Permillia says as she turns to me. "She was single and traveled a lot. When y'all were dating and then married, she'd take off for weeks chasing down leads. That was another thing that ruffled your feathers." She smiles briefly, then lets it fall.

A bulb glows in the back of my mind. "What investigations?"

"Claire liked the controversial kind, diggin' up dirt on folks, exposing corrupt politicians. She liked catchin' preachers coming out of motel rooms with their pants around their ankles." said Permillia; she laughed again, then let it wane, "I warned her once that she had to quit pissin' folks off because someone was gonna get mad, real mad."

"You think something like that might have happened? Maybe pushed someone's hot button once too many?" I ask.

"Can't say for sure, but she stepped on a lot of toes."

"And you think I'm somehow involved?" I don't need to turn my head to know that Permillia is staring at me.

"Why…" Permillia starts with a gasp. "Jonesy! I know you have a mean streak, but I could never see you hurting Claire, much less killing her."

"But you think I'm involved, don't you?"

Permillia takes a deep breath, stares across the kitchen, and then lets it out in a heavy exhale. "Yes, I think you might be involved somehow, helping her, I'm sure." She raises an arm, waving me down as if already knowing I will argue the point.

"Which I was," I say slowly, the words barely coming out of my mouth. The light in my head is now brilliant white and pulsing with awareness. I *had* been helping her. In what fashion, I do not know.

"What?" Sheila and Permillia blurt at the same time.

"It's just a powerful sense or feeling. Like déjà vu, but to the nth power." I glance over to Permillia. "I can't explain it. I see what I would call 'memory flashes'. Some are clear enough to make sense of, but the rest are like wisps of fog on the highway. Before I can see them, they're gone."

I feel a twinge in my eye. I've been feeling these for the past week, and they always herald a vague memory, but this one is stronger. Numbers coalesce deep inside my mind. "I bet if you call," I close my eyes and pull an image out of my brain before it fades, reading off the numbers as they swim before my eyes, "we'll all be surprised." I repeat the number twice before Sheila says, 'Got it!' and drops the pen she used to write the number on the back of her hand.

A surge of adrenaline lifts my spirits. The stuck cogs in my brain are loosening up, sliding into place.

I climb to my feet, ignoring the popping in my knees, and walk over to the old, corded phone beside Permillia's faded Lazy Boy recliner.

"Whose number do you think it is?" Sheila asks.

"Don't know," I lift the phone from its cradle, "but we're about to find out." Sheila reads off the numbers as the ones in my head disperse into nothingness. On the fourth ring, the call connects.

"Yeah?"

I don't know what I was expecting, but a man's voice is the least of them. A spike of fear runs down my spine. "Who's this?" I ask, shrugging in answer to Permillia's pantomiming.

"Jonesy!" the voice says with a relaxed drawl. "Let me hand it to you, son, you're a slick joker. If that fuckin' bum hadn't gotten himself thrown off the bus, your plan might have worked. We would've checked up on you, you know, just to make sure you were all right, that you were being taken care of." He laughs hard and ragged into the phone, close enough to the mouthpiece for me to hear his smoker's rasp.

It is time to dump the call. Dropping the phone away from my ear, I speak casually into the handset. "Sorry, man, I think I got the wrong number," I finish with a light smile and return the phone to its cradle as nonchalantly as possible. I clap my hands together and chuckle, hoping it sounds natural. "So much for my memory returning. At least I now have the phone number for *Aaron's Sub Shop*."

Permillia and Sheila laugh. At least the tension in the room was broken. I walk to the front door, pull the curtains aside, and peer out the window. "What were we talking about?" I ask, staring up the street.

"You doubted that someone could go missing if they were well known," Sheila answers. "Then you had your 'epiphany,'" she says with a slight smirk in her voice. I can't tell if Sheila is being sarcastic or coy—strange time to hit on me.

I close the curtains and run a hand over my head. "Yeah, missed that one big time." I walk over to Permillia's well-used recliner, drop into it, and grin. "Anyone wanna guess how long my sub's been ready?"

"Maybe that number's not as wrong as you think," Sheila says. "Maybe there's something there that can help you."

I lace my fingers behind my head and lean back in the chair, staring at the ceiling as if I'm considering the idea. "That's a thought. I might swing by and…."

The phone's sudden ringing interrupts me. As the phone rings, Permillia rocks forward as if she is about to climb to her feet, then stops.

"Son, are you going to answer that phone?"

We lock eyes on each other as she makes a half-hearted wave toward the phone. Damn, she didn't believe a thing about the sub shop.

I let the phone ring a few more times before grabbing it. There is no need to say hello or any other greeting. The earpiece is blaring by the time I curl it toward my head.

"… piece of shit had better not hang up on me again!" the caller snarls. "We want that package, and we want it now. We'll give you an hour to put it back where you found it. Otherwise, it's gonna get hard to hold the hand of that pretty little waitress if she ain't got no hands to hold on to."

He is about to say something else when I rip the phone cord out of the wall and throw the phone across the room where it crashes in a cacophony of shattering plastic and ringing bells. Permillia and Sheila stare back at me, stunned.

"Get up!" I order, motioning them to get to their feet. "We've gotta go, all of us!" Neither of the women moves. "Are you deaf?" I shout. "We need to leave—now."

Sheila edges out of her chair, but Permillia waves her down. "No sir," she says and crosses her arms over her chest. "I'm not going nowhere. I'm old and I'm tired, and I'm not lifting my butt off the ground until you give me enough reasons to do so."

"Listen to me." I walk over to Permillia and crouch in front of her, so we are eye to eye. "The man or men who did this to me," I say, outlining the fading bruise on my forehead with my finger, "and screwed up my head is the same person I just called. I have no idea why I can only remember his number and not my own." Still crouching, I shift my position to look out the front windows. "And I have a bad feeling that he's the same person or persons that Claire was investigating and that he is probably responsible for her disappearance."

"And," Permillia says while trying to stifle a yawn, "you know this, how?"

"I just do. Trust me on this. I don't know where I've been prior to last week, but this feeling is like a damn midnight fire-alarm screaming in my head, warning me to get myself really lost, really fast."

"But why do *we* need to leave?" Sheila asks. Her dark brown eyes are large with fright, her slender arms trembling.

Permillia continues to shake her head. "Jonesy, slow down! Who is this that you're talking about and how do they know where you are?"

"They're bad dudes, killers, and they won't let a few loose ends get in their way."

"But they don't have a clue where you are!" Permillia argues.

"They called me back, for Christ's sake! Permillia, almost everyone has Caller-I.D. on their phones. Within minutes, you can have anyone's address with the click of a mouse." I stand, ignoring the popping and cracking in my knees, and hurry to the window. I pull the curtains apart. "They're coming."

"You don't know that."

"I do. Somehow, some way, I *know* this, know that he, them, they—whoever they are—are coming. And they will not leave any witnesses behind."

"Permillia, I think we should do as he says," Sheila says, rising from her chair.

"Maybe you're right," Permillia replies as she stands. "But Jonesy, I think you're holding out on us; you haven't told us everything you know. And you can start with that phone call."

"Sure. Later. Now's not the time." I move to the other side of the window and stare down the other end of the street, looking for cars that appear out of place. "We need a place we can hide, someplace way off the beaten path."

"I'll go get E-Lee up. I'm sure he knows some place we can go."

"Oh shit, forgot about him. He's in danger too."

Five minutes later, a groggy E-Lee joins us in the living room. "Mom says we need to find someplace out of the way for a few hours." He yawns and stretches. "I think I know a place. Let me make a quick call, and we can be on the road."

"Make it quick. I don't know how much time we have."

The room quiets as E-Lee steps out to make the call. The clock over the stove ticks the time away while the wind stirs the dead leaves in the yard.

Two minutes become five, stretching to almost ten before E'Lee returns.

"Damn, kid, how long does it take you to make a phone call?"

"Sorry about that. I was trying to get hold of a friend. It's all set. Y'all just follow me."

"Where are we going?" I ask, putting on a coat that E-Lee provides me.

"Just down the road. Let me grab my keys, and I'll take my truck. You can ride with mom." He walks back across the room toward the rear of the house. Sheila and Permillia pull their coats on, cinch them tight and head out the door. I button my jacket and glance around the tidy living room. I sure as hell didn't mean to get anyone else involved. Hopefully, we'll all be back someday to have a cold beer and talk about the future, whatever of it remains. I open the front door and descend the steps.

The wind hits me with a cold, hard blast, lifting my collar and chilling my ears. If I hadn't been concentrating

on keeping my face out of the wind, I might have noticed
the man before he put a gun to the back of my head.

Chapter Twelve

Nothing gets your attention like the feel of cold steel pressed to the nape of your neck, the ratcheting clack of a hammer drawing back, and a gravelly voice whispering in your ear, "Make my day, Jonesy, run for it."

I freeze in my tracks with my hands dangling loosely down my sides, fingers twitching. *How did they get here so fast?* They must have been watching everyone I was associated with..

"Now, Jonesy, don't do nothing rash. It'd be a lot easier to take you in breathing than to have to get answers from yonder lovelies."

Without moving my head, I flick my eyes to the left, where Permillia and Sheila kneel with their backs to a man that could dwarf a phone booth. Both women have their fingers laced behind their heads and their faces pointed at the ground.

"So, how about putting your hands behind your neck and lace your fingers together. Cool?"

I do as I am told and feel the gun move from the base of my skull. Relief floods my brain, knowing the barrel of that widow-maker is pointing somewhere else. Lightning flashes in the clear sky as pain explodes behind my right ear, sharp enough to make me bite my tongue and blur my vision. I stagger and fall to my knees. I stare at the sidewalk, waiting for my eyesight to clear. As the cold gray concrete swirls into view, I see the first fat red blood spots hit the ground, followed by a heavier trickle.

I gingerly test the side of my head to see if I'm missing a section of my skull and have yet to die. Thankfully, the side of my head is still intact, but my hand comes back red.

"You bastard." I hiss as new shards of pain lance through my head.

"That, son, is an attention-getter. Now, no one told you to stop moving. Get your ass up and keep on walking toward the edge of the road. I've got a ride that's gonna be pickin' us up any moment now."

The pain diminishes from paralyzing to merely incapacitating, but my vision is still narrow and pain-streaked. "Leave the women out of it. They don't know anything."

"Well, we'll find out soon enough, won't we? Now put your hands behind your neck."

He backhands me when I don't move. Again, pain flares behind my eyes, forcing me to sprawl forward. I drop to my knees, leaning forward in a spreading pool of blood. The cold steel presses against the base of my skull once more. "Lace your damn fingers *now!*"

"Okay, okay," I whisper. Balancing as best I can, I get one hand behind my neck. The man grabs my wrist and twists it to within a hair of snapping it.

"Give me your other hand before I shatter your wrist."

I feel a cold metal ring snap over my wrist. Handcuffs.

The man leans against me, driving a knee into my back. "Jonesy, you're gonna make me very popular in a few minutes." He grabs my free arm and wrenches my wrist sideways to force me into compliance.

My running is over.

"Nothing personal, you know, just business." He is trying to snap the remaining cuff on my right hand when I feel him turn. "What the fu…" he mutters, then I hear a sick crack, like the sound a bat makes when the ball connects with the weak spot, shattering the handle. The man topples beside me, his close-cropped blond hair already streaked with crimson highlights. The gun he jammed to the nape of my neck, a silenced nine-millimeter, skids just beyond his outstretched arm.

I see a yellow Louisville Slugger bat splattered with blood drop to the ground and E-Lee sprinting away.

Instinct again takes over, roaring into control from the lair it sleeps in. As I scramble after the weapon, time seems to stand still. I see the man with the barrel chest rotate toward me; the gun aimed at the women, not wavering. He shouts, "Warren!" His lips move slowly, his words hanging in the air. He then sweeps the weapon towards me as I scramble for my tormentor's gun, the one loose cuff clattering on the sidewalk.

His weapon roars, breaking the time-warp feeling and sending a slug into the turf just ahead of me. It explodes the lawn in a spray of dirt and grass. The second slug stitches a nice little crease across my left shoulder, passing between my shirt and my skin, close enough to burn. The third whining shot passes over my head like a quarter-ounce lead hornet.

I lift the weapon while threading my finger through the trigger guard. The human phone booth is about to squeeze off another round when Sheila pivots and kicks hard, driving her foot below his right knee. The man bellows in pain as his knee crumples. He stumbles to the side and brings his weapon around when I fire the first of four quick shots; the silencer made each one sound like the tweets of a sick bird. *Choirp, choirp, choirp, choirp.* My first shot catches the man in the left shoulder, spinning him toward me. The second and third strike his chest dead center. My last round sails high and wide. He manages one wobbly step before the gun falls from his hand and he crumples headfirst to the ground.

I struggle to my feet, my head swimming from pain and adrenaline, my vision muddy. "Get up!" I scream at Sheila and Permillia. "Get the hell out of here!"

Sheila helps Permillia to her feet, and then they sprint for her car. "E-Lee, you drive." I close my eyes and hold on to his shoulder as the world wavers. "Don't stop for no one; not cops, not school guards… no one!" I drop the clip from the weapon, verify that it is still loaded, and snap it back in place. I hand the weapon to him. "Ever shoot a gun before?" He nods. "Good. Take this one. I'm going after dead-and-ugly's piece."

"What're you going to do?"

"Gonna wait and see who else shows up for the party."

"Jonesy, they'll just try to kill you again."

"Probably. Y'all go on, get the hell out of here." I pause at the sound of an engine racing our way, not sparing the horses. "They're after me, not you."

E-Lee turns toward the sound, nearly a half mile away, on the far end of a barren field. Nothing between the car and us but barbwire and saplings.

"Hide that piece and get going!" I give him a shove and then hobble toward the dead man. E-Lee starts in a quick walk that turns to a dead run when the cloud of dust comes racing up the street like a V-8-powered tornado.

Dead-and-ugly is just that. Dead and ugly. I don't recognize him, but his pockmarked face, heavy eyebrows, and cracked and missing teeth would be hard to forget. I pick up his revolver, a heavy, long-barreled .357 magnum—a killing weapon. I glance up when I hear Permillia's old Chevy firing up in a cloud of blue-gray smoke. E-Lee slams the transmission into gear and speeds out of sight.

The approaching car is about one hundred yards away. I rip open the man's coat to rifle through his pockets, finding the additional rounds I knew he'd be holding, then dart toward the rear of the house and the far trees, ignoring the throbbing in my skull and the possible concussion.

As I sprint away, I slap open the chamber and reload. I pause behind the house, peering around the edge to see who has arrived. It is both good news and bad. By the Sheriff's emblem on the door, I figure they aren't here to kill, though I can't be certain.. But I am still being hunted, that much I am sure of. I hear a door open and muffled shouts as they inspect the two corpses on the ground, then lots of excited radio chatter. If I am going to make a break for the tree line, it would have to be now. They will tire of the bodies soon and start nosing around.

Not wanting to be caught with a weapon I'm sure can be traced to a murder, I wipe it clean and toss it into the bushes behind Permillia's house.

Getting to the trees is going to be close. If I jet now, run straight as an arrow with the house to my rear, the run will be several hundred feet, about a dozen seconds of me being wide-ass out in the open. I take a deep breath and a second one for good measure, then dart into the open. I haven't gone ten steps before I hear shouting behind me and the sound of one of those big V-8s revving. A patrol car shooting dual rooster tails as it rounds the corner. Within seconds, he is ahead of me and swerving to block my path. I turn right, heading for a thin stand of woods on the far side of the property. They won't hide me, but will prevent their cruiser from driving up my ass.

The cruiser shoots past, attempts to brake and turn, but only accomplishes getting itself stuck in the soft dirt, the tires digging a nice trench before running out of grip. *Finally, a break!* The unexpected change of luck inspires me and spurs me on. I double my effort, watching the thin grove of trees draw close. Past the woods is a small clearing, a dry creek, and a stand of pines. Once I get there, I can disappear, vanish into the trees, and reappear at my discretion.

Or so I thought.

The other deputy is coming from the other side of the house and running like a fuckin' holster-and-badge-wearing deer. The dude is flying and isn't even black. *How in the hell can he run in all that gear?* I reach down deep and drag up the last of my energy reserves. My breath is coming harder; the hiking boots, lightweight as they are, feel like land anchors. I'd be long gone if I were in a pair of sneakers. But I'm not, and I wasn't. The deputy is closing like a black-booted cruise missile.

"Get 'em, J.D.! Shoot the bastard!" the deputy in the stuck cruiser shouts out the window as if the man chasing me needs any additional inspiration. He closes on me.

I've run over eighty yards flat-out in a pair of hiking boots. My lungs burn as if I've inhaled a cloud of gasoline, and a stitch is running up my side. The deputy pulls within a few feet and is just starting to breathe hard.

I suck up the last of my adrenaline and manage a meager burst of speed. Now my head is pounding, black spots dance before my eyes. The thin grove of pines draws close.

"Take him down, dumb ass!" the man from the cruiser yells. The deputy mutters something and falls back.

Hot damn! I might make it after all! The pines are fifteen yards away. My view of the world is improving when everything around me explodes and a small pine splinters. Another cannon blast causes the dirt in front of me to erupt in a small geyser.

I jog to the right and another pine is sacrificed, its sappy pulp plastering my face.

"Next one caps you in the ass, Cowboy!" The deputy shouts.

Time's up; game over. I quit running, throw my arms in the air, drop to my knees, and wait to be cuffed.

Chapter Thirteen

"Cuff 'em, then help me get my cruiser un-stuck."

I hear the unmistakable sound of handcuffs being readied. The deputy jerks my arms behind my back and secures them.

"He's taken a pretty good whipping. You want me to call EMS, you know, to pretty him up or something? His head's bleeding out, and I don't want that shit all over my car."

"No!" snaps the older, fat officer. "Forget about that piece of shit and help me get out of here. We were only ordered to cuff 'em and stuff 'em. Nobody said nothin' about him breathing." The men laugh.

The deputy reaches down, grabs me by my belt and cuffed hands, and pulls me off the ground. "C'mon friend," he laughs, "time to take a little ride."

I stagger to my feet, not putting much effort into walking. The more I wear this sonofabitch down, the better chance I have of getting away. I slump against him. In return, he jerks my wrists higher, kicks my feet out from beneath me, and lets go. I smash to the ground face-first.

The deputy drops to one knee and gets in my face. "Listen up, boy. When I tell you to do something, by God you do it."

I comply as best I can and rock to my knees. My head is swimming. I dry-heave several times, managing only a thick string of sandy drool. Finally, I lift my head and stare up at my tormentor. He is young, maybe late twenties, with a flattop haircut. His narrow, washed-out gray eyes stare at me over an upturned nose.

"You wanna try this again?"

I nod gingerly, not wanting to stir my brain more than necessary. Once again, the deputy steps behind me and yanks up on the cuffs. I step forward, glad I'm able to regain my balance, and wobble toward his cruiser.

"Wait here," he orders and opens the rear door. He pulls me around, then shoves me in. I barely avoid catching my head on the roofline as I sprawl on the back seat. He slams the door, locking me inside.

The interior of the car reeks of nervous body odor; the dash is marked with coffee stains. I stare out the rear window as the deputy strolls away, whistling and adjusting his county-issued ball cap.

The deputies high-five each other, point at me, and act out their capture. You'd have thought they just collared Osama Bin Laden. The young deputy stands behind the stuck cruiser and pushes while the driver works the gas. Before long, the car inches forward.

The driver stops his cruiser and climbs from his car. Unlike the deputy who chased me down, this officer has a round stomach and a red face. No way he could chase anyone on foot. He mumbles to his partner too low for me to hear and jumps back in his car. My driver follows suit.

"Alrighty now!" the young officer says with obvious delight as he slams his door shut. "Time to go answer some questions." He picks up the mic to his radio, speaks fast into it, quicker than I can understand, cranks the wheel to the left, and digs a nice trench across Permillia's front yard. We had just hit the hard-packed clay road when he smacks his hand on the dash and mashes the brakes hard enough for me to slam into the driver's cage.

"Watch it, boy, nobody wants you getting all bruised up." He laughs, climbs from the car, and waits by the hood.

Staring through the mesh divide, I spot a third cruiser flying up the street, then sliding to a stop. The young deputy marches to the third cruiser. Another animated conversation follows. Then he jogs over to me and yanks the door open.

"Get out, boy." He turns and stares over the roof of the cruiser. "Sheriff, here's the present I promised you. Sorry that we didn't have a chance to put a bow on him."

The Sheriff nods briskly, his heavy eyes never leaving me. "Lock him in my car and then brief me."

"No problem, Carl." Stepping back, the deputy opens the door and motions for me to climb out of the cruiser. Carl. That's who Sheila said is looking for me. And here he is, ready to take possession. Is this check-and-mate? With my hands locked behind my back and enough pain in my body to bring pleasure to a dentist, there is no escape route. I duck into the car, pulling my legs in before the deputy slams the door shut. Slumping against the seat, I gaze out the window just enough to see the fat deputy wiggle his fingers at me. "Toodles," he says with a smirk.

A shadow passes by, then the driver's door opens. The Sheriff climbs in without acknowledging my presence. He pulls the mic from its clip, calls the dispatcher, and advises that he is '10-21' or some other jargon. He replaces the radio on its hook and drives out onto the dirt road. The radio crackles with reports from officers in the field, occasionally switching to frequencies used by the fire and Emergency Medical Services.

Clay pings off the bottom of the car as the driver speeds down the hard-packed dirt road. I slept on the way to Permillia's house, but I'm certain we aren't heading toward town.

The open fields transform into stands of pine and oak trees, and farmland surrenders to forest. We have traveled at least a half-hour when we pass a sign advising we were now entering Blackroot Swamp State Park. The cruiser slows abruptly and then turns down a fire-access road, the car bouncing and bottoming out as the suspension tries to keep the car level over the seldom-used road.

We drive another mile before the Sheriff takes another hard turn and slides the car to a stop at the edge of a black-water lake. The wind ripples the lake's oily reflective surface. He throws the car in park, shuts off the engine, and sits there for a few moments. The engine makes metallic tinkling noises as the hot parts cool. The driver climbs from the car, walks to the cruiser's rear, and opens the trunk. A moment later, he pulls my door open.

"Get out."

I climb from the car, taking my time, trying to figure out his angle. I can't see any good coming from being dragged to the middle of a swamp, a dozen miles from the nearest house, by a man with a gun in one hand and a shovel in the other.

"Turn around and lean against the car."

I do as ordered and feel the barrel of the pistol press against the base of my skull. The Sheriff works the lock on the handcuffs. "Now, don't get any ideas in your head about trying to make a run for it. This time of year, there ain't a soul around for miles and miles. No one to hear a gunshot."

I remain motionless, feel one, then the other cuff drops from my wrist. Then the pressure against the back of my skull is gone as well.

"Move," the man motions with the shovel toward a stand of water oaks, their broad, winding limbs climbing over each other while curtains of Spanish moss hang from their folds.

When I hesitate, he slams the shovel's blade down on a fat oak tree; the handle giving off a deadly crack. "Now, before I split your head open like a melon!" I drift to the right, keeping my eyes on him. If he is going to kill me, it will not be from a blow to the back of my head. The sonofabitch will have to see my staring eyes cursing him all the way to hell.

"Go on now," he throws the shovel about twenty feet ahead of me like a javelin, then wags his service weapon at me. "I've got something for you."

I glance in the direction he points. A black bundle is on the ground. Keeping one eye on the Sheriff, I approach the bundle. "What the hell is going on?"

"Just some loose ends that need taking care of. Nothing personal, you know. But you've caused more trouble than you can ever imagine, and there's some folk around here that don't appreciate it."

"You're out of your godforsaken mind. You know that, don't you?"

"Possibly, yeah, but I'm not paid for my brain. I'm paid to get things done. Now put that coat and hat on so we can do a little modeling. Call it a 'photo shoot'!" The

Sheriff's laugh lacks warmth, and his hard, gray eyes never leave me for a second. "I think you'll find they fit you just about right."

I stare at him, hoping to stall for time, then look down at the coat and hat I had previously worn. "Where in the hell did you get these?"

"Don't worry about that. It's none of your damn business."

I am shivering. The cold, wet forest is zapping the last of my bravado as I reluctantly slip the old leather coat, then put the hat on my head. "What's the shovel for?"

"What the hell do you think it's for, boy? It's for your grave, dick-weed. Now pick it up and start diggin'."

"No. There's no way you're going to make me dig my own grave." And there wasn't. He will have to put a bullet through my brain before I touch the handle of the shovel.

Carl walks around the front of the cruiser. "Fine. I'm not one to argue."

I back away, now wishing I had picked up the shovel. At least I could have attempted to brain him with it. "You're just going to shoot me in cold blood?"

He shrugs. "Just business."

"C'mon, at least face me like a man!" I yell, feeling the thin coating of bravado beginning to shatter. "Drop the piece and let's go mano-a-mano. Damn it, Carl! We used to hang together!" The words are out before I realize I'm saying them. A memory of the two of us in high school storms out of the black hole in my mind. We are sitting on the tailgate of a pickup truck, the body of a deer on the ground beneath us.

A slight smile, almost too thin to be noticed, parts his lips as he gives the briefest of nods. "That's what makes this almost difficult."

I am about to ask 'Why?' when I am driven off my feet by a sledgehammer blow to the chest. Pain explodes from my sternum, radiating out my arms and down to my gut as I am blasted off my feet, and land on my back with the coat twisted around me. Glancing up and trying to speak, I see smoke drifting from the barrel of Carl's weapon. The light above me fades as consciousness leaks from my body. I can barely make out the shadow looming over me.

"Those were fun times," he says before firing again.

Chapter Fourteen

My vision is still blurry as rockets of fire swarm around inside my skull. Carl is standing over me, firing his service revolver toward my head, the bullets slamming into the ground just inches from my right ear. The rounds pass close enough for me to hear their titanic whine as the lead splits the air and smashes into the dirt. Grit and mud spray out like a horizontal geyser, coating my face with black debris.

I blink the dirt out of my eyes and try to focus on the long-branched water oaks swaying in the stiff wind, their beard-like Spanish moss trailing behind. I pull my vision horizontally with the ground, watch Carl holster his weapon, and then walk back to his patrol car. He disappears for a few minutes before returning with rope and a concrete block.

What the hell is he doing? I glance at the pond, and a memory unlocks in my head, black-and-white snapshots of dead fish and fowl. The pond is deep, cold, and polluted with dioxins and a cornucopia of waste chemicals. No one swims or fishes here, not in the past thirty years. Just being here is enough to get you arrested or diseased.

It is also an excellent dumping ground for bodies.

I attempt to rise on my elbows, but shards of pain pierce my chest and shoulders. The best I can do is a weak lift of my head.

Carl's shadow drapes over me once more. He lifts my legs and wraps a length of rope around my ankles.

Before I can twist my legs free, he ties them to a cinderblock and drops my legs to the ground. Moving with a wrestler's grace and speed, he rolls me over and once again secures my wrists behind my back with handcuffs. I try to scream, to shout, anything that might catch the attention of a lost hunter, but only manage a hoarse whisper. Carl grabs me by my bound ankles with one hand and the block with the other, dragging me toward the bank.

He pulls me over limbs and rocks. The pain ebbs as self-preservation takes over. I twist and spin like a bass trying to slip off the hook. The Sheriff pauses and wrenches my legs higher, putting more pressure on my shoulders and neck.

He doesn't stop, but at least he's tiring. I hear his breath coming harder, his pace slowing. But the pond is drawing close, approaching quicker than the fatigue is wearing him out. I can see the water out the corner of my eye as he angles toward reeds that are standing tall in the wind like sentries guarding the bank.

"Carl," I croak in a weak voice. "What's going on?"

My question gets his attention. He stops and lets go of my legs. He drops a knee on my chest, pressing out any further comment and igniting another unbearable wave of pain. Lightning bolts blister my vision. He pulls a strip of cloth from the inside pocket of his coat and ties it around my head, then over my mouth, gagging me with an old sweat-stained rag.

I thrash my head against the ground, hoping to dislodge the cloth.

Twisting hard to the left, I can make out a small shack, maybe fifteen feet long by twelve feet wide, sitting by the water's edge. Carl marches over to it and pauses. I watch him spin the dial on an old, rusted lock. He forces it to release, hooks it to his belt, then pries the swollen door open and enters. A moment later, he steps out and glances up both sides of the pond. Carl pulls a knife from his belt, the blade gleaming under the sparse streaks of sunlight penetrating the cloud cover.

Glancing over his shoulder, he drops to the ground and slices the rope holding the concrete block to my legs. Before I can move, he rolls me over, grabs me by the cuffs and my belt, and tosses me into the shed. He slams the door shut and replaces the lock through the hasp. Seconds later, I hear heavy footsteps walking behind and past the shed, toward the pond's edge. Then there's the sound of a large splash.

Footsteps jog by, followed by the rumble of the cruiser starting and leaving. Then the swamp is silent except for the whisper of the wind through the trees and the call of a lonely bird. I lay on my back on the soft dirt floor of the shed and cast my gaze across the dark, old planking.

I thought I would be using the last of the oxygen in my lungs by now and swallowing mouthfuls of the polluted pond. Instead, I lay on my back, trussed up like a deer but thankfully breathing because of the bulletproof vest sewn into my coat.

Taking deep, measured breaths, I try to relax my body and ease the pain. The pain flattens to a dull throb that runs from my head to my feet. Sitting up, I press my face against a stud and use it to drag the gag out of my mouth. I then close my eyes and rest.

The streaks of light dissolve into nothing. The next thing I know, the beams of yellow illumination are coming from low on the sides of the shack, not from overhead. I've fallen asleep. I roll to the side and rock to my knees. My head aches as a wave of nausea washes over me. I bite my tongue to clear my vision and crawl to the door. Reaching out with my foot, I give it a shove. Despite its frail appearance, the door barely moves. I'm about to shove it again when I hear movement outside. A dog is circling, growling deep in its throat. Is this why I was saved? To be fed alive to a hungry pack of dogs?

The dog scratches the door, its growl deepening.

I lean against the wall and climb to my feet. The rope binding my legs loosens. I inch to the rear of the shed, scouring the floor and walls for anything I can use as a weapon, though not sure what I can do with my arms cuffed behind my back.

There is nothing. The building is empty. Not even an old rusty screw I can spit at the first idiot to burst through the door. I retreat to the far corner where the wood is as black as coal and crouch, ready to head-butt either man or beast and wait.

The growls cease, and the only sound is the wind whistling through the trees. The dog has either wandered off or is waiting to attack the moment I get free.

I count to one hundred before moving again. Sinking back to my knees, I sit on my heels and feverishly work the knot holding my feet. After what feels like an eternity, the rope falls off my ankles, and my legs are free.

I still don't have the full use of my hands, but my legs are untied. I can kick, jump, and run. I prowl the shed's dirt floor, stopping at the locked door to listen.

Silence.

I press my shoulder against the door, adding pressure. It creaks forward, then stops when the latch on the padlock catches with a soft clink.

I back away from the exit, allowing it to close the half inch it has opened. Once again, I drift around the perimeter of my enclosure, studying the wood slats. I can either try to kick the door open or batter my way through the wall. But who or what waits outside? The dog hasn't returned, and neither has Carl.

"Screw it." I take several quick steps toward the door, ignoring the lingering pain in my head, back, and chest, and launch a clumsy kick at the center of the door. I expect it to shatter when my two-hundred-pound frame crashes into it. The door shudders and holds, but the recoil casts me backward. I stumble and land flat on my back in a cloud of black dust.

The pain vaporizes my breath, leaving me gasping. I grit my teeth and roll back to my knees. There is no way I will let a door on a fifty-year-old shed stop me. I stagger back to my feet, take several wobbly steps, and charge again, this time slower. I kick the door halfway up, anticipate the recoil, and land back on my feet.

"Take that, bitch," I grunt, spin around, and hit the door a third time. The door lets out a sharp crack as a deep fissure runs down the center.

I kick the door a half-dozen times; it starts to warp and flex on its hinges. I pause, resting against the side of the shack to catch my breath. I've only been at this for a few minutes, but I am spent.

Backing to the rear of the shack, I begin another run. I take a quick, hard step, then skid to a stop. Someone is coming. Fast. I hear the deep rumble of a large vehicle powering toward the shack, crushing the brush surrounding the pond, the suspension creaking over the unlevel ground. I press against the wall, just to the left of the door, and peer through a small crack. My view is to the right and away from the approaching automobile.

I move along the wall, looking for another crack or hole big enough to give me a better perspective. Sonofabitch! The planks are just far enough apart to allow light in, but not enough for me to get a glimpse of the outside.

The vehicle is almost to the shed.

I stand to the side of the door again. If someone is foolish enough to open it, I am going to drive a shoulder against them, slamming the person into the wall and, hopefully, to the floor. Then I'm going to stomp the fool's face to mush.

The vehicle rolls to a stop just shy of the shed. The motor idles as the car door opens on groaning hinges. Footsteps approach at a rapid pace.

The latch on the outside of the door squeaks as the lock is manipulated. The door jerks open, but no one enters.

I remain pressed against the wall, my muscles tense, eyes fixed on the opening.

Someone is moving around the outside perimeter, shuffling through the leaves, cursing low under their breath. I am about to rush through the door when the growl returns. A shadow looms just outside.

A big shadow.

It looks like a small bear, but I've never heard a bear growl. The shadow continues to linger outside the shack, moving back and forth. The movement stops as the shadow pauses, then bolts through the door.

Chapter Fifteen

The thick black snout stops short of my stomach; heavy dark eyes stare at me as saliva drips from its muzzle.

"What the hell are you two doing here?" I sputter as a tall, gangly man wearing thick coke-bottle glasses steps inside the door.

"We were looking for you!"

"Why? I mean, how in the hell did you know I was here?"

The man, more of a kid than anything else, trots over to me. "That's a long story." He grabs me by the shoulder and spins me so that I face the side of the shack. Seconds later, I feel the cuffs release and fall to the ground. As I rub my wrists, he retrieves the binders. "C'mon, we don't have all that much time." He hurries out the door and waits for me to follow. The pony-sized lab turns and joyfully bounces after its master as if it is going for a walk in the land of cheese-covered squirrels.

Not wanting to linger, I hustle out the door to where a familiar, battered El Camino sits idling. I open the door, and Orville jumps in without hesitation. The owner slides behind the wheel and drops the truck in gear before his door closes. He guns the engine, and we race forward, bouncing across the field that borders the pond.

I brace myself with a hand on the roof as the truck lurches and careens over stumps and depressions. "You got any seatbelts in this crate?" I shout over the rumble of the motor and the grind of saplings dragging against the vehicle's bottom.

"Nope," he says as we ford a dry ditch on the back side of the pond. "I cut 'em out a few months back to use as tow straps when the transmission blowed up."

"Wonderful," I say, though not feeling the least bit happy.

Orville is taking the rocking and dipping in stride. His one-hundred-pound frame lies across the seat, his head lolling in his master's while his tail swishes back and forth in absolute contentment. We continue our trek through the brush and scrub oaks before exiting onto a lonely strip of highway. A passing trucker swerves into the opposing lane, his horn blaring as we fishtail across the road.

"Whoo-eey!" Robbie howls when the truck's rear quits trying to pass the front. "Now that's what I'm talking about!" He rubs his dog's head vigorously, massaging the mutt's neck and ruffling his ear. Orvy moans with contentment and tries to stretch out, pushing me against the door.

"I guess 'thanks' are in order?"

"Aw, shoot, it was nothin'! Orvy should thank you! It's been a long time since he has found someone alive. You made his day!"

"He's a rescue dog?" I now have more respect for the slouching mongrel.

"Sure is! Best in this part of Alabama. We use him a lot to find little kids and whatnot. Usually, they wander back home, so there ain't nothing for Orvy to find." He pauses as we run up on slower traffic, then flicks the truck around an old Lincoln Town Car driven by a fossilized human traveling at least twenty-five miles under the posted limit. Robbie waves, but the old woman stares at her knuckles that are clenching the top of the wheel like pigeon talons on a statue.

"But we don't always find 'em doing all that well. If they get caught up in the swamp, especially in the winter, it's bad news. And lately, we've been looking for older kids." Pausing, he glances toward me, the jovial life-ain't-nothing-but-huntin'-and-fishin' fading, "Teenagers, mostly girls." He turns, stares straight ahead, and doesn't speak for a few moments. "Actually, nothin' but girls."

A screeching alarm explodes to life in the back of my head, pulsating like early-warning radar after an ICBM launch. I mute it but let it flash in the background, waiting for the next tumbler to fall in the lock that keeps my memories sequestered. I want to ask if he's found any nine-fingered dead blondes but hold back.

"Damn," is all I can say. We drive on for a while, the old two-lane blacktop stretching toward the horizon, passing acres of dead farmland, the spring planting still months off. "So where we heading?"

Robbie points down the dark highway. "I've got an old hunting place up on the Ocochassin River. It's secluded, way off the beaten path. House looks like it's about to be swallowed up by kudzu, but it's actually in good shape."

"So," I say as I stare at the hills growing more prominent in the distance, "you haven't told me how you knew where to find me."

Robbie scratches the underside of his chin and adjusts himself in his seat. "Yeah, well, I had a clue something was up out there. It was really nothing."

"What do you mean 'a clue'?" I ask, not liking how this normal jabberwocky is getting tongue-tied.

"You know, 'a clue', a tip." He refuses to look my way. Instead, he rubs the dog's ears and pats Orville's shoulder.

"No, I don't know. I'm a bit fuzzy on this whole 'tip' thing. Could you enlighten me a bit?" More alarms sound in my head. This cat knows lots more than he is letting on and it is pissing me off.

"Man, I don't know how to put this in a way you'll understand."

He's getting nervous—a bead of sweat rolls down the side of his head.

"Try me. I'm a bright dude."

Robbie steps hard on the brakes; the vehicle slows and veers to the right and up an old dirt road covered with pine needles. Seventy-foot pine trees line both sides of the road. The mufflers rumble as he steps back on the gas and powers up an incline and deeper into the woods.

"If you can wait just a few more minutes, I'll explain everything."

"And where are you going to do that?" I ask without looking his way.

"My cabin. That's where we're supposed to meet up."

"Who?" I wonder why this clown is keeping things close to the vest.

Robbie doesn't answer at first; he keeps driving up the winding dirt road. "Permillia, E-Lee, your girlfriend."

"She ain't my girlfriend."

"That's not what I hear."

"You hear wrong. Let's just leave it at that."

"Whatever," Robbie adds, navigating a pair of ruts deep enough to snare the axles.

We slow even more as he fords a section of badly washed-out road; the truck bottoming out as we skirt several gullies the rain has carved. The road settles down, and I reach over and put my hand on the gearshift.

"Hold up a minute. Before we go another hundred feet, I want some answers, and I want them now."

"You'll have to wait. Carl will explain everything."

"Stop this thing right now before I jam the transmission in park!" Robbie tries to push my hand off the gearshift as I snatch it down into low gear. The engine howls as the rear wheels lock and the truck slues sideways.

Robbie jams the brakes to the floor, and we skid to a stop, his hands white-knuckled on the steering wheel. Orville lifts his head, glances between us, and whimpers.

"What the hell is your problem?" Robbie snaps, turning toward me. "I just had the transmission rebuilt!" His voice notches up a few octaves. "Fuck you and the horse you rode in on." Robbie shoves his door open and throws a leg out of the truck. "I'm through with you and Carl and all this crap! I never wanted any part of it." The boy is practically spitting on me. "C'mon, Orvy!"

The mutt sighs and rises.

Feeling like a real shit, I reassure the dog with a quick pat on the head, then reach over and grab Robbie by his coat sleeve. I pull him back inside the truck. Robbie resists before tumbling behind the wheel. He's trembling, his eyes watering as he stares at his hands. "Just let me and Orvy get back to fishing and hunting, and y'all can solve all these damn murders by yourself."

"Robbie, chill out for a moment. I wasn't trying to blow your transmission up. I just wanted you to stop for a moment so I could wrap my head around everything. I'm tired and want to get this—whatever it is—over with."

Still looking at his hands, he takes a deep breath and regains some composure. "Could've fooled me." He slowly turns my way. "My cousin says you're dangerous and go off half-assed all the time."

I smile and shake my head. "Speaking of your cousin, you still haven't told me how you knew that bastard locked me up. Did he also tell you he took a couple of shots at me, one hitting me in the chest?"

"You look pretty alive for someone who's been shot in the chest."

"Yeah, well, lucky me. Someone took the time to sew a bulletproof vest inside my coat. You don't know nothing about that, do you?"

Robbie shakes his head. "No," he says with little conviction. "I don't know why you were locked up or shot or nothin'." He stares out the windshield, puts the truck in gear again, and we gradually move back up the road. "All I know is that I got an email with coordinates. It's how me and Orvy know where and when to search. That's how we are always notified."

"But how'd you know I was in the shed and the lock's combination?" I stare at him, trying to force the truth from him.

"Because this time there was a note sent with it. It had the combination and a code the sender used advising me to hurry. That usually means the 'drop' is fresh. We've found a few alive that way."

The fatigue in me is turning into a hard chill. There's far more going on here than I understand, and I'm getting a deadly feeling that I'm smack-dab in the middle of it. I ride with my eyes half closed, trying to conjure up answers to my growing list of questions, urging my mind to clear, to open up whatever is being shielded from me.

"So, who's sending them?" I ask, almost to myself.

"I don't know. They come from all over—yahoo, Hotmail, Gmail. Just about any place you can get a free email address. But no address is used more than a few times." We drive on, the road angles higher, and the brush grows thinner. The hill was timbered in the recent past. Various scrub oaks and pine saplings have replaced the lost trees.

"And they always have the same info?"

"Pretty much. They all have coordinates and dates."

"Could Carl be sending them?"

Robbie shrugs. "Anything's possible. Carl's a dick and all that, but he's not a killer."

"I didn't say he was killing anyone. But someone wants you to find these girls, and I think this same person sent you the email about where to find me."

Robbie chews on his fingernails and doesn't comment.

"And you don't find that fishy?" I ask.

After a moment, he nods almost imperceptibly. "Yeah, a little."

"All I know is I'm gonna get some answers from that sonofabitch next time I get within arm's reach of him."

"Well, that won't be long now."

"Why do you say that?"

"We're here." Robbie says and points out the windshield.

We crest the top of the hill to where a small, rough-hewed cabin sits hidden amongst the pines and kudzu. And peeking out from the corner of the house is an easily identifiable set of blue lights.

Chapter Sixteen

I am out of the truck and marching toward the cabin before the vehicle rolled to a stop. A sheriff's cruiser waits on the far side, backed deep into the kudzu that hangs over the shack. Robbie is yelling for me to wait as my march becomes a run. The door to the cabin is just opening when I hit the wooden front porch.

"You sonofabitch!" I roar and charge at the man standing in the door frame. I cock my arm and swing at the Sheriff the moment I'm in range.

Carl intercepts my blow, twists my arm behind my back, and slams me face-first into the wall, knocking the breath from my lungs.

I snarl, "You tried to kill me, you no good piece of shit!" Carl grinds my face against the wall..

"If I wanted you dead, you'd be burning in hell where jerks like you go when their miserable, useless lives are over," he spat. "Besides, I already have enough on you to put a bullet in the back of your head without explaining why." He smashes my head once more against the rough siding and retreats into the cabin.

I stumble from the wall, head hurting. I wait for the streaks of pain to fade from my vision. I stagger through the door. Carl is to the right, leaning against the bar that separates the den from the small kitchen, his weapon holstered, but his hand lingers just above the grip, fingers twitching on the trigger guard.

"What the hell are you talking about?" I lean against the doorjamb and run my blurry vision around the small room, trying to determine if this is another setup.

"Murder, kidnapping, prostitution, racketeering. You name it. The only reason you're not locked up, and the key thrown away, is because I need some answers, and I need them now."

"If you wanted answers out of me, why didn't you just beat them out of me when you had me locked up in that damn shed?"

"Because I didn't have time for all that. If I'm going to save the life of your girlfriend…."

"She ain't my damn girlfriend!" I snap.

"… and your other friends, I had to put you on ice for a while."

"Well, you didn't have to shoot me! You could have just told me to shut up and chill until you came back."

"And let you get loose to go off and kill again?" Carl says, chuckling and shaking his head. "I don't think so."

"I haven't killed anyone!" I shout and take several quick steps across the room, my fist balled up tight and rising.

Carl draws his weapon and has it cocked and aimed before I see his arm move. I freeze without taking another breath, shocked at his speed.

"Watch it, boy. This time I'm not planning on aiming where you can stop a bullet. You ain't superman. Just someone I owe a now paid debt to. And as far as you not killing anyone, the evidence begs to differ."

Carl's eyes lock on me, the gun not wavering, the barrel pointing to a fleshy and unprotected part of my gut. I force my fingers to unlock and then release the breath I'd been holding. I retreat across the room to put distance between us. I turn to Carl; his body language has relaxed a hint, but the cold steel of his weapon hasn't changed. The Sheriff is still pointing the barrel at me; the hammer still set to kill. Holding my hands to show I'm not planning anything, I lower myself into a chair by the front windows.

"Carl, what's going on? Why this damn charade? You know as well as I do I haven't killed anyone." At least I felt fairly certain I hadn't killed anyone. "Man, we used to be…." I pause as images of us, like movie projector frames, unwind in my head. We are at the beach, posing atop a dune as a couple of girls laugh. Seconds later, I give Carl a shove that sends him toppling down the backside of the dune. The girls laugh harder, then the image dissolves like a film burned by a projector. "… friends."

A trace of a smile skates across Carl's face; his eyes flicker, losing some of their edge, then revert to their hard glare. "That was a very long time ago." He lowers the gun, sliding it back into the holster but not snapping it shut. Carl spins a barstool around and perches on it with his hands clasped, elbows resting on his thighs. He stares at me for some time without talking.

"Why'd you kill the hotel owner?"

"You mean that sick bastard behind the counter?"

Carl nods.

"I didn't kill him."

"Evidence says you did."

"What evidence?"

"One being a videotape of him shaking you down. We know he needled you out of a wad of cash. You looked none-too-happy."

"Lots of folks have pissed me off and I haven't killed any of them." Carl doesn't look persuaded in the least bit. "What happened to him?"

"You took a beer bottle, smashed it over his head, then sliced his throat with the neck. You then left him behind the desk where he bled out."

"Not me," I counter. "That fool was alive the last time I saw him,"

"Fingerprints on the bottle match fingerprints we have on file—your fingerprints, amigo."

"I had a couple of beers in my room. Somebody must have grabbed them from the garbage."

"And who might that be?" Carl asks, his voice hinting that he doesn't believe a damn thing I'm saying.

"Same sonofabitch who beat the shit out of me and threw me from a moving car!"

"Once again, who might that be?" he asks.

"I have no clue." Clenching the armrest of the old chair, the wood creaks under the pressure. "I can't remember shit since before last week. I'm just now getting any memories back at all. Ask Permillia and Sheila. They can vouch for me." I just realized that I didn't see Permillia's car when we arrived. "Where are they?"

Carl ignores my question and stares at me with utter condescension. "How do I know that they're not covering for you or that you're not making this story up?"

"Oh, for Christ's sake! You can't believe that I'm pulling this shit out of my ass as I go along, can you?"

Carl shrugs.

A bulb flickers in my head. "You said there's video of the man shaking me down." Carl smiles but says nothing. "What about the video of him being murdered?"

Carl's smile widens. "Funny you should ask. Apparently, someone pulled the plug on the camera just before the murder."

"Oh, c'mon, give me a break." I'm not making any headway. If anything, Carl appears more convinced of my guilt than ever. "Carl, about what time did the pervert at the hotel get offed?"

Carl's right eyebrow piqued with interest. "Coroner puts T.O.D. at about ten this morning."

"You sure?" I ask.

"Coroner says around ten this morning, give or take thirty minutes."

"I wasn't there and can prove it." I stretch, walk over to the door and stare toward the dusty road and the scrub oaks that line it. Robbie's battered El Camino is parked out front, but the lanky driver is nowhere to be seen. "Where's your cousin?"

"Why?"

"Because I was with him around eight this morning, caught a ride from the motel into town. Then I had breakfast around nine to nine-thirty. After that, I walked over to the bus stop. I was there until ten-thirty-ish."

"Why, trying to find a ride out of town?"

"No, you stupid prick, I was…." I pause and ask myself, what do I tell him he'll believe? The truth is what I lead with. "I was requested to meet someone there."

"Requested?"

"Yes, damn it, requested, asked, ordered. Whatever. Some fool slipped a note in with my breakfast, asking me to meet him or her at the bus stop a little after ten this morning."

"Who was it?" Carl asks, leaning heavily on his elbows, eyes becoming disinterested.

"No clue, they never showed."

"Have any idea what they wanted?"

"No. Like I said, whoever wrote the note didn't show." I'm about to tell Carl about the box and the threat but hold back.

"You sure?"

"Yes, damn it. If you don't believe me, ask your cousin. And you can ask Permillia about the coffee shop. Hell, you can ask the guy behind the counter at the bus station. He took a phone call for me. I'm sure he remembers me."

"Who called you?" Carl inquires, continuing the Q and A.

"What?" My brain hurts: the circling conversation is killing my head. I take a breath and realize I have just given up more information than I intended.

"The phone call! You said the person didn't show, and you didn't know what they wanted, but now you say someone called you. I want to know who called and what they wanted." Carl is now standing, his hands flat on his hips.

I lean back in my chair, rocking it on two legs, and stare at the ceiling for a moment before answering. I have just done a fine job of painting myself into a corner. Now I have to figure a way out. Taking a deep breath, I release my air at a measured pace, then let the chair settle to the floor. "He wanted me out of town."

"So, you were trying to leave." Carl accuses me, his eyes narrowing.

"If I was, we wouldn't be having this conversation." Carl nods in agreement.

"Like I said, I wasn't trying to skip town."

"Fine, whatever," Carl says quickly. "Why would someone want you out of town? To cover up your murders?"

"Goddamn it!" I ball my fist. "How many damn times do I have to tell you I haven't killed anyone! Ask the damn attendant if I was at the bus station. He should be able to identify me. Hell, I can even tell you what he was doing. He was circling the classified ads, looking for another shitty job."

"There's nothing I'd like to do more, but that's not possible."

"Why?" I ask, feeling the nerves in my back tighten.

"Someone bashed his head in with a mop handle. We found a blood-soaked John Deere cap, along with blood-soaked coveralls. We pulled the security tapes, and you'll never believe who we saw wearing similar coveralls and a hat with a John Deere logo."

"Surprise me," I say sarcastically. "I don't suppose the video showed who killed the attendant?"

"No," Carl replies after a moment's hesitation. "The attendant was killed in a maintenance area behind the ticket desk. Unfortunately, the cameras weren't working at that moment."

After shifting my stare to the ceiling, I walk to the front window, press my head against the glass, and gaze at the darkening sky. Rolling my head to the side, I peer at Carl from the corner of my eye. "Don't you find that suspicious? All the cameras capturing me all over the station, but the ones that would show the murder inexplicably quit working? Even if I'm as stupid as you think I am, I'm pretty sure I would have disabled the ones in the lobby as well. Plus, I've been with Permilla or locked in a damn shed since around eleven this morning."

Carl shrugs.

"Carl, I'm being framed." As soon as the words leap out of my mouth, I laugh and shake my head, realizing how stupid I sound.

"Framed? Wow, I don't think I've heard that before," he counters, a wry grin splitting his stoic expression. "Oh, Mr. Officer, I'm being framed, I'm being framed!" He sings and dances a little jig.

"Don't be such a dick. I'm serious. Someone is trying hard to set me up and has been for some time."

Carl sits back on the barstool and stares through me. "The way I figure it, you're involved—whether you had anything to do with them or not—in four murders and a disappearance."

"Four murders?" The number stuns me. "At last count, it was two. I guess I'm a bit more proficient at it than I thought. So, who else am I accused of killing?"

"A week ago, we found a burned-out car registered to you. There was a body in the trunk that had been shot through the head. His teeth were pulled, and the flesh was charcoal. We still haven't been able to pull an I.D. on the poor bastard."

"That one I know of."

Carl's eyes widen in surprise, and then he regains his composure. "Really? Interesting. We'll have to discuss that later."

"Who's the last one?"

"The last one we know of is a Kenneth Alcorn, twenty-seven, of Daytona Beach. A drifter. Alcorn had a few brushes with the law, primarily loitering and petty theft. You stabbed him in the throat and stashed him in a garbage bin at the bus station. We figured the attendant walked in on your attack and that's why you bashed his brains in."

"When the hell was I supposed to be doing all this? I can account for almost every minute of my day starting around eight this morning. Unless I can bend space and time, there ain't no way I could accomplish all that."

Carl spreads his arms. "It's not up to me to explain. It's up to you."

"Whatever happened to 'innocent until proven guilty'?" I shake my head. "According to you, I'm a one-man crime wave. So, illuminate me on the kidnapping. I'm just dying to hear about this one."

"You ready?"

"Sure, hit me with it."

Carl leans forward, his eyes narrowing on me. He splits his lips in a shark-like, teeth-baring snarl. "This one I know you're involved in." His hand dips down to the Taser hanging on his belt. "Claire contacted you three, maybe four weeks ago."

"Claire? You mean my ex?"

"Of course 'your ex'!" he stammers. "I told her to leave you the hell alone, that you're poison, that messing with you was gonna get her hurt. But she wouldn't listen to me, said that you—of all fuckin' people — was the only person she could trust."

His outburst stuns me. Ice water runs down my spine as my internal warning springs to life. "Assuming this is true...."

Carl's charge from halfway across the room interrupts me. "It's true, damn it! She sent you something, a package or a letter. Where is it? What'd you do with it?"

"... why the hell do you care?" I continue, ignoring Carl's ranting, but not the smell of alcohol on his breath.

"We were... an item," he mutters after a moment, his anger diminished.

That surprises me. "You and Claire?"

He ignores my question. My memories are fragmented and sparse, but what memories I have made me doubt Claire would be interested in this straight-laced, boring-ass cop. Unless she was toying with him. And from what I have learned so far, that I can believe.

"Jonesy, her cell phone records show that she's been calling you for weeks, day and night. You were working on something for her. I need to know what in the hell it was."

"Why? If she didn't go to you with it, it must be something she didn't want you involved in."

Carl closes in on me, the pistol in his hand. He appears more relaxed, but I can sense his mind is broiling under his calm exterior.

"Because," he says, "she's missing, and you're involved. Now I didn't risk my own life to buy your worthless ass a few extra days for nothing."

"That's what that little show at the pond was about, wasn't it? I'll be a sonofabitch! You faked my execution."

He ignores me.

"Permillia said that you saw Claire's body. So, you're going to tell me everything you know, and you're going to tell me now. Otherwise, I'm going to make your last few hours painful, very painful."

"So, you have been talking to Permillia," I say as a storm of fury builds. "You already know I couldn't have committed these murders." My breath is coming hot and fast. I want to grab the Sheriff by the lapels and bash his teeth out with my head. He must have sensed it as his hand tightens on his service weapon. We lock eyes, and his are manic, cold, and dangerous.

I calm the rage inside me and raise my arms in resignation. "Okay, fine. Where do you want me to start?"

"From the beginning."

Collecting my thoughts, I breathe in as deeply as possible, let it out slowly, and start talking.

Chapter Seventeen

I spoke for almost an hour with only a few interruptions, mostly on specific items Carl wanted to have clarified or for him to refill his glass of Jack Daniels. I began with my first memories, the items I found in my pocket, and running into Sheila. Then I recounted my trip to and events at the Dream Land motel. I finished with today's travels and the shootout at Permillia's house.

For the most part, Carl is silent, nodding as I tell my story. When I finish, I ask for a beer. Robbie, who has been listening and petting a very muddy Orville, fetches an ice-cold Bud from the fridge, and tosses it to me. Carl waits for me to drain half the beer before asking questions.

"There's something I don't understand." He says.

"Join the club," I reply and finish the icy brew. The bitter taste is refreshing.

"You haven't explained to me how the clothes you wore ended up at the station with the attendant's blood all over them."

"Before I answer that, can you tell me what this Alcorn dude was wearing when he was found?"

Carl stared at me for a moment with his hand cupping his chin, sizing up where I was going. "Just skivvies and a tee shirt. We found his duffel bag in a dumpster."

Staring out the window, I tap the empty beer can on my leg.

"Jonesy, I'm not a fool. I know you haven't told me everything. How's this Alcorn guy involved?"

I hesitate before answering, watching the trees sway in the late afternoon breeze. Searching for the right words, I turn back to Carl. "As you thought, there is a package, a shoe box. I didn't know about it until someone put a card with my toast, telling me to be at the depot at 10:15. The note had the time and J18 on it. At first, I figured it had something to do with a bus or parking spot. I didn't realize it was a locker.

"Once I figured that out, I remembered the key. I still have no clue how I ended up with it, but it fit. I found a box inside with my name on it. No return address or anything else. Just my name. I shook the package to see what might be in it. It sounded like papers. But I never had the chance to open it. I hid it in the station, figuring I'd come back for it. Up to now I haven't had the chance."

"So how does the drifter figure in?"

I explained the phone call, the bus ticket, and my plan to slip away. "I thought my plan had worked until Mr. X—the same guy who called me at the bus station— called me at Permillia's house, telling me that my plan with the drifter had failed, that the dumbass had caused some disturbance and gotten himself thrown off the bus."

"How'd these people know where to call you?"

Laughing, knowing what I was about to say would be poorly interpreted, I gave up trying to choose my words and just told him straight-up. "I called him."

"You what?" Carl practically exploded. "I thought you had this amnesia thing going on?"

"I do, but random memories are surfacing, and that is one of them. I didn't know who I was calling, just that it might help. Instead, it has made shit worse."

"I'll say it's made things worse," Carl mutters as he scratches the bottom of his chin. "Those men work—or worked—for Milford Parson."

Carl must have noticed the blank expression on my face. "Son of Rockford Parson, the senator and former ambassador to Panama?" Carl shakes his head. "Damn, you are denser than a stump. Anyway, Milford is the black-sheep of the family; daddy's been trying to straighten him up for years. The boy's into interstate trucking, ties with organized crime, you name it. If you've stepped on his toes, you've done stirred up a whole hornet's nest of trouble."

"Not just me, but Claire as well."

"Yes, her too," Carl echoes in a whisper. "Christ, what has that girl gone off and started? You sure she's dead?"

"I'm sure whoever I found is dead. A bloody red and black hole in the middle of your forehead is usually fatal. But as for it being Claire?" I shake my head. "Hell, I don't know, man. I don't have any current memories of her, and only a picture to go by. Add to that, it was dark and raining. Only light I had was the zippo, and I only had a few seconds to look at her. I quit talking and offered a resigned smile. "When I later went back and there wasn't any blood, or crime tape… I don't know."

Carl is pacing around the small room, his eyes fixed and faraway. "I need to know whether or not it was her."

We sit silently in the room, watching the wind stir the leafless trees outside the cabin. A wall clock slowly ticks the minutes away as the sun dips lower on the horizon. "I need to get that package and open it," Carl says, breaking the silence. He stares at me as if I have all his answers.

"I'm sure they tore that damn station apart trying to find the box. I wager the attendant caught them and they killed him to keep him quiet. I assume the station's locked up tight?"

Carl nods it is. "We've secured the building. All the inbound buses have been rerouted and the forensic boys are crawling all over the place." He removes his Sheriff's Department ball cap and scratches his head. "Any chance you hid that box well enough that it hasn't been found?"

"I don't know. Maybe. I didn't have much time to think. I just stuffed it in the first place I could think of."

"Where's that?"

I smile, thinking about how much fun the men searching for the box would have retrieving it from its hidey-hole, and tell Carl about the location.

"And that's the best you could come up with?"

"If I'd known my ass was being hunted up one side of town and down the other, I'd come up with something else. If your goons hadn't run me down, I'd be on my way to retrieving it."

"First, they ain't my goons. They're damn good deputies doing their job."

"Then tell me something. How the hell did they know where I was? They seemed to show up minutes after Milford's men."

"We got a tip that there was trouble out there, and I sent a couple of deputies to check it out. Nothing more than that." Carl set his gaze on me. "Did you kill those men? Brain one with a bat and shoot the other? We could tie you to those deaths as well."

I wave away the accusation. "Get real. It was self-defense, and you know it." I walk to the door, lean against the door frame, and watch the last vestiges of the sun fade beneath the top of the pines. "I've opened up and told you everything I know. Now it's time for you to come clean."

"What the fuck do you mean?" Carl snaps.

"Oh, come on! Don't play all innocent and blameless. You're up to your eyeballs in this… whatever the hell it is."

"Just because I save your ass for a few more hours don't mean I'm messed up in jack-shit."

"What about the kids Robbie keeps finding? He says he gets an email with G.P.S. coordinates. I find it fascinating that you send him the same damn thing to find me! Interested in shedding some light on that?"

Carl draws his gun and races across the room, his face turning a deeper scarlet with each step. Pointing the Glock between my eyes, he says, "Shut the fuck up, damn it! You don't know what the hell you're talking about. Keep running your mouth and I'll make sure it extends out the back of your head!"

"Do it! Pull the damn trigger." I force my words through clenched teeth. "But if you do, you'll never find out if Claire's dead." I grab him by the wrist, pulling the gun against my forehead. Carl barely resists. I spread my arms wide, giving him a clear shot. "I guarantee you that if she's alive, you'll never see her again. The reason she came to me is that she doesn't trust you. She's scared of you, or what you have become." I stare straight down the flat-black muzzle and into Carl's accusing eyes.

"There's no way in hell you can know that!"

Gotta point there, you bastard. "Guess the only way to know is to find Claire,"

Carl jerks the gun away and holsters it. "I thought you said she was dead."

"I said 'I thought she was'. But I think I have an airtight way to find out."

"What are you talking about?" Carl asks, his eyes softening but coated with a wary veneer.

"One thing I didn't tell you is that before I discovered the body, I found a finger. A severed finger." The fiery blush vanished from Carl's face, giving way to cold shock. "In my pocket, wrapped in a cigarette pack. There was also a photo with it, a picture of a blond chick with a bullet in her skull."

"Was it her?" Carl asks.

"Claire or the woman in the alley?"

"Either."

"I don't know. The image looked a helluva lot like the woman in the alley, but whether that woman is Claire…." I shrugged.

Once again, a heavy silence settles over the room. The clock over the stove continues to tick away the minutes.

"I assume you have her prints on file?" Robbie asks.

Carl stares at Robbie before nodding.

Robbie shakes his head. "I figured you did."

"Carl, you're a real piece of shit," I snort. "What do you do, collect D.N.A. on everyone you date?" I wave off the statement. "Forget it. Let's match what you have with the finger."

A glimmer comes into Carl's eyes. "Which finger was it?"

I concentrate on the body's position and her hands. "Right index finger, I think. But it could have been from her left hand. I only had a split second before the lighter went out. Why does it matter?"

"She keeps breaking the nail on her right index finger. She has a habit of poking people in the chest to get her point across. So, she keeps that nail short, saves on breaking it."

"I can't recall the length."

"If you've left it somewhere, it's no good now. It's probably been eaten by maggots or just rotted away."

I shake my head. "It should be fine."

"What'd you do, stuff it in a freezer?" Carl scoffs.

I allow a fleeting smile. "As a matter of fact, I did."

Carl's body language changes: it is now almost hopeful. He crosses his arms and cups his chin. "Where'd you leave it?"

"A safe place. It'll keep for a while," I say. "Why, you wanna go take a print now? See what you can find out?"

"Of course!"

"Your 'knowing' might kill her."

"What the hell is that supposed to mean?" Carl's voice was cold, on edge again.

"You know what the hell I mean." I was tired of this pussyfooting around. "Someone's knocking off kids around here, and you know something. I'm not telling you a damn thing until you open up on what Claire was working on." I advance on him in two quick strides. We now stand toe-to-toe. I'm half expecting to see his hand reach for the Glock. Instead, he sighs heavily, drops into a chair, and stares out the door.

"Robbie, your radiator's leaking, boy. There's a huge-ass puddle under your truck. Before you fry the motor, go fill your radiator."

"My truck's not leaking," Robbie argues before Carl slams a palm down on the arm of the chair. "Go put some damn water in your truck before you blow it up."

Finally taking the hint, Robbie sighs and starts for the door.

"Boy's the greatest tracker you ever seen. It's like some kind of weird E.S.P. That geeky kid can track with his eyes closed. It's the most unbelievable thing you ever saw. But when it comes to machines, kid ain't got a clue."

I step out of the way to let Robbie pass. The moment he does, I shut the door and turn the deadbolt.

"Okay, talk."

Carl leans back in the worn leather chair. He takes his hat off, pulls his weapon out, and sets it on a small table. "And if you don't mind," he points toward the kitchen counter, "there's a bottle of Jack up there. How about tossing it to me?"

"Want a glass?" I retrieve the half-full bottle.

"Nope. Sometimes you just gotta take it like a man."

I toss him the bottle, which he catches with ease. He unscrews the cap, takes a quick slug, then a second that makes him grimace. "Good stuff, that Jack. Mighty good, in fact."

"Let me give you some background on what has been going on, then I'll tell you what I know." He tips the bottle once more, coughs, then sets the bottle on the table and talks.

Chapter Eighteen

"Y'know, a sheriff don't make all that much money."

It is a statement, one that doesn't elicit further comment. I offer a quick nod of agreement.

"Oh sure, we get a company car, insurance, a few friendly perks," he chuckles, then lets the laugh die. "But it's also twenty-four seven. Neighbors are always knocking on my door or stopping me in the store to ask what they should do because their dumbass, drunken, shit-for-brains husband done slapped them around a bit. I tell them to file a report, get a restraining order… yada, yada, fuckin' yada." He waves his hand around as if conducting his own personal pity party.

Carl rolls the bottle around on the edge of the chair arm, threatening to spill the liquor. "Women only want you because you make them feel safe," he finishes in a child-like voice. "But they're afraid of your gun, of your attitude," he sneers, stares down at the bottle, then continues. "Scared of every damn thing that makes you a good cop." Carl lifts the bottle and drains another half-inch.

"And then someone like Claire comes along. She in all her southern charm and acid-sharp journalistic mind." Carl stops talking and gazes through me, his hand clenching and unclenching around the neck of the bourbon. "Woman could hold her liquor about as good as anyone, used to drink men under the table to get a story. I don't know how she did it, but I saw her do it more than once."

Carl's eyes take on a faraway expression as he pauses.

"That's all fine and dandy," I prod, "but you're wasting time." I stand, pull back the cheap curtain, and watch as the last of the day's light slides out of view.

Carl nods and sighs. "Like I said, me and Claire started seeing each other, casually at first. I knew I was in over my head the first time we met up. She suggested Simeon's down on Lake Plantain. Expensive joint, you know?"

I shake my head. My current memories didn't offer any kind of recollection.

"Well, it is," Carl continues. "They have valet parking, coat-check, tuxedoed maître d`. I spent more that evening than I do in a month. But I didn't mind. With Claire on my arm, I'd gladly mortgage my house."

"And did you?" I ask, feeling confident this man would drain all his accounts and those of his kids, if he had any, to keep up with this woman.

He smiles sheepishly. "My savings, my truck, my 401k plan…" he trails off, leans forward, and massages the top of his head with his hands. "It was all gone before I knew it, maybe thirty, thirty-five grand in all."

"Did she drain you on purpose?" I am feeling a cross between sympathy and disgust. The thought of a man driving himself to bankruptcy for a woman leaves a bitter taste in my throat.

"No, not really. I was happy to pretend we were on the same level." He leans back, puts a cap on the Jack Daniel's, knocks on the right armrest with his fist, and laughs. "Then things went downhill."

Carl's eyes droop, the quarter bottle of bourbon hitting its stride. If I can keep him talking, I can peel back a few more layers of this mystery. "So, what happened?"

Carl makes a fist and a movement like he is jacking off.

"She dumps you and you revert to being twelve with a Victoria's Secrets catalog?"

He snorts, "No, jerk. I hit the tables in Biloxi and Cherokee, gambled the last of my 401k, cashed in the few stocks I had… lost my house." Carl takes a deep breath, holds it, and leans back hard in the chair. "You know what makes for good hyena bait?"

That stops me in my tracks. "We're still talking about you and Claire, right? You're not taking the goofy-trolley down some fucked-up memory lane, are you?"

He smiles, not answering my question. "Broke cops. They make the best damn hyena bait. I was put on a fishing line and tossed out like a badge-wearing shiner." Carl is now in his own world, having slipped from the conversation in the past few minutes. He pantomimes baiting a hook, casting a line, and then reeling it in.

"You can handle the first few nibbles; you've got your principles and all that crap. Y'know what I mean?"

I respond with a slow shake of my head, having no idea where he is going. "They sting at first, don't let a worm tell you different." he cackles, then wipes the side of his mouth with the sleeve of his shirt. "I was broke, catching rides for a week, telling everyone the motor in my truck soured. Told them I was thinking about buying something new, something with a little panache. But after a while, that story fell apart." He glances at me and crosses his arms over his chest.

"Then deputies from my department show up to serve the eviction papers! Can you believe that shit? No courtesy call, not even a fuckin' kiss." Carl's face quivers in anger and turns scarlet. He again clenches the bourbon bottle by the neck, draws it back like he is going to hurl it through the window, then drops it to the floor.

He's quiet for a few minutes, the muscles in his arms contracting and twitching.

"That's when the hyenas showed up," he says in a quiet voice. "I could hear 'em sniffing around the edge of my yard, nosing around my garbage can, watching me from the shadows." He pauses and makes direct eye contact with me, his eyes clear and narrow as he bares his teeth and grinds them from side to side.

Damn, if he doesn't look like a hyena, it sends tingles up my spine. Carl sighs and loses focus once again.

"So, who called in the hyenas?" I ask; not sure where he is leading, but I suspect it's a career-ending event.

"You should know." He slurs and crosses his arms over his chest.

"Nope, don't have a clue. Maybe you should chill for a few minutes, lay off the Jack until your head clears."

"Like you care," he snorts and reaches down for the bottle, finally grabbing it on the third attempt. He spins off the lid, and another quarter-inch disappears.

"I don't. But if you pass out, I'm not going to get another thing out of you until you sober up." Carl cradles the bottle to his chest and strokes it like a baby. "These hyenas, do they happen to be part of the Mutt and Jeff routine that ambushed me earlier?"

Carl tips the bottle toward me in confirmation, then clutches it to his chest. "The same. Cop gets into money trouble, and his problems are just beginning." Carl tries to lift the bottle to his lips. I dart forward, trying to snatch it from him. He rolls to the side and tucks it between himself and the arm of the chair.

"And they, what, make you fix a few tickets, turn a blind-eye on a couple of hookers working out of the truck stop?"

"Somethin' like that," he slurs, his tongue thickening

"Something like what?" I press, sensing that I am getting close to what is going on. But I will get nothing else out of him. The bottle drops from Carl's grasp and rolls across the floor, pouring out the last of the liquor. "Sonofabitch," I growl. Carl's eyelids close as he slumps in the chair.

"C'mon, don't do this to me!" I snap my fingers in front of him, then slap his cheek. Carl's only reaction is a soft snore. "Shit!" I try to shake him back to consciousness without success. Jack has won this battle, and I won't get anything out of him for another eight hours.

I walk over to the door, unlock it, and lean against the frame with my fist on my hips. I'm thinking about what to do next when I hear a deep, menacing growl. Robbie, standing just outside the door, calls to his dog and then to his cousin.

"Carl's out like a light, man. He's practically comatose."

"Well, we've got company coming." Robbie rocks back and forth on the balls of his feet, eyes dancing between the distant headlights and the cabin.

"Who's coming?"

"Help me toss Carl in my truck," Robbie says without answering. He rushes through the door and tries to pull Carl upright. "C'mon, I can't do this by myself."

"What's the hurry? Just let him sleep it off."

"No!" Robbie snaps. "We can't leave him here. They'll kill him the second they see him."

"Who?" I run over, grab Carl's weapon, and slide an arm around the drunk officer's shoulder. Together, Robbie and I drag Carl out of the cabin and shove him into the truck's cab as Robbie whistles for Orville. The lab jumps into the bed of the El Camino; the hair on the dog's neck stands up, its ears lowered, and the happy-go-lucky gait is gone.

Robbie fumbles with his keys as the headlights, which the trees obscured only moments before, are now pushing over the hilltop. I see several flashes burst from the approaching vehicle, followed by two more. His side mirror explodes in a glass shower as something slams into the pillar behind my head.

"Anytime soon would be good!" I turn and stare out the back of the cab. The other vehicle slides to a stop about forty feet behind us; the doors pop open and disgorge a quartet of shadows.

Robbie stabs the key in the ignition, twists it forward, and floors the accelerator. The motor backfires like a howitzer, causing the shadows to duck. Robbie wrenches the gearshift into drive and punches the accelerator to the floor. The truck leaps toward a black wall of trees lining the horizon as a swarm of lead-based hornets scream past my window.

I grab Carl's sidearm, bracing myself out the window, and fire off a trio of rounds. There's no way I could hit a

cruise ship the way we were rocking. But I had to slow
those guys down. We swerve around a tree stump large
enough to park a tractor on and rocket downhill toward
the woods, the truck twisting and turning blind corkscrew
maneuvers. We flash across a cleared field illuminated
only by a half-moon. Heavy brush and thickets scrape
along the fenders as we drive without lights.

"Can you see where the hell you're going?" I yell
over the engine's roar and the truck's crashing through
the undergrowth.

"No better than you can!" Robbie hollers back. The
truck's rear jumps out behind us, casting Carl face down
across my lap, his head resting between my knees. I can't
help him, not without being thrown from the seat. He'll
have to ride that way until he revives, or we lose our
pursuers.

Robbie gathers the truck back up and again floors
the accelerator. We crest a small hill, and I there's the
sensation of being airborne. We slam down hard; the
suspension bottoming out as bits of crap inside the truck
bounce off the ceiling. Suddenly the ride smooth's out,
and our speed increases.

"Where are we?" I ask, pushing Carl back to an
upright position.

"We're on Dogger Creek Bridge Road. It runs the
backside of the cabin, then to the river and back into
town."

I glance over my shoulder to check on our chasers.
"I think we lost them."

Robbie nods and flips the headlights on.

I gaze out the windshield, watching the needle-
covered road bend to the right, deeper into the woods.

"That was some hellacious driving back there, man." I reach over Carl and give Robbie an appreciative squeeze on the shoulder. "Damn good driving. You saved our ass big-time."

Robbie smiles. "Ain't nothing to it. Me and Orvy's done that drive lots of times. Usually not while being shot at."

"Your dog!" I gasp, having forgotten about the mongrel in our escape.

"Relax," he says and flips a switch on the dash that illuminates the bed. "Orvy knows what to do."

I glance back, and there's the dog curled up beside the spare tire and the cab, his snout resting between his feet. He glances up at me, yawns, and curls back up. "So, where are we heading?"

"A place that's safe."

"Safer than your cabin?" I ask as we drive along the moon-swept road.

"Hope so," he says with little conviction.

"I thought Permillia was supposed to be at your cabin?"

Robbie nods slightly before answering. "That was the original plan."

"Where did they go?"

"Don't know. Carl must have sent them on."

"Any idea why?"

Robbie shakes his head. "He must have had his reasons." He turns up the radio volume as Van Halen's Runnin' with the Devil blares from the speakers. How so fuckin' apropos.

Chapter Nineteen

We drive for over an hour, winding down one back road after another with only the sound of the engine for conversation. Finally, we bounced along a rutted drive that terminates at an abandoned farm. A rusting windmill lists hard to the south, creaking in an icy wind. The barn and original homestead are barely visible in the moonlight. Both roofs are caved in, and dark, glassless windows peer from the house toward the drive.

"Where are we?" I'm completely and utterly lost.

"The old Winston Fulmer farm. Old man Fulmer got busted back in the forties for running moonshine. His kids took over and never did nothin' with it. I don't know who owns it now, but it's been abandoned for as long as I can remember, maybe thirty years or more."

Robbie picks his way down the choked drive, past the dying barn, and toward a row of decaying chicken coups.

We pull up beside a pile of tin that could have been a shed an eon ago. Robbie cuts the motor, and we sit for a few minutes listening to the tinkling of the engine as it cools.

"I take it this is where we're to meet up?"

Robbie nods as he squints toward the darkened hen houses. "This is our fallback position."

"Could you guys not find another place to meet, somewhere not so desolate?" I ask in a hushed voice, not sure why I am whispering.

"Permillia's son suggested it. We've shot some quail here before, nice big fat ones. We ain't never seen another person. There's also no cell service. Heck, you can hardly get a radio to work here."

We sit for a moment. I turn and stare at the driver. "So… what's next? Do you know where they are?"

"They're supposed to flick a light back at us."

"Well, they haven't." I open the door. "Let's go find out what's going on." I stretch, my back popping and cracking. Holding the door open, I point to Carl. "I guess we'll leave sleeping beauty in the truck." Robbie chuckles and pats Carl's shoulder in agreement.

I hear Orville jump from the bed and disappear into the tall grass.

The moon is waning, a weak sliver of white, providing just enough light to see by. We push through the bramble and skirt pieces of rust-frozen equipment.

"Place is eerie as hell." I say in a muffled voice. "All we need is an owl hooting in a dead oak tree to be part of many slasher films."

"Place is spooky enough without you conjuring up the dead," Robbie whispers back as the sound of a door being shut startles us.

"Shh," I say, motioning him down. Staying low, I side-step over rotten wood planks and approach the closest chicken house. I keep to the dark shadows, allowing the rustling brush to cover my footsteps. Robbie glides up to me, quieter than a ghost in spectral slippers. With a tilt of his head, he shows a section of siding thirty feet away that has been pulled loose from the structure.

I give him a thumbs-up and drift along the edge of the house, keeping out of sight. I hold my breath and concentrate on hearing sounds from inside the building. The coop is quiet. I slip my fingers under the galvanized sheeting and pull it open. As soon as the opening is wide enough for my shoulders to fit through, I peek inside.

A heavy piece of cold steel meets me halfway in and presses against my forehead. Before I can react, someone grabs me by the front of my coat and jerks me into the dilapidated building.

The stealth I was trying to emulate is lost when I crash into stacks of metal barrels and sprawl on the dirt floor. Robbie's squawk of concern finishes our attempt to arrive undetected.

"Jonesy!" a woman's voice cries out. "Thank God you're alive!"

A yellow glow-stick warms to life, held high by Permillia. "E-Lee, put that gun away before you kill someone."

"Okay, mama," he says, retreating out of sight.

Permillia holds the light higher so Robbie and Orville can navigate the maze of overturned fifty-gallon drums and pipes. "Son, what in the world have you got us involved in?"

I climb to my feet. "First, let me say that I'm damn glad you're okay. I didn't know what had happened to you." I pause and brush dirt off the front of my pants. "And I'm really sorry I got you involved in this… crap. It seems that the more people I come in contact with, the more people that get sucked in. All I wanted to do was find out who I am and what was going on."

"And what've you figured out? Anything?" This time, Sheila asks the questions, trudging from the shadows, shaking a second and third glow-stick to life.

She hangs the tubes from a galvanized pipe running the length of the building. The room glows in the diffused, hazy chemical light of the sticks. She stands with her hands crossed tightly over her chest, hugging herself. Apparently, it is her favorite way to stand.

I shrug and reply. "A little, but not much. I'm still not sure what all's going on, but I have a much better picture than I did. And what I know is this: someone around here is killing, or trying to kill, girls, young women." I hear gasps of surprise. "Claire must have stumbled onto it and asked for my help. I think that's the main reason she's gone missing, and for someone punting me out of a moving car."

"You have got to be kidding!" Sheila says, her voice low and laced with disbelief. "How do you continue to come up with this crap? If they were finding bodies of dead women around here, I think we'd have heard about it."

I righted a rusted orange drum and sat up on it. It made a dull ring when my heels tapped on the side. I cringe at the sound. For people trying to hide, we've made enough noise to attract the attention of a deaf mute.

"Not if it's being swept under the rug, you wouldn't."

"But there would be people looking for these women, for Christ's sake!" Sheila's eyes take on a haunted gaze. "People just don't disappear," she finishes, her voice dropping to a near whisper.

"Tell that to Claire," I counter. "And they can disappear if no one knows they're missing. If it were local kids, then yeah, the entire town would stomp through every creek bed, pond, and hillside. They'd unplow a farmer's field if they thought someone might be hidden beneath the cotton and soybeans. But I don't think these are local girls."

"But you don't have any proof?" Sheila's eyes regain some fire, challenging me.

"Unfortunately, I do." I nod to Robbie, who has stayed out of the festivities by sitting against the side of the building, hiding in the dark. "Tell them what you know."

Robbie shakes his head.

"Tell them now, boy." I kick a scrap of wood in his direction; it bounces off the wooden crate he is sitting on.

Robbie climbs to his feet with all the speed of one approaching the gallows.

"What he says is true," Robbie begins hesitantly, cupping his hand over his mouth. "There's been bodies… girls' bodies." His voice is a near whisper, as if the muffled words would lessen the impact. "All but a couple of them dead…strangled, I think. Me and Orvy have been finding them for about a year, first only one or two, but a lot more lately."

Sheila walks forward. I can almost feel the heat from her as she glares at Robbie. "These girls, how do you find them if no one knows that they're missing?"

Robbie glances my way, and I motion for him to continue. "One day, I got a call from the Sheriff's department, didn't know who it was, never found out. But they knew me and Orvy and what we do. They said there's a missing teenager in the woods and that they knew the area where they believe she was. They asked me if I wanted to run Orvy out there, just to 'help them clear part of their grid', you know, eliminate some areas to search. I figured Carl told them to call, so I said, 'sure, we hadn't had time to do much searching lately and it was a nice day to be in the woods'. I thought nothin' of it." He casts his eyes around the room, the whites looking sick and yellow in the dim light. He licks his lips and takes a deep breath.

"But when I looked it up on the map, it was like way out in the middle of nowhere. I just kept thinking, how in the world did they get out there? There ain't no road, barely even trails for them to follow. This person was about as deep as you can get in the Blackroot Forest. I knew a few old logging roads we could start down, so we headed off." Robbie quits talking, bites his bottom lip, and sits back down on his crate. With a sad and excessively long sigh, Orville drags himself up, traipses over to his master's side, and drops his head at Robbie's feet, his brown eyes staring up at his friend.

"You found someone, didn't you, Robbie?" Permillia asks, her voice gentle.

"Yes, ma'am," he says in a whisper.

Permillia clasps her hands as if praying and holds them to her face. "Did you recognize her?"

Robbie shakes his head and doesn't speak for a long minute. "She…" his voice cracks when he tries. "She was too beat up… her face caked in blood, her eyes were open and staring up at the sky. Flies were buzzing around her."

I look over at the women. Sheila is shaking, staring at nothing. Permillia's hands cover half of her face as if she is in pain. It is my turn to ask questions.

"Robbie, what else did you see?"

He turns to me, his face wet with tears. At first, he just shakes his head, saying nothing. Then a weak smile parts his lips. "I, uh, didn't see anything for a while." Robbie squirms a bit. "I fainted and didn't wake until I heard Orvy whining. I then jumped to my feet and ran as fast as I could until I found my truck." He brushes his hand nervously over his head, straightening his hair. "Then I called Carl about what I had found and gave him the G.P.S. coordinates."

"What did he do?" I ask, curious how deep his involvement went.

"I'll tell you what I did," Carl says as he makes his way through the makeshift door, answering for Robbie and startling the shit out of me. "I got Robbie the hell out of there and called the coroner. After that, I went back to work."

Chapter Twenty

"Who the hell was it?" I sputter, still in shock at Carl's sudden wobbly appearance.

"Don't know." Carl catches his balance against a pole supporting the rusted roof. The yellow glow sticks reflect eerily on his bloodshot eyes. He staggers to a drum beside Robbie, rights it, and sits. "And we never found out. Her prints didn't come up on any database, dental records the same. The coroner listed her as a Jane Doe. We ran a composite of her on the wires but never got a hit. Eventually, her body was cremated and buried in the county cemetery."

Sheila covers her face with her hands, then pulls the fingers down far enough to stare over the tips with dark-lined eyes. "And what about the other girls? Were they treated the same, just burned like trash and thrown in the landfill?"

Carl's shrug answers the question. "Some… most… were done just that way. Not buried in the landfill, but out in the county cemetery. We never had a hit on any of them. And believe me, I busted my ass trying to figure out who they were."

"You didn't try hard enough," Sheila replies, forcing the words through a tightened jaw.

Carl dismisses her comment with a wave of his hand and leans forward, resting his elbows on his knees. "After they found the fourth kid, they took me off the investigations and the State folks took over."

"How'd you get involved?" I toss my question toward Robbie.

Before the boy can answer, Carl puts his hand over Robbie's chest, pushing him back and out of the line of questioning. "I got him involved, that's how. They asked me to drop the investigations, but sometimes I don't hear too well. And I needed some help. Nobody knows these woods, streams, and rivers like this kid. And I didn't just drop the case as ordered. Do you think I'd let the State boys run the show, cover everything up, and let more girls die? Hell, we even saved a couple." Carl nods toward Robbie and gives him a 'thumbs up.' The Sheriff then yawns and droops.

"What happened when you talked with the girls?" Permillia asks. "Surely they had more information."

"You would have thought so," Carl says. "The ones that could speak English were too terrified to talk. The ones that couldn't…." Carl trails off, not adding anything else.

The sensation of a timer ticking down grows stronger. I asked my questions as fast as possible, hoping to swerve into some form of the truth before Carl passed out again. "Answer a couple of questions for me: Who is killing these girls, why are they being killed, and how were you able to find them and nothing gets leaked to the papers?"

Carl glances up, his eyes like twin stop signs. "Actually, that's four questions, but here's your answers." He sits up straighter, pulls at his shirt to smooth out the creases, and tries to focus. "The first girl was suspicious as hell; I mean, how the hell do you get beaten to death that deep in the woods? That was strange enough. She was obviously not from around here, and I don't just mean Waynesville. I'm talking not from Alabama or the Good ol' U.S. of A."

Carl has our attention. No one bothers to speak or move. "This girl looked Asian, not like the cutie-pie Barbie dolls we have around here. She was very thin, almost gaunt. And definitely, not some college kid tossing off her degree for cheap shits and giggles." Carl stretches and yawns. "Coroner put her age in the mid-twenties."

"What didn't get in the coroner's report—and this bugged the shit out of me—is the fact that she'd had multiple partners that day or previous night."

"She was a hooker?" I didn't expect that little nugget.

"Don't know, most working girls have their johns use protection. But this kid had either partied hard or been used to party with."

"Sex slave?"

"That's my guess, but I couldn't get Mitchell—that's Derek Mitchell, county coroner—to comment on it. Hell, he wouldn't even put the D.N.A. we found into his report. He just filed it with the State. When I brought it up, he said that the files were sealed and out of his hands."

"What about the other girls?"

"Same thing. All were foreign—Hispanic, Asian, Middle Eastern—and all were beaten, strangled, or drowned. Some all the above." A minuscule shudder runs down Carl's back. I don't think he wanted us to notice it, and he played it off well. The man might have a shred of compassion in him.

"And the coroner. What did he report?" I ask, even though I already know the answer.

"Same thing. Cause of death, either blunt force or strangulation. No report on toxins or assault. After a while, I quit pressing."

"Where's this guy now? Maybe if we drag his ass out here, we can get him to talk."

Carl snorts, letting a sick smile crease his face. "Nothing I'd like to do more. Unfortunately, there's one problem."

I feel my gut sink, a feeling that is happening more and more lately.

"That being?"

"We can't find him. He disappeared about a month ago. I've tried to locate him, but he's just vanished, gone."

That nagging, tingling instinct flares to life like a long-forgotten memory awakened by a scent. I walk a slow circle, scratching my head and stirring the dusty floor with my foot.

"What are you thinking?" Carl asks, rising to block my path. "I've seen you do this before while working a case."

"I'm not sure… just trying to sort out some things." I stare over his shoulder into the gloom at the rear of the building. "Did y'all ever I.D. that body you found in that burned-out Crown Vic?"

"What are you talking about?"

"The burned-out Ford at the stadium. There was a body in the trunk, burned to a crisp. Toasted along with the car."

"You think that's our old coroner? He vanished long before that car showed up."

I rub my hands together hard, warming my palms. "Don't mean they didn't keep him on ice, then cut him loose along with the car. He could have been dead since he disappeared. Nice way to destroy the body and throw everyone off track."

Carl shows his acquiescence by pursing his lips and nodding slowly. "Last I heard, we still had nothing on that body. All we have is that the car was registered to you. Kind of funny, huh?"

"Yeah, a real gas," I say while continuing to circle. "Was Mitchell feeding you info?"

"Yeah, some," Carl confirms. "But once the State boys took over, it was like pulling teeth to get anything out of him. He clammed up tighter than a nun's…." He pauses when he notices Permillia and Sheila glaring at him. "Never mind. You get the point."

I have nothing to add, and neither does Carl. We sit in silence for the better part of twenty minutes. One by one, we sink to the ground until we are all either sitting in the dirt or leaning against a drum or wall. No one speaks. We listen to the wind brush against the sides of the building.

Carl breaks the silence. "We need that damn box, Jonesy. I'd bet my ass against a box of doughnuts that it has all the answers. I hope you did a better job of hiding it than you let on."

I nod and glance at the tired, worn-out faces, hoping that Carl is right. "Is the station still locked up tight?"

"I'm sure it is. We'll keep it sealed up like a drum for the next few days."

"Well," I say, turning to face in the station's direction, "how are we supposed to get in? Can anyone pick a lock?"

"Like you don't know." Sheila snorts.

"Like I don't know—what?" Even though this woman is hot in a pouty, needy kind of way, she is starting to bug the shit out of me.

"Jonesy, how many times did you break into the liquor cabinet at the bar when you were out of money? How about all the time!"

"Really?"

Sheila rolls her eyes and stares at the ceiling. "Really!" She laughs with no joy, her words heavy with scorn. "It wasn't hard to find who had been draining the bottles, because you'd be passed out in the lobby, sleeping on a bench."

"That doesn't sound a bit like me," I say, winking at Permillia. She doesn't crack a smile. So, I clasp my hands, crack my knuckles, and survey the room. All eyes are on me. "Well, I can't go back for it. So far, I haven't been able to shake the bastards chasing me."

"I might have a way in."

I turn to Permillia, the last person I would have expected to speak. "You? How?"

"There's a dumpster shared by the bus station and a couple of businesses. A.J.'s garbage service collects there during the week, around three in the morning. It's one of their first stops. They always drive down the alley behind the station on their way through town. You can jump off the truck as they pass the rear of the station. There're no lights back there, you won't be seen."

I cross my arms over my chest, rub my eyes with the palms of my hands, and think about it. "Sounds possible. But how do you know this?"

"For one thing, E-Lee worked a summer with them a while back. And A.J.'s been coming to the diner for years.

He's a good guy and owes me a big favor—I've comped him a few meals over the years. And he's always trying to find good help for his overnight shift. I'll call him and tell him to put you on his crew for tonight. He won't ask questions. Then you break in and get the box."

"But that still doesn't get him into the building," Robbie says.

Carl steps forward. "Yeah, it does. There's a roll-up door by the maintenance bay on the backside of the building. Like Permillia said, there's enough cover there to hide anyone trying to pop the door open." He kneels and sketches a quick diagram on the dirt floor. "I've driven around the building many times. You should be able to get in without being seen."

"Okay," I say, rubbing my palms together, trying to siphon off heat from the friction. The building is getting colder. "Just a couple of minor, nagging problems."

"Like what?" Carl asks, having turned my way.

"I don't have any lock-pick tools with me, and I'm not sure I can remember how to do it."

"You'll remember. You were too damn good at it to forget. What about your car? You used to always keep burglar tools in your trunk."

"That's possible, except for the fact…."

"That you don't know where your car is?" Carl finishes for me.

I shake my head. "Not a clue. Couldn't even tell you what color, make or model it is."

"So, what do we do next?" Permillia queries, twisting around and stretching.

"For now, E-Lee, Robbie, and Sheila need to stay here, keep quiet and try to stay warm. E-Lee's got a gun.

Protect yourself. Don't be afraid to pull the trigger." After a moment, I glance at Carl, who agrees with me with a quick tilt of his head. "The three of us will drive down the road to the first spot we can get a cell phone signal. If she can arrange everything, we'll return and drop Permillia. Then we'll head toward town."

"How are you going to get into the building?" Sheila asks, her voice calm but tired.

"Don't know. Guess I'll cross that bridge when I get there." I lean toward Carl. "You ready?"

He takes a deep breath and claps his hands together. "As ready as I'm gonna get."

The three of us exit the rear of the building and climb into Permillia's Chevy. I drive out slowly with the lights off, concentrating on winding my way down the overgrown field without colliding with the mounds of abandoned equipment and debris. The feeble light cast by the moon helps us navigate. We then turn onto the old highway as clouds swallow the last of the dying moonlight.

Chapter Twenty-One

There is no conversation as we drive, each to our thoughts. Ten minutes after we leave the farm, Permillia leans forward over the front seat and says, "I've got a good signal. I'll call A.J. from here."

I pull over and turn up the heat. The air is turning colder, brittle. The chicken house has to be below freezing. Permillia's call is quick and to the point with scant explanation.

"Everything set?" I ask, surprised at how easily she is able to complete her task.

"Yes, he said to be at his place by midnight, and that he'd have a set of coveralls hanging on the back of a truck. He said, slip them on, so you'll match. He'll give you the basics. Once he drops you off, you're on your own. He won't be coming back."

"He didn't ask questions?"

"No," Permillia answers, sinking back against the seat and folding her arms in her lap. "Like I said, he owes me more than a few favors. Plus, he gets a few hours' work out of you and doesn't have to pay nothing. To him, it's a win-win situation."

I look up in the mirror. Permillia appears to have aged twenty years since just this morning.

"Good, then we're almost set." I look over at Carl, who is just snapping his phone shut. "Any word?"

"I called a friend who's gonna take a quick look at the bar and a few others. We'll figure something else out if we can't locate your car. But you're resourceful. I'm sure you'll do what needs to be done."

Turning the wheel hard to the left, I accelerate and spin the car. We drive in silence back the way we came. Less than thirty minutes after we exited the farm, I escort Permillia back to the old chicken coop and returned to her car. Before leaving, I take another slow, careful look at the barren farm. It is just as quiet and dead as when we arrived.

"C'mon," Carl urges from the passenger seat, "I'm cold and we've got a pretty good ride to town. We'll take a route that should throw off anybody trying to follow us. A.J. has a good-sized salvage yard you can hide in. Just keep your ass hidden until it's time to go."

"When or if I get the box, where do you want to meet?"

Carl shakes his head. "Don't know just yet. Use the payphone near the bathrooms and call me on my cell." He pulls a bent and wrinkled business card from his wallet. "Number's at the bottom. But stay low 'cause you'll be visible through the lobby windows. I'll figure out where to meet later."

"Sounds like a plan," I say as I drive out of the farm for the second time.

"Follow this road until you come to the intersection with Hwy 9. I'll tell you what to do then."

I do as instructed, following Carl's convoluted directions that have us traveling along back roads, barreling across cracked and worn roads that might see a dozen cars a day.

During the hour-long odyssey through the brambles of the county, a building or road sign knocks a cog in my mind into place, and two pieces of a bazillion-piece jigsaw puzzle match-up, giving a snippet of an image. Not enough to see the entire picture, but enough to keep my mind fighting to join the parts.

Twenty minutes before midnight, Carl motions for me to stop and points across a patch of flat, cleared land. "Kill the lights and head south through there."

"South?" I ask, having lost my sense of direction under the black and gray sky.

"To the right, toward that far tree line."

I gun the engine and slog across a plowed-under field, bouncing and rocking toward a wall of corrugated metal that runs for hundreds of yards across the horizon. I bring the car to a stop just before the fence.

"I take it that this is the place."

"This is it. Drive around to the far side and park. There's a patch of woods where we can ditch the car. You'll find his truck's closer to the office. Just keep to the shadows and wait. I'll find A.J. and see which truck he wants you in."

"You know A.J.?"

Carl's eyes glitter in the sparse silver light. "Yeah, I know A.J. Most of the sheriffs in this part of the world know him. Not that long ago, quite a few missing cars ended up here. Most were missing fenders, hoods, engines — you name it."

"A chop shop?"

"And then some." Carl opens his door. "C'mon, we're wasting time. Go find a place to hide. I'll come looking for you when he's ready to roll."

"Alrighty, then." I follow him as far as the first truck. I clap him on the shoulder in a way that feels as natural as breathing and tell him to be careful. The touch makes him stiffen and pause. He tips his head in acknowledgment but doesn't comment.

We find three trucks lined up head-to-tail; the coveralls that Permillia mentioned are resting on the rear of the first truck. I slide into them and retreat into the shadows of discarded garbage bins.

The uniform is a gray, stained jumpsuit with A.J.'s Sanitation stenciled over the left side of the chest. On the right side, 'Nate' is stitched in red embroidery. The uniform smells as if it has never been washed and is about a size too large. I toss my coat behind the bins, stuff my hands in my pockets, and try to stay warm.

The only sound in the frosty night air is the rustle of dead leaves and the creaks from the corrugated metal fence. I hear a cough and stick my head out from behind the garbage bins. A chill, not having a damn thing to do with the weather, rifles down my back, freezing the blood in my spine. It's the man from the alley that was tossing garbage bags on the loading dock, the one with enough steroids coursing through his body to barely qualify as human. His arms bulge, stretching the fabric of his sweatshirt to its limit. A knit cap is pulled tight over his head, stopping just short of his Neanderthal-ish brow. He leans casually against the last truck and pulls a phone from his pocket. The weak green light from the screen accents his hard, angular face. I make a mental note to never tangle with this freak and withdraw deeper into the shadows.

Fully relaxed, Mr. Steroids talks and laughs with the ease of someone waiting for a bus. He parks a cigarette in his mouth, playing with it while he talks, then pulls a silver lighter from his pocket. The man flips it open and spins the wheel. The lighter flares to life in a small explosion of oily yellow light. Steroid-man turns away from the sudden brilliance and stares straight at me. My heart pauses as I a stab of pain blossoms in my head, as if a six-inch roofing tack had penetrated my right eye. A new memory sputters to life and plays in my mind, jerking and snapping as if the projector reels are too tight.

The flash envelops me, takes away my breath and sense of location. My eyes shut tight from the pain, and the video begins its choppy playback. We are….

…. in the pool hall. I am….

…. crouched behind the bar, less than a dozen feet away from a young blonde woman. I clench half of a broken pool cue in my hand while blood seeps into my eyes from above my forehead. The calm-looking blonde sits at a table, but her fingernails—bright red nails— betray her nervousness as they tap on her glass. She lifts her gaze as a fit, muscular, and casually dressed man in a bomber-style leather jacket approaches. His well-groomed blond hair is parted on the side. Behind his back, he holds….

…. bolt-cutters. Python-arms drops beside the blond and runs off a string of questions. The woman shakes her head at each one. He pulls her right arm out and holds it flat against the table. The man in the bomber jacket places the cutter's jaws over her index finger and snaps them shut. She screams and falls back against the booth, her mangled hand clutched to her chest. She drops her other hand to her lap, pulls a cell phone from her pocket, and dials. A silenced pistol shot cuts the conversation short.

The vision stops abruptly. I stumble from my blind and trip over a discarded bumper. Python-arms spins around with cat-like reflexes that seemed to defy his chemically engorged muscles. A fat revolver magically appears in his hand as if conjured out of thin air.

"Jonesy!" he laughs. "So damn nice of you to finally show yourself." He breaks into a wide grin. "I thought that was you earlier. Didn't recognize you dressed as a farmer." He starts in my direction, the revolver not moving, the steel looking dull and deadly under the cold moonlight.

"Tennico," I say, almost as a statement.

His smile broadens. "I heard you were claiming to have lost your mind or something. Hopefully, it ain't all gone. We still ain't found—" I hear a sickening crack, and the gun tumbles from his hand as he collapses headfirst.

Carl steps from behind the garbage truck holding a cracked length of two-by-four. "Wilson Tennico, thug, drug dealer, and all-around bad dude." He rolls him over with his foot while holding the cracked lumber cocked and ready to swing again. Satisfied that the man wouldn't be pulling himself back off the deck, Carl grabs a pair of rubber gloves from his coat pocket, pulls them on, and picks up the gun. "Serial numbers have been filed off. Not surprising."

"I know him," I say and walk around the prone man. "He's also involved in all of this. Said he was looking for me."

Carl snaps his phone off his belt, dials a number, and talks quickly as the trucks rumble to life. "Okay, Jonesy, time for your midnight ride. A.J. will be with you in a few. The instructions are simple. At each stop, grab the cans that have his initials on 'em and toss the contents in the back. Jump back on and ride to the next location. I'll have my guys pick this fool up and run him in. We'll catch up in a few hours."

"Okay, sounds simple enough."

"It is," he adds. "Just don't fuck it up." He glances over his shoulder at the sound of the revving engines. "Good luck." He holds out his right hand. The handshake is quick and straightforward, but also encouraging. Maybe things are moving for the better.

I retrieve my leather coat and toss it to Carl. "If you don't mind, keep this for me. As far as I know, it's the only thing I own." Carl starts for the car with my coat under his arm. I say to him, "One more thing." I need to tell him about my vision.

"Tell me later." He yells back, carrying my coat over his shoulder and waving me on. He reaches down and drags the moaning bad guy into the shadows.

Chapter Twenty-Two

The ride through town and residential neighborhoods proves uneventful. A.J. complained that one of his drivers has yet to show up and that his replacement will delay the route of one of his trucks by at least an hour. I can only assume it is Mr. Tennico that has failed to show.

We turn back toward the town's main drag; the buildings becoming familiar. The bus station is about four blocks away, or about twenty-five minutes' can-time. Braking hard, the driver turns left, and we lurch into the parking lot behind the bus depot. My compatriot, a wiry black kid about nineteen years old, takes the cans on the left side of the street while I handle the cans on the right. As I grab the last of the containers, a heavyweight falls against my leg. I glance down and notice a small two-pound hammer. I slide the handle through a loop on my coveralls.

The truck slows to navigate between two large metal bins and a tree whose branches overhang the drive, blocking the glare of the streetlights. This is the best time to disembark. I jump from the truck and hit the ground running. I crouch in the shadows as the truck slows for its next stop. The lone garbage man jumps from the back and races for a pair of cans behind an auto parts store. I do a double-take when a second man returns with him. Well, I'll be damned! Permillia set this up right. The truck moves forward, turns left, and disappears. I hear its engine rev as it powers back onto the main drag through town.

I count to thirty, waiting to see if we have a tail. The way things have been going, I was sure I'd hear an engine idling up behind me or possibly the click of an automatic pistol being drawn. Keeping low to the shadows, I slide along the rear of the building, pulling the sledgehammer out as I move. The lock on the roll-up door is old and rusted and offers little resistance. It breaks the instant the hammer hits it.

It is now or never. Grabbing the base of the door, I lift it just enough to slide under; the metal creaking and rattling with each inch. When the gap is knee-high, I enter and let it drop. It closes with a muffled clang.

I cringe, not believing I just let it bang shut. The noise seems to echo inside the bay for an eternity. When no black-booted killers spring up from behind the crates of supplies or rappel in from ropes tied to the ceiling, I climb to my feet and pick my way through the dark room, illuminated only by the weak red glow of the emergency exit light.

Pausing at the double doors leading to the lobby, I brush ten years of dust and grime from the now opaque glass and survey the room. It is gloomy and empty. The Red Barron Pizza clock casts a red hue on the walls. Quietly pushing the doors apart, I slip through, holding one by a finger until it closes with its partner. I sweep the empty chairs and corners with my eyes, prepared to leap back through the doors and into the cargo bay at the first hint of trouble.

The air remains still, the room silent. Staying low and clinging to the shadows, I avoid any errant shafts of moonlight. Officials have stretched yellow and black crime scene tape across the building's entrance. It's unmolested. Good, no one has been here since the murders.

The supply closet is just down from the bathrooms and past the lockers, far enough back from the windows to power up the cigarette-sized penlight Carl gave me. Pressing the button on the bottom, I guide the beam up and around the hallway.

The signs of murder are everywhere. Bloody boot-prints lead from the supply room, fading as they head out of the station. The room itself resembles a slaughterhouse. There's blood on the floors and walls. The box of women's pads—along with every other box— is torn apart, the contents scattered.

Glancing up and smiling, I recall how I lied to Carl about the package's location, not sure how much I could trust him. I am confident the box hasn't been found. Climbing the end of the metal rack, I push the acoustic ceiling tile up, slide the insulation to the side, and reach inside.

Nothing. I swipe frantically to the left and right. My heart races as I panic. I climb higher, and the shelving shifts, the metal braces bending and groaning. Stretching my arm through the insulation as far as I can, I probe the surrounding tiles.

Again, nothing. I ascend higher, my head nearly to the ceiling. The shelving shifts abruptly, the brackets giving way as the stanchions pull free from the wall and the storage rack collapses in a shriek of tearing metal and falling supplies. In desperation, I grab the metal rim that supports the acoustic tiles, pulling the rig free, and together we slam to the floor. The fall knocks the wind out of me as pink insulation spills from the space above.

It takes a few minutes for my head to clear and my eyes to focus. I shine my light up at the gaping hole in the ceiling. And just inside the remaining framework, inches from where I had been searching, is the package. I stagger to my feet, tripping over buckets and bottles of cleaning supplies. The ceiling is a good ten feet above me, the rack I used to reach it crumpled.

Ignoring the pain in my back and head, I run from the room and through the dark depot lobby to the maintenance bay. There is a stepladder leaning against the wall. I grab it and sprint back through the lobby, keeping to the shadows as best I can.

I spread the ladder apart, climb, and retrieve the box. I dash to the payphone, dial the number on the card and try to calm my breathing as I wait for Carl to answer.

Carl doesn't say hello, congrats, or any such greeting. "Get out! Now!" That is all he says as the line goes dead. I turn toward the front lobby windows. Headlights are approaching and getting brighter by the second. I dart for the maintenance room, lift the door far enough to see out, then scan the rear of the building.

No one is approaching from this direction, but the sound of heavy engines racing toward the station is increasing. I hold the box under my arm like a football, lift the door far enough to escape, roll out of the building, and come up running. Behind the station is an eight-foot-deep creek bed, mostly a wet-season drainage ditch that only holds water after a sustained rain.

A thick row of bushes and small trees line the ditch. I dash for the depression, diving through the brush as a vehicle roars around the rear of the building. The headlights pass just over me. I press my stomach hard against the ground and gaze through the foliage. More vehicles charge up to the closed depot. Doors open, and men jump out, their hard-soled shoes pounding the asphalt in staccato fashion as they circle the building and block all exits. I remain flat on the ground, peering through the brush at the cars. They are all unmarked, the occupants not wearing uniforms or visible side arms.

Who the hell are these guys? I push backward and scramble along the creek bed, away from the station. After progressing about a hundred yards, I keep flat to the ground and push up through the tangle of vines and saplings. I'm almost at the pavement level, but hidden in the shadows. More cars have joined the blockade. I study the group long enough to determine that they are no longer searching the building and are now expanding their search perimeter toward the ditch.

Several vehicles have backed away and are now driving around the perimeter, their searchlights probing the tall grass.

A deputy's cruiser moves away from the pack and casually drives down the road before the driver cuts the lights and coasts to a stop a block away. The interior light glows as the deputy sits behind the wheel.. If I were going to make my escape, I'd have to pass the car without being seen or heard.

I approach silently, trying to manifest enough courage to proceed. My heart is pounding, blood pressure rising to the catastrophic failure point. Ain't nothing to it but to do it, I whisper and begin crawling. If only the moon would dip behind the clouds, I could easily pass, but it is brighter now than it has been all evening, just beaming cold white light all over the city.

The patrol car is less than twenty feet away, and the driver's head is focused down. The undergrowth is sparse, its protection ends directly in front of the patrol vehicle.

I inch as close to the barren area as possible, contemplating what to do next. Do I dart across the opening on my hands and knees? Or do I press myself as flat on the ground as possible and slither by?

The moon makes my decision easier as it dips behind a cloud and throws a welcoming shadow over the gully.

I slither to the edge of the thin brush. My heart is racing. The moment I feel my heart slow just a beat or two, I intend to slither through the open expanse. I am counting down from ten. I'm about to scramble through the gap when a gloved hand covers my mouth, and someone holds me down and whispers' Shhhhhh' in my ear.

Chapter Twenty-Three

"Do you have the package?" the shadow asks.

I'm no chump, so I won't give up information without knowing who I'm giving it to. "What are you talking about?" I ask through the glove covering my mouth.

"The package!" the person hisses in my ear. "The one you were supposed to get, the damn box we're all risking our lives for. Do you have it or not?"

The glove moves away.

"Who's 'we'?"

"It doesn't matter. Me and my partner were sent to get your ass out of here. In about ten seconds, my partner's gonna radio we have movement over here and you're gonna have a whole lot of hurt raining down on you."

I feel the person move off to my left and climb the embankment.

"I've got it," I reply, not thinking I have an option. One pistol shot, shout, or radio call, and it'd all be way over. Tucking the box against my body, I climb the hill toward the waiting patrol car staying on the driver's side to block me from view.

The back door opens, and I scramble inside and pull it shut. The driver folds the paper he has been reading, places it on the seat, and reverses the transmission. We back away from the ditch, then turn back toward the station.

"Hey, what the hell is this?" I demand. The driver glances up in the mirror, and his reflection stops the blood from flowing in my veins. "You!" I almost shout as the doors lock with a loud 'c-chunk.' The driver is the deputy that chased me around Permillia's house. His partner is riding shotgun.

He is grinning, but his words aren't. "Stay down and shut up." He snarls. "Me and J.D. are putting our lives on the line for you. Carl says you're worth it. Personally, I'd rather drive you back to the bus stop and let those boys have a go with you. There wouldn't be enough left of you to make a decent chum bag out of."

The car accelerates and passes the depot without hesitation. I hear the passenger—J.D.—talking into the radio, saying something about a shift change and paperwork. His communications aren't questioned, and we don't slow.

"All right, you can sit up, we're clear," J.D. announces over his shoulder.

I do as I'm told and stare out the windows at the dark world passing by. "So, where are you taking me?"

"That depends. Carl said if you've got the package, we're to meet him out on route fifty-eight. If you don't have it, he said to drop you off somewhere out of town."

I pull the box out of my coveralls. It is now flattened to about half its former size. "I've got it, but don't know what's in it."

"Well, it better be worth it." The officer riding shotgun says. "Carl's career is toast after this, and he's a good man, despite the shit he's gotten himself wrapped up in. If this turns out to be some wild goose chase, I'm gonna track you down and boil the skin off your bones."

"It's worth it." At least, I hope it is. There's no telling what's in the box until we open it. "Trust me. This is going to be well worth it."

"We'll see. You can bet your ass on that." The driver makes another call on the radio as he pulls onto the highway. He opens the throttle and pushes the needle toward triple digits. I lean back against the seat, wondering if this is just another damn rabbit hole I'm tumbling down. When the last of the town disappears and we don't pick up any undue attention, I let myself relax. A few radio calls later, we are traveling down a solitary blacktop, the moon sliding closer to the horizon and daybreak.

I cradle the squashed box like a baby. As bad as I want to rip this box open, I hold back, waiting to examine the contents in private. I glance out the window and recognize a stretch of pasture and barbed wire. We exit the road at high speed; the vehicle bouncing and rocking as we race toward the rear of the property and the cover of trees and brush. Carl appears behind the chicken coop and motions for the driver to pull his car hard against the rear wall. As the engine dies, he and Robbie throw armloads of brush over the top to camouflage the sedan.

"C'mon, let's open that box up," Carl says when I climb from the vehicle's rear. He pulls the corrugated metal door open and waits. I step through, noticing that the glow sticks are now exhausted, and that someone has taken the time to wall off a small area of the coop with scraps of lumber and metal sheeting. In the center of the makeshift room hangs a small gas lantern. Permillia and Sheila lay against one wall, curled up in dusty sleeping bags. A small camp stove burns in the corner, the burner glowing blue and orange. On the burner, a pot of coffee sits in the middle, the flames providing a small circle of heat.

Robbie pulls the door shut and drags a small wooden desk with him. The deputies follow with a laptop and several battery-powered lamps. After securing the door, Carl hands me a thermos filled with strong black coffee.

I sniff the steaming black liquid. The aroma borders on heavenly. "Thanks, I'm gassed, and this is just what I need." While I savor the hot drink, Carl readies our makeshift 'command center,' setting up the laptop, a scanner, and lights, all powered by a car battery.

Carl holds his hand flat, palm up, fingers flexing toward him. "The box, Jonesy. It's time to open it. I'm sure you're just as curious as I am to get at it."

I nod and toss the box on the old, cracked desk. "Be my guest."

The sheriff pulls a pair of latex gloves from his pocket and a small knife off his belt. He slips the gloves on, then runs the blade's tip around the end of the box, carefully peeling the top off. Tilting it, he shakes the contents on to the desk. Out slides an unlabeled CD, a cheap journal, and an envelope of pictures.

"Is that it?" Carl pats the bottom of the box. This time a folded note with my name on it tumbles out.

Carl spins the note around with the tip of his knife. "It's addressed to you," he says and slides it my way.

"Yep," I respond and reach for the paper.

He flips it out of my reach and holds it down with the tip of his knife. "Hang on a bit, put these on." Carl reaches into the satchel he'd brought with him and retrieves a second pair of latex gloves. I put them on and unfold the note.

Jonesy, thanks so much for helping me. I'm worried that Milford's men have gotten to Carl, and he's no longer trustworthy. I know I should have gone to you first! Together, we'll bring these bastards down. Everything we talked about is on this disc and in the notebook. Take a look at it and let me know if you can verify it through your sources. I'll meet you later tonight. By this weekend, you and I will be on every morning talk show!

Love you!

Claire

She finished the letter with a series of X and O's.

I hand the note to Carl, who reads it with little reaction. After a moment, he snorts, throws it on the desk, and glares at the letter.

"Was she right?" I ask.

Carl doesn't look my way; he rests his cross gaze on the unfolded message. He sighs and lets a half-grin slide across his tired face. "Maybe, I don't know." This time he turns toward my way. "Those jackals I mentioned earlier and those men at Permillia's, they all run with Milford. Actually, they run for Milford. He's their handler."

"And who the hell is he?" I ask.

"Milford Anthony Parson, the third. Ring a bell?"

I shake my head. "Nope, but I guess it should?"

"You might say that." Carl sighs. "You ready for this?" he asks, a flicker of sadistic humor returning some spirit to his eyes.

"Hit me with it."

"Are you familiar with the Brice-Parson cookie company? They package those crappy donuts, cakes, and pastries for vending machines? They're in every local government office in the county and across the state."

Ah, something I could recall for a change! "Yeah, got that damn dumb-ass looking clown sharing a slice of cake with an elephant?" Everybody is staring at me. "I only know 'cause I've been living off them for the past week."

"The same."

"And the part I need to ready myself for?"

"By any chance, do you remember Claire's maiden name?" The smug satisfaction gives more life to his eyes.

"It is…" I can feel the answer on the tip of my tongue, dancing around like a hopped-up mirage on speed. And then it hits me like a velvet-gloved anvil. I cover half my face with my right hand and stare around my fingers at Carl. "Parsons. Damn."

"Give the man a prize!" barks the heavy-set deputy.

Carl continues. "She pissed off her old man by going to journalism school, and her first project was exposing conditions in his plants. Just about destroyed his senatorial hopes. But if you toss enough cash around, you can win an election with a goat. Still, give her credit for having more balls than her worthless older brother."

"And that would be Milford?" I ask, taking a sip of my coffee.

"Man, you're on a roll!" The deputy laughs and claps me on the shoulder.

Carl spreads out the box's contents and locks his gaze on me. "He hates the name and insists everyone call him Trey. You don't dare call him Milford, or God forbid, Millie to his face. The boy has a severe case of Napoleon complex. He likes that a nine-mill stuffed up one of your nostrils makes him a very big man.

"His father condemned him for dissing the name and refused to call him Trey. Said Milford is a prestigious family name, and he should be proud of it. They never saw eye to eye, always fighting. Only thing they had in common is that they'd screw a dead nun if they thought it'd get them ahead. Old man Parsons screwed over so many people. It's amazing he lived as long as he did. Apparently he forgot that adage: 'For every ass you kick on the way up, there's twice as many asses you have to kiss on the way back down'."

"I take it Millford's father is spoken of in the past tense?"

Carl nods and smiles. "You could say that."

"How long?" I ask, feeling some familiar detective cogs slipping into place.

"Two years?" he says to himself. "Yeah, that's about right."

"What happened?"

"You mean what happened first?"

That brought me to full attention. "You mean more than one thing happened to him?"

The deputies laugh, and J.D. takes over the Q and A. "Well, there were three good probable causes of death, and any of them could be the reason. If the cold hadn't killed him, the drowning or beating damn sure would have. Or the loss of blood. Forgot about number four."

"They tortured him?" I stammer. "What the hell for?"

"Well, a couple hundred million in cash and assets will make a boy do all kinds of crazy things." Carl picks up the notebook and starts leafing through it.

"You think Milford did this?"

"Son, ain't no thinking to it. He hated his old man and couldn't wait to get his hands on the estate." Carl tosses the notebook on the desk, opens the laptop, and powers it up.

"So, what happened, exactly?" I ask as the sheriff's logo brightens on the laptop screen.

"Nearest Mitchell could figure…."

"This would be our missing county coroner?" I ask, interrupting.

"Yeah, the same one," Carl answers impatiently. "Anyway, the prevailing theory is that they stripped him naked and left him in the trunk of his car overnight to soften him up. Whatever they were fishing for, they didn't get. Mitchell figured they spent the better part of the day beating him and clipping off fingers and toes. We found his ten little piggies on his blood-soaked kitchen floor. Only found six of his fingers. When they ran out of digits, or when he passed out from loss of blood or shock, they tossed him in the swamp. It'd be hell trying to swim with no fingers or toes. Not to mention the fact that they tied a concrete block to his legs."

I felt my guts twist. I'd puke if I had anything inside me to offer besides coffee. "He used bolt cutters, didn't he?"

Carl stops typing on the laptop and stares hard at his deputies but doesn't look my way, his words coming out slow and calculated. "How the hell did you know that?"

"It's kinda like this," I begin, telling him of my vision several hours earlier.

Chapter Twenty-Four

Carl stares at the laptop display, which has now switched to a screen saver of badges, weapons, and patrol cruisers. His hands clench the desk hard, turning the knuckles white and strained. The muscles in his jaw tighten as the deputies cast accusing glances at me.

"These memories," Carl says, his voice barely controlled, "seem to have a random way of showing up. Is that right?"

"Seriously? I can't control this shit in my head right now. I think all that Jack has turned your brain to mush. If I thought taking a chainsaw and slicing my head open would help my memories and find Claire, I'd gas one up and let you go to sawing."

Carl backhands me. I land flat on my back, a hot stove-like burn growing on the left side of my face. I'd forgotten how quickly he could move. Much to my surprise, the deputies jump between us, pushing their boss away from me.

Robbie, who always seems to be a non-person and is usually completely invisible, helps me sit up. I work my jaw from side to side. I'm glad Carl pulled his punch. Otherwise, I might be spitting out blood and teeth. Pushing myself up on my knees, I use the desk to help get to my feet. "We'll settle up on that cheap shot later," I say, seething, knowing that my vision hasn't cleared enough for me to connect with a ten-foot length of two-by-four, much less a fist.

Carl shakes his arms free of his men and yells across the room. "If you'd told me this earlier, we could've dragged Tennico's ass back with us! I guarantee you we'd have that punk spilling his guts by now. We'd be on our way to finding Claire."

"First, I don't think they have her!" I fire back, my vision clearing and my blood heating. "If they did, we wouldn't have just spent the night going back for this damn box." I can feel the red haze of anger pulsing in my skull. "Second, if you don't remember, I tried to tell you this. But you told me to go on." I unclench my fist when I see the hate in Carl's eyes fade. Then his words hit home. "Where is Tennico? I thought you were going to round him up."

"We lost him," Carl said. "Had him cuffed in the car, unconscious. By the time my men got there, he was gone. Don't know if he came to on his own, or if someone found him."

"Don't worry," I respond, feeling my anger and adrenaline taper off. "I think I know where Tennico works during the day. Just grab his ass tomorrow and ream the answers out of him."

Carl rubs his hands over his head and through his hair, the fire now quenched. "I know where he works," he says flatly. "We'll pick him up first thing." Igniting a penlight, Carl opens the notebook and thumbs through the pages.

"What is it?" I ask, staring down at the small, spiral-bound book.

"It's a ledger," Carl replies, staring at the pages as he works a flashlight from side to side. "Nothing but cookie brands—I guess — with dates, times. There are numbers in the margin, but I don't know what they reference." Closing the ledger, he says, "You used to be good at seeing patterns. See what you can make out of it." Carl flips the notebook around and shoves it toward me with the back of his hand. He then pops the disk into the laptop's CD tray.

Good at patterns? Well, that's something new and positive for a change. I click on my flashlight, open the book, and thumb through the first few pages. It is, as Carl said, nothing but column after column with names, dates, times, and numbers. After glancing at a handful of pages, I jump about a third of the way back and then to the end. It's the same from cover to cover.

"Hell, it could be anything—deliveries, orders, maybe even bathroom cleaning assignments." I drop the book back on the desk, close my eyes, and rub them. My eyelids feel as if I lined them with grit. "Man, I'm beat. I need to close my eyes before I tackle this." I sit on the edge of the desk and let my gaze drift to Carl, realizing that he hadn't said anything in the last ten minutes. He is concentrating hard on the laptop with his right hand stretched across his brow, as if trying to shield his eyes from a bright light. "What is it?"

"Video clips. Milford must have filmed every deal he made, must have blackmailed every damn elected person in the state and a hell of a lot of prominent businessmen. Audio ain't so hot, but I think we can clean it up later." Carl rotates the computer toward me. A grainy video is running, showing a stocky, casually dressed man sitting in a shabby office with a well-dressed man who is accepting several large bundles of cash. They shake hands over two drink tumblers filled with a dark liquid. After the man leaves, Milford lights a cigarette, takes a deep drag, and beams.

"Jefferson Monk, the junior state senator from Altamore Springs. He's on the state's transportation board," Carl informs me without looking up from the screen.

We spend an hour scanning videos, while Carl takes notes on a pad. Carl shuts the machine down and sits on the corner of the desk. "That little bastard has been a very busy boy. It looks like he's accepting payoffs from every person involved with interstate commerce, inspections, regulations… you name it."

"But isn't this going backwards? Shouldn't Milford be giving the cash and not getting it?"

Carl turns, surprised by the unexpected voice from the shadows, and slips off the desk, landing on his side in a cloud of dust and explicit language. Permillia steps out of the gloom, yawning and smiling.

"Ain't nothing right about this whole damn mess," I answer, fighting not to yawn myself. "He has something on these guys, something that they'll pay to keep quiet."

"Well, it can't be cookies. What they sell isn't all that great. Definitely not Keebler or Oreo's. Those stale crackers aren't worth bribing folks or killing for."

"No, but something is," I mumble as I leaf through the book again.

Carl brushes his hands off and joins the conversation. "That's awful heavy-hitting for a piss-ant cookie company. Where do they reach… Georgia? Florida?" Carl perches on the edge of the desk and crosses his arms over his chest. "We need to study that ledger, see if we can make sense out of it."

"Uh. Carl?" It is the older, fat deputy. "I think this explains quite a bit." He tosses several pictures on the desk. "Here's Miss November, Miss January, and a couple I don't recognize." The pictures land face up.

"Well, fuck a duck and call her sweetie," Carl whispers as he sorts through the pictures. He glances at his deputies and then at me. "This would be worth killing for. They've got half the damn judicial system compromised." He tosses incriminating pictures my way. "Here's Judge Oversby, Solicitor Camble, and Sheriff O'Neal of Logerston County.

"Shit, look at this one!" Carl throws a photo to his senior deputy, who catches it and smiles like a kid who just discovered what those magazines in his daddy's locked cabinet have between the covers.

"I thought you'd like that one." Carl laughs hard, coughing as he tries to catch his breath. He turns the photo toward me. "Pastor Adoris of the Waynesville First Baptist Church. He's a big-time bible thumper, likes to stand by the pool hall and shout at you when you exit. Got a big-ass horn on top of his truck that he uses to broadcast his hell and damnation spiel at truck-stops. I wonder how much this cost the church."

I pick up the nicely focused color picture and shake my head, fighting laughter. Tied to a four-poster bed is Pastor Adoris. A tall, leggy brunette stands beside him with a whip. The man's face is twisted in ecstatic bliss. I stare at the photo for a moment, wondering when the question hiding in my skull will divulge itself. I don't have to wait long.

"I wonder where they shot these." I muse. "Do any of you recognize the setting?" Carl's deputies purse their lips but only shake their heads. Then deputy J.D. nods and stares straight at me. He cracks a wide smile.

"You know, don't you?" he says to me, more of a statement than a question.

"The Dreamland Motel," I answer, the location gelling in my brain. The room differs slightly from than mine, but there is no mistaking the cheap, scarred furniture, the cracked and torn orange leather cushions, and the aqua-blue walls.

"Sure as hell is." Carl confirms.

"Well, that answers another question." I spread the pictures out. The majority of the photos were shot at the motel.

"And what question is that, son?" J.D.'s partner asks.

"Why they offed the old man. He was a loose end, and with Claire stealing this shit, they didn't know how far we could track the story back. Kill him, blame me, and that has you guys running around chasing shadows."

The officer's glance at each other, then nod in unison.

"My guess," I continue, "is that they caught that old creepy bastard with some kid. It's either twenty years in the slammer with a bunch of big ol' boys who don't take kindly to crimes involving kids, or a nice, comfy hideout for the senators. All the old coot had to do was keep his mouth shut, and they'd protect him, possibly tossing him a bone or two. I bet the old fool got a bit too greedy and tried for a little insurance on his own. Maybe he tried to blackmail the blackmailer."

Carl picks up my train of thought and creates the next unspoken connection. "Let me see that ledger." I hand it to him. He turns about halfway back and pins it to the desk with the pages facing up. "What does that look like to you?" When I stare at him, he continues. "The writing, look at it closely. Sure as hell looks like the weak scrawl of an old person, doesn't it?"

"Man, what I would give to have a sample of that sick bastard's handwriting," the thick deputy offers.

"What would you give?" I ask, curious what the man would give up.

"Huh?"

"You said you'd give up something if you had a sample of his writing. What would that be?"

He thinks about it for a moment, then lets a sideways grin part his lips. "I'd give up my old lady for that new, hot waitress at the truck stop!" He nudges J.D., who laughs and nods in agreement. They high-five each other.

"Well studly, I'm about to make your dream come true. Carl, is my coat still in Permillia's car?"

"Yeah, why?"

"I'm fairly sure I have a copy of the registration in my chest pocket. He filled out the bottom and signed it."

Carl snaps his fingers twice and points toward the door. J.D. is moving before the second snap quits echoing. I turn my attention back to the pictures; the photos sparking diffused memories like a blurry watercolor painting. Each girl is in close intimate contact with a state rep or other person of influence. The girls are redheads, beach-blondes, raven-headed beauties—each one stunning.

And then the pattern solidifies.

"Christ, is it that simple?" I mutter to myself.

"What do you have?" Carl asks, his eyes brightening as he leans on the desk.

"Maybe nothing, possibly just a weak hunch, but let me see that journal again."

Carl slides the book over to me, and I thumb a dozen pages into it. "About when did you find the first girl?"

At first, he stares at me, then cocks his head to the side. "What are you getting at?"

"Do you have to answer every damn questions with one of your own? About what month and date that you found the first girl?"

Robbie answered for him. "August 9th, two years ago. I'll never forget it." Robbie goes on, but Carl waves him down with a quick patting of the air.

"You see a pattern, don't you?" Carl now stands with his hands on his hips, staring down at the book.

"Maybe," I mutter. I swing the light back and forth, scanning and flipping page after page.

And there it is. Not exact, but close enough.

"Check out this date. August 6th. There is an order for Singapore Sweeties. First girl was Asian, right?"

"Yeah, she was," Carl confirms after a moment.

"And the delivery is to Hancock Motor Freight." I close the book over my finger to save my place. I stare at Carl to see if he caught the implication. His expression is blank.

"Why in the hell would a trucking company be ordering cookies?" J.D. asks, returning with my coat.

His partner answers for him, staring at him as if he is a complete moron. "They ain't ordering cookies, you nimrod."

"It's girls, isn't it?" Sheila asks, finally making her way into the circle of light. "He's trafficking in girls, sex."

Carl glances her way. "That's how it looks. He's running a prostitution ring under the cover of the cookie company. I bet he has a few other actions going on as well—drugs, money laundering, extortion."

I tap the book with my right index finger. "This is what Claire is investigating." I grab the pictures and shuffle through them. "I don't know how she got this stuff, but she knew it could get her killed."

"Or did," Permillia adds, her voice quiet.

There is a long, dark pause as everyone stares at her.

"Damn, lady, way to brighten the mood!" The fat deputy laughs.

Permillia shrugs.

"Jonesy," Carl sits back down on the desk with his hands resting on his hips. "We need that finger. I can have my deputies retrieve and print it. They know how to access my personal files to see if it's a match. If it's Claire, one mystery down. If not, at least we have a reason to bust that Tennico bastard."

I nod and tell them where they can find the digit. Carl orders the deputies to get on it ASAP, then find Tennico and drag his ass back here—unconscious if necessary.

Chapter Twenty-Five

The deputies leave, and we finish the last of the coffee. The final few drops are burned and taste like cooked rubber. I grimace and toss the sludge on the floor. Carl stretches across the desk on his back and his eyes close. He snores immediately. Permillia drapes her sleeping bag over him, covering the sheriff like a flannel-stitched flag. She, Robbie, and Sheila rub their hands together, trying to stay warm as the temperature drops below freezing. Their breath hangs in the still air like silver clouds. I take Sheila up on her offer to stretch out in her sleeping bag, close my eyes and allow the bag's warmth to breach any walls I have erected against sleep.

Sleep doesn't come easy. My mind is a tempest of thoughts and images. They twirl and merge like a mad kaleidoscope of fragmented memories. Despite being drained and exhausted, I worry I am too tired to sleep. When my eyes don't slam shut like a death-row cell, I am confident I have many long hours ahead of me. That is my last thought until I wake to Sheila gently rocking me.

"What is it?" I stammer.

"The deputies are back, and whatever they told Carl, he's not thrilled with it."

I push the sleeping bag off, figuring I'd slept an hour at best, and climb groggily to my feet. "What time is it, and how long has Captain America been up?"

Sheila smiles briefly, the first genuine smile I've seen. "It's around seven-thirty. The deputies showed up about fifteen minutes ago. They woke him and have been huddled ever since.”

“Any idea what’s going on?”

Sheila shakes her head while keeping an eye on the deputies. “No, but Carl became very upset as soon as they started talking.”

“Well, hell.” I rock first to one knee, then the other, dragging my stiff body upright. I could easily have used another dozen hours of sleep. Yawning and rubbing my eyes, I start toward the men. They ignore me and converse in hushed voices, their heads down. “What’s happened?” I ask. They ignore me for a moment, then Carl turns, his eyes blazing, seemingly on fire..

“Tennico’s dead. We just found most of him.”

“What?” I stare from one man to the other, hoping this isn’t some sick gag. “Tell me I heard you wrong, but did you say, ‘most of him’? Are you saying that there’s a large section of him missing?”

“Someone fed him feet first into a chipper last night. They shredded him up to his stomach before the engine seized. Next time they try to mulch someone, they should check the oil,” Carl says flatly.

“Christ, that’s….” My breath crashes from my lungs. I drop to the desk. “Shit, where did you find him?”

Carl smiles a humorless smile. “I think you’ll appreciate this. 911 took a call about a man screaming and the sound of an engine racing behind the bus depot. When the first units arrived, they found the chipper engine smoking and the top half of Tennico’s body. Bastard was still twitching.”

“Christ, still alive? Did he say anything?”

"He wasn't really still alive. His body just hadn't accepted the fact that it was dead. Paramedics pronounced him a few minutes after they arrived."

"What about the chipper? Any idea where it came from?"

"Not yet, but you could rent one of those almost anywhere, or just steal one from a construction site."

Changing direction, I aim my question at the deputies. "What about the finger? Did you guys have time to print it?"

"Yeah, we got it. But so far, no match."

"So, it's not Claire?"

Carl shakes his head, his lips drawn tight. "No, thank God. But we still don't know whose it is or why you had it."

"Sorry, can't help you. There are still big gaps in my memory. And as for how I ended up with it, that's anyone's guess."

The deputies stare at me without comment. Carl turns his attention to a place over my shoulder, scrubs his face with his hands, and sighs. "This just keeps getting more and more unbelievable. Why grind him up where we can find him? Why not just sink him in the swamp?"

"Hell, as a warning, pure and simple. Also, to let us know that they're still on our heels, maybe closing in," I say, catching Sheila and Permillia in my peripheral vision. They have been following the conversation and are visibly shaken.

"We can't stay here much longer. We need to move on as soon as possible," Carl says, resting his hand on the butt of his weapon.

"But the big question is, how do we avoid these bastards, and for how long? Hiding out here is a short-term fix. And returning to town is out of the question. Any ideas?" I look from Carl to his deputies, the women, and to Robbie and E-Lee. They all shake their head.

Silence fills the room, leaving only the puffs of wind against the tin roof to disturb it.

"Couldn't we just leave the box where they could find it?" Sheila asks, breaking the silence and walking over to us. "Once they have their evidence back, won't they just leave us alone?"

The fat deputy laughs hard enough to make his round gut bounce. "Little girl, you've seen what's there. Even if you hadn't seen the box, they'd think that you had. And think about the way they off'd everyone that hadn't seen it. No, they'd make you disappear just as easy as all of them girls. Us, they grind, filet, burn, shred… you name it. If we're lucky, they'd just cap a bullet in our head and that'd be that. But you, well, it wouldn't be so pleasant."

"But you don't know that for sure!" Sheila cries and her eyes take us in, searching for confirmation.

Permillia slips an arm around Sheila's shoulder. "They do, sweetie. And you know it." She squeezes Sheila's shoulder gently. "We'll just have to take a little vacation, maybe head down to Panama City, maybe Biloxi, until all this blows over. Me. You, Robbie and E-Lee, get out of this cold, wet weather and go someplace fun."

"But I can't. I have to work… got bills to pay." Sheila wipes a tear off her cheek, one about to have many followers. "Plus, I'm broke." She says with a wan smile.

"Don't you worry none about that. I've got some cash on me, and we can stop by an ATM or two along the way. We'll have fun, maybe go get me a tan!" Permillia smiles openly, showing her mouthful of white teeth. "And when we come back, all this," she waves her arm over her head, "will be over. Then we can go back to being just another sleepy ol' town. Boring but sleepy."

"What about our jobs? We just can't up and leave! I'll get fired."

"Trust me, girl, we ain't gonna lose our jobs. I've been serving coffee in this town long enough that almost everyone owes me a favor or two. And I can assure you that ol' Belinda Rutledge, she of the too-tight jeans and ill-fitting wig, won't be firing you. Her daddy's been getting free coffee and pie since she was a little girl. I'll call her and say that you need a break and will be back in a few days, maybe a week. She knows I take care of her daddy, so don't you worry."

Sheila nods, then turns to me. "What about you?"

"About me? What do you mean?" The concern in her voice catches me off guard.

"What are you and Carl going to do? They'll kill you if they catch you—both of you."

"Well," I say, fixing her with my best grin, "first thing we're going to do is not get caught."

Her face brightens briefly, more of a flicker on her lips than an actual smile. "And how are you going to do that?" she asks, brushing hair out of her face and sweeping it behind her ear.

I hold my hands palms up and shrug. "That I don't know. We'll just have to figure it out as we go." I take a deep breath, then relax. "But I agree with Permillia. You guys should all leave town. Now. Don't go home, don't pack, just hit the road. Call us when you're a couple of hours out of town to let me know you're safe." I hand her the crumpled business card Carl gave me earlier. "And don't worry about money. I have a couple grand in my coat. Grab it and take it. That should tide you over for the week and then some." Sheila's eyes drop to the ground as she stirs the dust with her foot. "Go on now, get."

Sheila nods in agreement, the stubbornness of her stance loosening. She surprises me again by stepping close and wrapping her arms around me in a fierce, protective hug, then buries her face against my neck. "Be careful, please." She pushes away but lets her hands linger on my wrists, her eyes focusing intensely on mine. "Despite all we've been through, I still care," she says; another flash of a smile skates across her face before vanishing. She lets go and turns.

I beam back at her and feel an unexpected warmth in my stomach. "We'll be fine." I put an arm around her shoulders and steer her toward Permillia. "You girls have fun. By the time you get back, everything will be settled down."

Permillia waits for us by the door as E-Lee returns from outside. "The sun's already up. We need to get going," he says.

"E-Lee's right. Thankfully, it's overcast. Permillia's faded, primer-coated car will blend in for a while. You guys need to hit the road."

"Listen to Jonesy," Carl affirms from across the room. "What he says makes a hell of a lot of sense."

"Mom, the car's running, let's go." E-Lee takes his mom by the elbow and guides her toward the opening.

"Okay, son, we're going." She follows E-lee out the door with Sheila in her wake. Sheila pauses, lingering for a moment, then turns to me.

"When this is all over, will you call me?"

"Absolutely. Once we're sure it's safe for you to return, we'll call you immediately."

"No, Jonesy. What I mean is, when this is over, will you call *me?*"

"That's what I meant," I say, breaking into an uncontrollable grin as the pressure in my chest increases. Sheila lets a genuine smile grace her tired, weary face. She hangs on the doorjamb a moment longer, her eyes glittering in the dim light. "Get on now, girl."

Sheila steps through the opening. A minute later, I watch the car drive through the tall weeds and brush, the brake lights flittering a few times as E-Lee navigates around the various piles of debris that litter the farm. The lights glow once as the car moves onto the empty road, then winks out. Within a few seconds, the engine's sound is just another memory.

Chapter Twenty-Six

I pull the door shut and tie it off with three feet of half-rotted yellow rope. It won't hold for more than a few pulls, but it will be enough to let us know they we've been located. After that, we'll be running and ducking, hoping to hit the tree line before a slug lobotomizes each of us. Satisfied that I've done all I can, I join Carl and the deputies standing with their arms crossed over their chests, their eyes drooping from exhaustion.

"So how do y'all want to handle this?" I ask.

J.D. perks up, flexes his arms, and caresses his sidearm with his right hand. "I say we call them out. Offer 'em a trade. What we have for your girl."

"Oh, they'll agree to that, sure enough," laughs Walters, the fat, older deputy. "We show up in good faith and they cap some rounds in our heads. They have all the evidence, and all we get is a six-foot deep piece of land and our heads stuffed with sawdust."

"Plus, we don't know if they have Claire," Carl adds. "I think we turn over what we have to the FBI, bypass the local boys. Milford might be a punk, but he's not stupid. He's got so much of the department in his back pocket that if we turn this over to them, it'll disappear. Then life will get much tougher for us."

"I don't even think that'll do any good."

Carl stares at me, his eyes pinching down to a hard squint. "Why do you say that? We've got him on goddamn video shaking down every damn official in the county. Not to mention a notebook detailing every killing in the past couple of years!"

"I know that, and you know that. But Mr. Parsons's attorney will argue that all we have is Milford accepting donations from local businessmen to help fund the charities he supports. And you can bet your ass that he has documents that can make it stick. Or will by the time this gets to court.

"As for the sex videos," I say, "did you see Milford with any of these girls, any connections?"

Carl shakes his head as if the action is painful. "All we got is a lot of red-faced officials with their britches around their ankles and a dead hotel clerk who got offed by some bastard he tried to shake down. That's what John Q. Public Defender will claim."

"We got the goddamn notebook!" Carl shouts.

"The notebook? It ain't nothing but a damn order and delivery schedule. We ain't got shit to tie Milford to these girls."

Carl's mouth quivers in anger.

"What we have is enough shit to stir up one hell of a damn hornets' nest." I say.

J.D., whose posturing has become decidedly meeker during my exchange with Carl, removes his cap and scratches his head. "So, what do we do?"

"Well, we obviously can't go arrest Milford and drag his ass in. He's untouchable, sitting high and mighty in his brick and stucco castle. What we gotta do is knock the supports out. Let his big, bad house come toppling down."

"And how in the hell do you plan to do that?" Carl asks.

"With the videos. We hit the weakest targets first, threaten to expose them to their wives, the media. Let one perverted bastard roll up the next guy in line. Most of these cats will fold like a house of cards. This way, we cut Milford's legs out from under him."

Carl crosses his arms and stares at the coop's metal roof. "I like it. But once we drop this little nugget, the word is going to get out like lightning. We'll have to move fast, and I mean fast. These perverts are going to hide behind a wall of lawyers. We'll need to drop our little H-Bomb where it will do the most damage."

J.D. snaps his fingers. "Commissioner Dayton! He's lucky not to be doing time for taxes. And I bet that chicken-shit fool will roll over before we even hit him with the video. And he's on the pardon and parole board. The last thing he wants is to be locked-up with boys he refused an early release."

Carl grins and nods vigorously. "Damn straight he is." He reaches over and takes the fat deputy by the shoulder. "Dayton should be leaving for work soon. You two drop by his place. Tell his housekeeper that you need to see him now, right this minute. Don't tell her why, just that it's important… something about a break-in at his office and his desk being ransacked. That'll get his attention. When you get him alone, tell him you collared a perp out at the Dreamland motel with a bag of videos and want to discuss the vid's before they get tagged into evidence. Tell him I'll do what I can to keep it quiet. I think he'll be very cooperative."

J.D. practically trips over himself, heading for the door. The fat deputy stares at him, then back at Carl. "Boy's eager to get going. Are you sure this is the best target? I mean, we're only going to get a few rounds off before they all start heading for the hills."

"He'll piss all over himself almost immediately. And he's got more dirt on folks than you could ever imagine. He hasn't been able to stay out of jail because of his sterling reputation. That little puss has the spine of a damn worm. But he is the most conniving, politically dangerous bastard I've ever seen. We get him and we knock the damn knees out of Milford's operation."

The deputies are halfway to the door when Carl shouts after them. "You guys be careful. If he suspects that there's something up, he might draw down on you. He ain't brave, but going to prison makes a prissy little man very unpredictable."

The men nod in unison, pull the rope from the door, and push through.

The door swings shut, and a cruiser engine cranks. Seconds later, the car passes by the side of the coop, barreling through the high brush. Carl walks to the far end of the coop and pries open the door, staring outside for a couple of moments before securing the door and returning.

"Okay," I say, "you've got my attention. What's up?"

"I'm not sure who I can trust, and don't want what I'm about to tell you to leave this room."

"Once again, you've got my attention. What's so important that you couldn't share it in front of your deputies?"

"I didn't show you all the videos."

"Why the hell not?"

"As I said, I'm not sure who all I can trust...."

"And you feel you can trust me? I'm honored."

"Cut the shit and pay attention because the battery's about to die." Carl powers up the laptop. The video is from inside the Dreamland Motel. A flabby, middle-aged man with a fringe of black hair clinging to the sides of his skull is reclining against the headboard. He is shirtless, allowing his round belly to lap over his boxer shorts. There isn't any sound, not that you need to know that the man is in a very animated conversation with someone off-screen. Finally calm, he reaches up between the headboard and the wall and switches off the lamp. The room is dark for a moment before another light spills across the foot of the bed.

A woman with shoulder-length black hair steps into view, reaches over to a lamp on the dresser, and turns it on. With her back to the camera and wearing a lacey, nighty that barely reaches below her ass, she sashays seductively up to the man, allowing a finger to slip along the inside of his thigh. His back arches as his eyes roll up in his eyes. He reaches for her, but she playfully dodges his grasp and produces a pair of fuzzy handcuffs from the nightstand. In one smooth move, she lifts his right arm, kisses the inside of his wrist, and snaps the cuff on. A second later, she has his arm cuffed to the headboard.

"Who the hell is this guy?" I ask as the woman walks around the bed, repeating most of the same actions, but this time sliding a finger over the man's belly and teasing the elastic band of his boxers.

"Just watch the video, and I'll let you know when it's over."

The woman's finger dances up the man's belly and circles his nipples. His back arches and his eyes flutter. He offers no resistance as she kisses the inside of his elbow, moving teasingly up his arm. At his wrist, she reaches beside the bed and picks up a matching pair of cuffs. Once again, he offers no resistance.

Now cuffed to the bed, the woman climbs beside him, drifting his way. She lifts his face as if to kiss him but aims it straight at the camera. She lets go and faces the camera herself. The playful kitten is gone, replaced with a frightened expression. She then mouths something to the camera, her lips moving without sound.

Chapter Twenty-Seven

The video continues for another dozen seconds before ending. I stare at the black screen, speechless. Then a locked memory cog drops into place. "Holy shit," I sputter. "It's Claire, isn't it?"

Carl nods in agreement. "I couldn't tell for sure the first time I saw this video, but when I watched it again, I knew, black wig or not, that's Claire. Did you catch what she mouthed?"

I have never been a lip reader and hate it when women would mouth words to me. I always think they are coming on to me. I am, more often than not, wrong. "I think she said for me to call her."

"That's what I thought as well. Any idea what she's doing?"

"No," I say and shake my head. "But she appears to be working this case dangerously. What about the guy? Any idea who he is?"

"His name is Anson Gilbert, president of New State Bank. Supposed to be a real up-and-up guy, pillar of the community, local Boy Scout leader and all that. Don't know what the hell he's doing at that flee bag motel. This would ruin any chance he had of running for the state senate. Not to mention his standing in the community. That's why we're heading there now."

It's time to abandon the freezing chicken coop. Being in a windowless room for hours has made me feel vulnerable. I wake Robbie and Orville and join Carl beside Robbie's battered El Camino. Orville assumes his position in the truck's bed as the three of us pile into the cab.

"We need to ditch this crate," I advise. "It's too well known."

"I agree," Carl says. "I've got a guy that has a used car lot. I help him operate under the radar, and I use his cars when I need to be inconspicuous."

Robbie threads his way through the abandoned farmland and onto the highway. Carl digs his phone out. After a dozen attempts, he reaches Michael Railsteen of M&R autos. It takes almost twice as long to convince the owner to part with one of his vehicles. It isn't until Carl mentions running a background check on all the vehicles on his lot that the man warms to the Sheriff's request for a new set of wheels.

We travel down more back roads than I can count, ending up at a rundown used car lot, its banners and pennants faded and tattered. A sign advertising a 'Summer Sale' sags off the front of the office trailer. The guy has a dozen cars lining the road, a dozen more cannibalized vehicles are scattered amid weeds and scrub oaks; some stripped to the frame. Robbie drives between a pair of dusty, grime-streaked Dodge vans and circles to the rear of the dilapidated mobile home.

Before we quit rolling, the back door flies open, and a fat, middle-aged man shuffles out the door and onto the shaky porch. He's waving his hands in the air and cursing. Wiry, gray-streaked black hair jets out from under a stained Redman tobacco hat. His tee shirt struggles to contain his gut and is in imminent danger of losing the battle. His jeans are grimy and wrinkled. He wears no shoes and doesn't seem to notice the freezing weather.

Walking sideways, he descends the steps, each one creaking and moaning under his weight.

"This is it, Carl. We're squared up," he yells, his quivering jowls flushing. "Don't forget, son, you ain't all that lily-white yourself!" He stops moving when he sees me standing beside Robbie's El Camino.

"Jonesy, you sonofabitch!" He breaks into a lopsided jog when he steps from the last board, heading my way as fast as his girth allows. "Man, I'm glad to see you."

Carl gives me another of his 'what the hell are you hiding now?' glares. I shrug, shocked by the greeting.

"If that woman of yours calls me one more time, screaming at me to find your ass, I'm gonna reach through the damn phone and yank her tongue out!"

I glance at Carl, whose eyes are now wide open. He slams the door to Robbie's truck and grabs the startled car dealer by his threadbare shirt. "Who, Michael? Who's been calling you?"

The fat man's face pales, and his lips tremble. He turns to me for support, as if he needs permission to answer. I motion for him to continue.

"Claire, you know," he whimpers, tilting his head in my direction. "Jonesy's ex."

The tee shirt tears as Carl forces him to walk backward, the man's feet scuffing up the dirt.

"When was the last time she called?"

"Y… yesterday morning sometime." He stammers. "Said it was important to find him."

"She's alive," Carl whispers as he lets go of Michael's shirt, and the heavy man falls on his ass at the unexpected release. "Where is she?"

Michael sits up, his brow creased, and his eyes flicker between the Sheriff and me. He licks his lips as beads of nervous perspiration dot his face. Carl steps closer, letting his shadow darken the man. "I…" he pauses and looks at me. "Don't know. She won't tell me, says she'll only talk to Jonesy. That's why she keeps calling. She says they're working on something together, and it ain't none of my damn business." Michael turns back to me, the color now returning to his face. "Ask him. He's the only one she told."

"Won't do no damn good," Carl replies. "Millie's men beat the hell out of him and left him for dead. Boy's got a convenient case of amnesia."

Michael pushes himself up to his knees and eventually gets to his feet. "You're shittin' me, right?"

I walk around the front of Robbie's truck and lean against the hood. "Last week, I didn't even know what my name was. It's coming back in bits and pieces. But there are still huge chunks missing. All I know is that Claire asked me to help her with something to do with Milford that involves prostitution and maybe the deaths of at least a dozen women."

The fat man props himself against the step-railing, cocks his head to the side, and looks straight at me. "Carl, tell you I used to work in the motor pool for the sheriff's department?"

Oh crap, another damn left turn in a week full of left turns. I would love for one of these fools to open their pie hole and talk straight to me. I've had enough of this damn cryptic shit. If this story has anything to do with hyenas, bait, or other loony crap, I will grab Carl's gun and relieve my head of any unnecessary brains. And if it feels good, I'll do it again. I shake my head and glance at the Sheriff from the corner of my eye. His expression is non-committal, but a little psychic birdie whispers in my ear that he is feeling anything but neutral.

"No, not that I'm aware of."

"Oh, yeah, worked there for eighteen years, until about a year ago. Ain't that right, Sheriff? I guess I worked until late March. Got fired for 'working on non-departmental vehicles', and 'unauthorized service on departmental vehicles' or some shit like that. That's about right, ain't it Sheriff?"

Carl turns toward Michael, his eyes hardened. "No, that's not right, and you know it. You resigned under a cloud of investigation for non-departmental work on paid duty hours and unauthorized use of department property."

"Oh, that's right. My choices were twenty-four months in the county lock-up with five years' probation and a $25,000 fine, or I could quit and stay out of jail but lose my pension, benefits… all them goodies."

Carl stares straight ahead without refuting his statements.

Cogs in my head are meshing, and answers to questions are now beginning to connect. A better picture of this puzzle is forming. I take a deep breath, savoring the sharp tang of cold weather and pine trees. I watch a buzzard circle beyond the tree line, its black wings silhouetted against a sterling cobalt-blue sky. Oh, the glorious feeling of puzzle pieces matching up.

"Carl, you had this poor sonofabitch installing G.P.S. tracking devices on non-county vehicles. Might these have been vehicles used by a certain cookie maker?" I shake my head and snort. "Why you devious bastard, so it was you tracking Milford's operations and radioing poor ol' Robbie to find the victims."

Carl slammed his palms on the hood of Robbie's truck. The sound is like a gunshot. I flinch, but Michael tries to break orbit. I've never seen a man his size jump like that before.

"I had to do something! And I'm sorry that Railsteen got caught up in the middle of all this. But I couldn't let these girls just keep dying in the middle of the woods, and no one tryin' to do a damn thing about it."

"What were you going to do to stop it?"

Carl's hands clench into fists. He stares at the ground and walks a tight circle in front of the truck. "I don't know; everything I have is circumstantial. And with Milford having the department and half the judges on his payroll, there wasn't anywhere I could go. I figured that at some point I'd be able to break free of Milford's grip and use this info to lock his ass up forever."

"And you didn't have a clue that Claire had her own investigation going on?"

Carl looks away. "No, but I knew she was up to something, because suddenly, everything just stopped. They changed their driving patterns, most of the cars remained parked, and no one ventured anywhere near the Blackroot swamp."

"I take it there's been no more deaths?"

Carl continues to stare toward the highway. "Not that we've found. Me and Robbie have hiked and driven throughout the woods surrounding the swamp and other popular dumping grounds. It's been quiet lately."

"At least that's something," I say and take a deep breath.

"Unless they're dumping somewhere else," the lot owner adds.

Me and Carl turn and glare at the fat man.

"What?" He asks, defending himself. "Just stating the obvious."

We sit in silence, no one saying a word.

"You think everything changed when Claire grabbed Milford's books?" I ask.

"I'm willing to bet that's what caused it." Carl answers. "So far they'd been able to act with impunity. They had me, and most of the county, in their pocket. But when Claire stuck her nose in and made an end-run around me, they must have gotten spooked." Carl rolls his head on his shoulders, then barks a hard laugh. "Man, as much as he hates her, I bet that cheesed Milford's ass."

Our conversation ends, the cold making it hard to keep talking. I glance at Carl. "We've gotta go. How about those wheels?"

Michael retreats into the trailer home and returns a few minutes later. He tosses a set of keys on the hood of Robbie's truck and points to a primer-painted 1978 Ford Granada sitting under a plywood carport. The car is covered with pine sap and dust. About as non-descript and boring a ride as you could find. If the car runs half-ass, it will be perfect.

"Try not to tear it up, will ya'?" Michael says.

I point toward Robbie and Orville. "What about the kid and his dog?"

"I'll stash his truck in the shed and give him something to drive."

"Robbie, you cool with that?" He shrugs, as does his dog. That was kind of weird. The boy needs to take a break from his mutt and hang with humans for a while. "Good. Carl, toss the man a card with your number on it. Call us if you hear from Claire."

We back Robbie's El Camino into the wooden carport beside the Grenada and lean the hood of a cannibalized car against it. No one will notice Robbie's vehicle unless they walk up and yank the hood away. It would be just another piece of junk rusting away in the back of a used car graveyard.

I take the box of evidence, now flattened to half its size, and wedge it under the seat of Robbie's El Camino, pushing it between the springs and seat bottom. No one will find it without taking the seat out and flipping it upside down.

Robbie and Orville follow the fat car salesman up the trailer's rear steps.

I snag the keys and walk over to the Ford; its interior faded and torn; its windows tinted gray to match the car. The door opens begrudgingly with the sharp squeal of fatigued hinges. I slide the key in the ignition and twist it. I'm surprised when the engine fires with a throaty rumble. I pull forward, and Carl and I switch seats.

"What did you do with the box?" he inquires

I explain how well it's hidden.

Carl takes a deep breath and stares out the window. "Guess that'll have to do."

I nod in agreement. "Where to?"

"We will head back toward town. Mr. Gilbert should be getting ready for work. Let's go screw up his day in a really profound way."

"Don't tear my car up, or you're paying for it!"
Railsteen yells as we drive off the lot. Carl flips him the
bird. Behind the tinted windows, we can ride in relative
anonymity to town. I keep my eyes glued to the side
mirror, watching the road snake out behind us, waiting to
see if we pick up a tail. Except for a state patrol car that
follows us a few blocks, and an old woman who glares at
us when we blow past, no one gives us a second look.

Chapter Twenty-Eight

We make one stop at a quiet 24-hour diner, Carl springing for two extra-large cups of coffee and some doughnuts. Steam billows from the lids, carrying the best aroma on the planet. The pastries are gone before we have traveled another mile, but the coffee is too hot to sample.

At around 8:15 am, we pull into the New State Bank parking lot, back into a space on the right side of the building. A tangle of overgrown bushes and trees shields us. We are just an anonymous, battered American sedan, one of millions sold over the decades, nothing that would garner more than a passing glance. But our position provides a wide open, unobstructed view of the building. Anyone entering or exiting the main or side entrance will be easily spotted. But if they enter from the rear, which is a possibility, we will never see them. It is a chance we decide to take.

I recline my seat and wait. The lobby won't open until nine, so we'll have to cool our jets until then. Carl twists toward the rear seat, reaches back, and returns with a pair of faded, stained baseball caps. "Here, put this on."

I take the frayed Budweiser hat, brush dirt and grime from it, and pull it down tight. "So, how do you want to handle this?"

Carl stares out the window for a moment without speaking. He then curls the bill of his hat as he slips on a pair of mirror shades. He glances at the space reserved for the bank president. "Well, since he's not here, I say we wait for him to show up and then corner his ass before he gets into the building. I want to keep this as quiet as possible. The last thing we need is for this to get nasty in the middle of the bank. Then we ask him what he knows about a brunette, the Dreamland Motel, and a rather telling video about him being handcuffed to a bed." Carl stares at the side mirror as he studies the road outside the bank. "And if that doesn't work, we play the video. He'll crack. There's no way he wants that video to get out in the world."

No argument from me. No sane man would want to jeopardize his life and family, not to mention his meticulously crafted career, if he can avoid it. But we aren't dealing with a sane man or men. There's no telling what Milford has on him. He might crack just as Carl predicted, or if he feels backed against a wall with nothing to lose, he might lash out and force us to do something we don't want to do.

The numbers bank clock change to 8:55. The lobby will open in five minutes.

Carl reclines his seat, resting his eyes just above the dash, his arms folded in his lap.

"How do you think he's going to react?" I ask.

"Don't know, but I suggest you be ready for anything. Hopefully, he won't do anything stupid."

I lace my hands behind my head. "And if he does?"

Carl reaches under his seat and retrieves a tranquilizer gun. "He takes a little nap."

"Where in the hell did you get that?"

"Robbie keeps it in his truck. Sometimes he'll tag an alligator, bobcat, whatever, for the Department of

National Resources so they can track it. This baby's strong enough to put a nine-foot 'gator on ice. It'll take down a big man in a heartbeat. One shot in the ass and Mr. Gilbert will sleep like a baby for most of the day. We toss him in the back of the car and take a ride out into the country."

"It won't kill him, will it?" I ask.

"Never has before."

"How many times have you used that on people?"

"Not many as of late. But it is always useful for crowd control. Get one son of a bitch running his mouth, pop a dart in his ass, and then it's night-night." Carl laughs and pats the gun. "We then grab the fool by his belt and throw him in the car. He'll wake up hours later confused and with a massive headache." The Sheriff leans back against his seat and clasps his hands behind his head. "Good times, man. Good times." He smiles, tilts the bill of his hat down, and stretches out. "Let me know if you see anyone show up."

"Sure thing." I sit up, take my hat off, and rub my head.

Sitting and watching the traffic while exhausted is brutal. The fight to keep my eyelids from slamming shut will feel like a twelve-round boxing match. I pull the tab on the coffee lid and sip. The brew is still hot after twenty minutes, and the aroma is almost better than before. With the sun fully risen and hot coffee flowing in my veins, I'm perking up.

I've been watching a steady stream of traffic pass by the bank when a black Lincoln rolls through the parking lot. The clock on the sign now read 9:18. I elbow Carl. "Show time." Carl sits up quickly, lifting the bill of his cap over his eyes. Together, we follow the progress of the luxury sedan as it drives around the building and slides into a reserved spot.

"Time for a little action, my friend," Carl says, tucking the tranq gun inside his coat and opening his door. Before I can put my coffee on the dash, Carl is out of the car and strolling across the parking lot.

"Anson!" Carl shouts amicably toward the bank president and raises a hand in greeting. Mr. Gilbert turns and waves, though his face shows he doesn't recognize the person calling his name. I hear the chirp-chirp from the Lincoln as the banker locks his car. He edges away from the Lincoln and moves cautiously toward the bank.

"Can I help you?" he asks Carl, but keeps his eyes on me as I climb from the car.

The banker walks faster.

Carl is now halfway across the parking lot, still waving his hand. "I just need a few seconds of your time, gotta quick mortgage question for you."

"Please come on in and give me a moment to put my briefcase down. Then we can talk in my office." Anson says with feigned friendliness.

"Actually, I'd rather we speak outside," Carl counters.t

The bank president continues toward the front of the bank, his briefcase drawn up close to his body as if preparing to use it as a shield. Carl picks up his pace and angles to cut Anson off. I trail a respectable distance behind them, not wanting to spook Gilbert any more than he already is.

"I'm sorry, that's not possible. I absolutely do not conduct business outside of the bank." He focuses on me, his eyes changing from worry to fear.

"We only need thirty seconds." I add and begin jogging toward him. Anson's face whitens. His plump face quivers as he lifts the briefcase high against his round body. He turns to run, but Carl expects this and moves to intercept. The Sheriff is now blocking the banker's path, standing only twenty feet away. I am bringing up the rear, but still a good hundred feet back.

"Jonesy, I've done all I can!" Anson blubbers. "You said that you'd leave me alone from now on!" The bank president snaps the locks on the briefcase open. Papers and folders spill at his feet. A gust of wind swirls across the asphalt, seizing the documents and scattering them in all directions.

Carl glares at me as if saying, *what in the hell is he talking about?* I shake my head. While we are flashing glares back and forth, neither of us notices the real reason for the briefcase opening. Thunder booms beneath a beautiful blue sky, and the driver's side headlight on our borrowed car is blasted out of existence.

"Gun!" Carl shouts, reverting to his police training and reaching for his weapon holstered behind his back.

"No shit, Sherlock!" I yell, dropping to the ground and rolling to the right, before springing to my feet and making a dash for a nearby dumpster. I hear the thunder boom again. Anson fires three more shots at me. Gilbert is screaming, his words raw and garbled. My heart pounds in my chest, my breath coming in ragged gulps. I circle the metal bin and peek around the opposite corner just in time to see the bank president stagger against his car, then collapse and slide to the ground. Carl stands a few feet behind the banker in a shooter's stance, the tranq gun in his hand.

Chapter Twenty-Nine

Carl runs to the fallen man and collects his gun. "C'mon! We've got to get him up and out of here before my department comes wheeling around the corner." Carl retrieves the keys from Gilbert's coat pocket and unlocks his car. "Toss him in the rear, quickly!"

Anson Gilbert is a tall, soft, heavy man. His rolls of flab make it hard to get a grip. It takes both of us to fold him into the rear seat. "Let's get the hell out of here," Carl orders as he climbs behind the wheel of the Lincoln. The doors to the bank open, and nervous patrons poke their heads out like rabbits wary of a lurking wolf.

I jog toward our borrowed car, then point down the street, away from the bank. "Did y'all see that?" I yell to the gathering crowd. "Damn, gang-bangers are having a running gun battle! They're heading north in a pair of black Escalades!" Several women hold their hands to their mouths, shocked by the thought of big-city warfare in their quiet, tiny corner of the world. Now the entire staff wants in on the action and pushes through the door to gape down the road. As they do, Carl eases out of the bank president's spot and circles around the building, away from the employees.

Still backing toward the Ford, I keep on talking. "I'm going after them before they hurt someone." I jump into the car, fire up the motor, and speed out of the parking lot. When I am out of sight, I do a quick U-turn, floor the accelerator, and head for the highway. Carl is sitting just off the road, waiting. I flash my headlights—well, actually

only one since the banker blasted one to glass dust—and
Carl flees up the road. I catch up with him several
minutes later. We drive another dozen miles before
veering off the road and into the parking lot of a closed
motel.

Perched up a hill, a hundred yards off the highway,
the building is locked behind a sagging, rusting chain-link
fence. All the motel windows are boarded over with
lumber scraps.

The Lincoln didn't stop to open the gates, but drove
through them, shattering the padlocked fence. The forced
gap is wide enough for my smaller sedan to pass through
without leaving scratches down the length of the vehicle.
I believe the Lincoln didn't fare as well. The tracks
continue around the building, disappearing into the brush
and saplings that infringe on the north wing of the
structure.

I stop inside the mangled gate and close it as best I
can. It won't stop anyone from running through it, but it
will make a hell of a lot of racket if anyone opens it.

Carl has pulled the Lincoln flush against the motel;
the trunk and hood are open. I swing alongside the black
sedan and park with the old Grenada facing out. I leave
the engine running in case we need another lightning-fast
escape. Carl is under the hood of the Lincoln, pulling on
wires. I throw my door open and jog over to him. He
glances up and answers my question before I can ask it.

"Gotta disconnect the battery. He has On-Star and
Lo-Jack, and who knows what else. As long as the car has
power, they can track him here. And odds are folks are
wondering where in the hell he's gone." Carl moves out
from under the hood, leans back, and stretches. "Done."

He walks over to the motel and kicks open the office door. The rotten frame shatters, and the door swings wide. I follow Carl and glance around the motel office. The windows are painted and boarded over; the room is dark and musty. A moldy couch sits half collapsed by the former registration desk. Carl points at it, then turns to me. "Let's get sleeping beauty out of the car and wake him up. Hopefully, he'll be a bit more accommodating than earlier."

Anson Gilbert is still where we left him, curled up on his side in the back of the Town Car. Carl takes him by the legs and drags him halfway out. We then pull him by his hands and feet and place him on the ground. "Grab one of his arms and help me sit him up."

Carl kneels before the slumbering banker. I mirror his position. "On three, pull him up and get him to his feet. We'll drag him in and wait for him to wake." We brace ourselves and prepare to pull the big, heavy man upright. "Ready? One… two…"

On a basic level, I know that a wounded animal can be more dangerous than a healthy one. That also applies to bank presidents. On 'three,' the two hundred and seventy-pound Anson Gilbert, President of First State Bank, became a wounded animal. Waiting until we pull him forward, he flings himself headfirst into Carl.

Catching us by surprise, the banker escapes my grip and throws a beefy shoulder into Carl, knocking the sheriff flat on his back. Anson then stumbles forward and around the Lincoln, heading for the still-idling Ford. Carl lets loose a flurry of expletives and climbs to his feet. I sprint around the rear of the Lincoln, trying to get to the sedan before the banker jumps behind the wheel.

Despite his girth and enough knock-out juice to stop a 'gator, the terrified banker has enough get up and go, to get up and be gone. He snatches the driver's door open about the time I bolt around the rear of the Grenada. I watch him dive into the car, pull his feet under the dash, and hit the lock button. He drops the car in gear, floors the engine, and shoots forward.

The banker spins the vehicle around and rockets away with the rear tires spewing gravel. I chase him as he drives the Ford along the front of the motel. I glance over my shoulder to see what Carl is doing and stop in my tracks. He has closed the hood to the Lincoln and is sitting on it.

"What the hell are you doing?" I shout. "Hook the damn battery up so we can go after him!"

Carl shakes his head and glances at his watch. "He's not going anywhere, at least not in that direction."

"How can you be sure?"

"Simple. They dug up all the old county sewer lines about three years ago. The old lines weren't worth a shit—literally. They had to dig down about a dozen feet to get the pipes connected with the new county sewer system. When I came out here last year on a homicide, there was still a…" we hear crashing metal and the sound of an engine racing, then dying. "Ten foot ditch, five feet across." Carl slides off the front of the car and starts walking toward the racing engine. "C'mon, let's go pry him out of the car. We'll put the damages on his credit card, consider it a business expense."

We reach the edge of the ditch thirty seconds later and stare down at the wreck. The car has nosed into a trench that is now only about five feet deep; the grill mired in about a foot of silt and mud. Steam rises from the pit as the engine sputters and dies. Anson staggers out of the car, collapses face-first into the muck, flails for a moment, and then lies still.

"Let's get him out before he drowns," I say, and jump into the gully. It was hard enough to pack a big man into the rear seat of a large sedan when the footing was secure. But dragging a two-hundred-seventy-pound banker up a hill and out of a slippery, muddy excavation proves impossible. After ten minutes of struggling, the three of us are slimed over with clay. We only rolled Anson onto his back and halfway up the bank.

"To hell with it," Carl growls, letting go of the banker's coat, then leans against the trunk of the Ford. "We'll just wait for him to come around and drag his own ass out."

I laugh hard, not because the joke is funny, but because I am beat. I let Anson down as gently as possible, then join Carl on the Grenada's trunk. Together we stare down at our beached whale in his three-piece suit. "You know, Carl, I actually feel sorry for the guy," I say. "This morning, it's just another day at the office. Now he's flat on his back in a thousand-dollar suit coated with mud. It's a damn sure bet this isn't how he saw his day unfolding when he got up this morning."

This time Carl laughs and nods in agreement, then sobers. "Just don't forget that he's caught up in this madness. I don't know how deep, but his fingerprints are all over it."

Anson squirms in the mud and tries to sit up but topples over. "How long is he supposed to be like this?" I ask.

"Hell if I know. With as much juice as I hit him with, most people are still unconscious. I can't believe he's able to shake it off."

I sigh, not knowing if it is true, but it sounds plausible. "He seems to be coming around a bit more. The wet and cold must be helping. Let's give him another five minutes, then try to get him up."

Without speaking, we watch Gilbert's stomach rise and fall as he breathes. I notice that one of his shoes is missing. I don't know when that happened, and I don't see it in the muck. He could have lost it back at the bank, it could be sitting in the middle of the parking lot, a lone testimony to what transpired earlier.

I clap Carl on the shoulder and hop off the car. "All right, let's try to get him up." Carl takes as much time as possible climbing down from the trunk. This time we had better success. After much coaxing, we get Anson to his feet and his feet under his body. We half drag, half push him out of the ditch. He doesn't fight us as we lead him back to the motel.

The bankers glances at me and mumbles, his eyes unfocused, his words thick, a mixture of dirt and water mats his hair and dribbles down his face. "Have you been sent to kill me now, Jonesy? Is that what all this is about?"

Carl shoots me one of his patented *what are you hiding now* expressions. I dismiss it with a quick roll of my eyes. "Anson, what are you talking about? We just wanted to talk, nothing more."

"Could 'a talked at the bank," he slurs.

"We tried that. You pulled a gun and tried to shoot me."

He shakes his head as vigorously as his anesthetized muscles will allow and stumbles. "The gun went off by accident, thought the safety was on."

"Four times?"

He doesn't respond.

"What the hell were you doing with it in the first place?" Carl growls. "You're damn lucky you didn't shoot yourself!"

The muddy, confused banker turns to Carl, his eyes clearing. "That's what I…" He pauses and cries. "What I planned to do," he sobs, "was kill myself."

Damn.

Chapter Thirty

Anson trails us to the motel, and the moldering office like a man resigned to the gallows. He walks with his head down, his hands stuffed in his muddy pockets.

"Is this where you're going to kill me?" he asks, switching his gaze from me to Carl.

Carl slams the door and wedges a broken chair under the knob. The room is lit by sunlight pushing through the wooden slats covering the window, the dark gloom almost as oppressive as the smell. "Sit your ass down." He points to the decaying couch.

"No. If you're going to kill me, you're going to have to look me in the eye." He stands as tall as his exhausted body will allow.

I lean against the abandoned front desk with my arms crossed over my chest; the desk shifts on its termite-assaulted frame. "Quit being so dramatic. What makes you think we're going to kill you?"

"Isn't that why you brought me here?" He is confused, expecting the damp and dusty room to be his grave.

"All we want to do is talk." I say. "You're the one who has decided it was time to eat a bullet."

"Then why did you come to the bank? You could have just called me, left a message. I would have gotten back to you."

Carl covers his mouth as he stares at the ceiling. I can't tell if he is stifling a laugh or a yawn. But the thought of us playing phone tag cracks me up.

"Like Jonesy said," Carl begins, "we have a couple hundred questions we need you to help us with. Questions that can't be asked over the phone. Now we've got a lot more time to get all warm and cozy with no one to interrupt us. Sit." Carl points at the couch and the banker complies.

The banker's eyes are focusing as he leans forward, his unease lifting. "What kind of questions?"

"You know anything about the Dreamland Motel?"

Anson's eyes narrow as he tries to remain neutral. He might have bluffed us this morning, but the drug makes it hard for him to concentrate. He blinks. "The Dreamland Motel?" Anson runs a hand through his stiff hair and continues. "I'm not sure I know what you're talking about."

The muscles in Carl's neck tense as he twists his head away from Anson. He walks over to a bank of windows and pulls back a length of plywood. The room brightens. I now see dust motes twisting in the yellow light.

Carl turns slowly back to the banker. "You sure you have no idea?"

"No, should I?" He holds his hands palms up and shakes his head.

Carl remains standing at the windows. He gazes at Anson out of the corner of his eyes. "Ever get handcuffed to a bed? Handcuffed by a brunette using pink fuzzy cuffs?"

"What in the hell are you talking about?" Anson asks, jumping to his feet and staggering. "If you're trying to shake me down, you'll have to do better than that!"

I want to clap. His bravado is first rate.

"Jonesy, can we do better?" Carl asks without even looking in my direction.

I smile, knowing how much the Sheriff is enjoying himself. "I think we can do better, sure," I reply.

Carl rubs the grime off the window with his sleeve. "Did you know that piece of shit running the motel had cameras in the rooms?"

"You're insane!" Anson blares. "I've never been to that motel!"

"Is that how Milford got his hooks in you? Did you decide to have a nice little tryst with a teller, decide to step out for some strange? Tell the misses and little Anson, Jr. that Daddy has to work late?"

"If you so much as mention this in public," the banker hisses, outraged. "I'll have your badge! This is slander!" The tranq has worn off. Anson rips his sodden coat off, throws it across the room, advances two steps, and stops. "I'll have you demoted back to a jailhouse cop! All you'll be doing is cavity searches for drugs."

"Please correct me if I get any of this wrong," Carl continues, ignoring Anson's outburst. "Milford says he has some cash he wants to deposit, say a cool hundred grand, but doesn't want questions asked. You tell him that anything over ten-grand has to be reported to the IRS. Milford then pops you with some nice, glossy eight-by-tens, nice close pictures of you and some young missy doing the horizontal bop?"

Carl stops talking, content to clean more glass with his sleeve.

"You liked her flat tummy. Is that it, Anson? How about an ass that didn't jiggle when she walked?" Carl quit staring out the window. "What'd you promise her? A nice raise, but not just from your dick?" He laughs without humor. He is on the hunt, breaking down his quarry, removing each layer of truth with each flick of his filet-knife tongue.

Anson stands with his arms folded, glaring at Carl, his jowls quivering. "You don't understand," he forces his words through a jaw clenched tight enough to snap bone.

"Bullshit!" Carl shouts, rounding on the banker, hands clenching. "I understand far better than you know! We break up domestic disputes that start from this shit daily." Carl steps forward, fists balled. He stops, takes a deep breath, and forces himself to calm down. "Your wife doesn't do it for you, but these young tellers do. You treat them nicely, give them little presents for jobs well done. For the ones that respond the most, you sweeten the pot, give them a nice little necklace, maybe a sexy ankle bracelet." He returns to the windows and removes another sheet of plywood.

Carl lowers his voice as he speaks. "They see dollar signs; you see a break from the boring life you live. And then you make the mistake of a century." He pauses, letting his claim sink in like venom from a cobra's bite. "You take one of those pretty little girls out to the Dreamland Motel, far away from the city and prying eyes, where discretion can be easily bought. And you get royally fucked, more than just in the common, literal use of the word. The old bastard filmed you, didn't he? I bet he told you to pay up or a copy would be sent to your wife. When you balk, which he knew you would, he turns it over to Milford. And then he pays a visit to your bank. But my question to you is this: did you fuck any of the girls Milford had killed? Or kill any of the girls you fucked?"

I didn't realize I'd been holding my breath until I let it out in a shocked gush of air. Before I can guess the banker's response, he provides it.

Anson howls in outrage and charges Carl, fast enough to make me leap off the desk and move to tackle him. But he only takes a few steps before Carl spins, Glock drawn, and rushes forward. He points his sidearm at the banker's head. The barrel doesn't waiver, nor does Carl's bitter voice. "If you want to die, I'll be happy to facilitate that for you. But not until you answer our questions. All you'll do with this reckless attitude is suffer until you assume room temperature." Carl fires a round that creases the man's trousers.

Anson screams and drops to the floor, holding the knee with his hand as he rolls around on the musty carpet. "You bastard!"

"Get your sorry ass up!" Carl yells. "I just put a hole in your pants leg. Next shot is going to hit meat."

The banker continues to wail as he lies curled up on the floor. Another round blasts the carpet beside him. "Get up. Now!" Carl barks.

With his tailored suit ripped and splattered with mud, Anson holds his hands up and climbs to his feet. "Please, I promise you. I had nothing to do with those girls!"

"But you knew about them?" Carl counters.

"No!" Anson wails. He quiets and works to compose himself. "Not initially, no." he adds correcting his statement. "I heard whispers about something going on… hush, hush rumors of girls with hard accents, willing to please, lining up to spend time with men. I heard the girls were young and not working girls. I didn't want any part of that."

Carl parks his weapon back in its holster, and the tough questioning continues. "But the visits to the motel didn't end; you still dipped your wick into some pretty little girls."

Anson whips his head back and forth. "Not with Milford's girls, no way. Like I said, I didn't want any part of that. I met one of my tellers out there a couple of times, but that's it."

I step out of the gloom. "But you joined in, didn't you? Once your image of yourself began to corrode."

Anson glares at me for a moment, then drops his head and shakes it slowly. When he looks back up, his lips are twitching. "Yeah, after a while, I figured, 'why not?' Half of the county is out there, and I am in deep enough with Milford that it didn't matter anymore." He glances around the room before returning his gaze to me. "I went out there only a few times, then I came to my senses and washed my hands of the lunacy."

"Tell me where I'm wrong," Carl asks this time, his prosecutor's tone gone. Just a simple matter-of-fact question. "How far does it go, Anson? How high?"

"You should have let me kill myself," he groans.

"No, we couldn't let that happen. We need Milford brought down, and you can help us do that."

Anson stares at the ground, shaking his head, refusing to listen. "You can't. He's too big, too unreachable. You'd have better luck pissing into a hurricane. He's bought the town. You're wasting your time. Tell you what, give me your gun and I'll take the bastard out myself."

I want to laugh. "You'd never get within a mile of him before his crew whacks your ass."

"I know that, you fool!" Anger flares in his eyes, and his fat cheeks burn red. "But at least I'd go out fighting, not having to face my family."

"What about all the families of the girls he murdered?" Carl explodes. "I'm sure they'd like to go home and face their family!" He is shaking. "You're just a big fuckin' coward!" Carl looks like he's about to pull his service weapon and brain the man.

"I know," Anson whispers.

Chapter Thirty-One

Anson trudges back to the couch and collapses on it, his face buried in the mildewed cushions. Carl follows, drags a chair with him, and perches on the edge of the seat, looming over the banker. "What did you do for Milford?" Carl presses. "How much money did he run through your bank?"

The banker rolls his head on the cushion and buries his face in his hands, showing the first signs of remorse. But it isn't for his wife, who will soon learn about his infidelity, or for the end of his marriage. It's for his true love, his position in society.

"You realize that this is going to destroy the bank, don't you?" he asks, his words muffled by his hands.

"Don't you mean it will destroy you?"

Anson nods. "Me, the bank, my marriage."

"Keep talking. You've got a lot to say, and we have little time."

The big man sighs, sits up, then leans back against the couch. "Milford had me make loans to a dozen local politicians, judges… you name it. All now in default. I've kept the loans off the books as much as possible, been juggling things as best I could. But I can't keep it up forever. We're set to be audited in a few weeks, and when that happens, all hell is going to break loose."

"And I assume you have records to back all this up?"

The bank president balls his fists and leans forward. "Of course, I'm no fool. I tried to protect myself."

"Speaking of protecting yourself," I say, entering the conversation, "why'd I spook you bad enough to take a shot at us?"

Anson leans my way. "Because the last time our paths crossed, you said the next time we met would be the last day I'm above ground!"

Carl glances at me. I point to my head and give him a 'can't-remember-shit' look. "Now, why in the hell would I tell you that?"

Anson swings his eyes away from me to stare over his right shoulder into the gloom. Carl, he hates. Me, he fears. "Because of that girl, that woman." He licks his lips and appears to shrink into his coat. "You said if I ever saw her again, you'd blow my brains out."

Carl stands. "This woman," he asks. "Was she about this tall?" He holds his hand at shoulder level. "About five and a half feet tall. Black hair cut to her shoulders. Whispery voice, devilishly intense blue eyes, and bright red fingernails? Did you have a nice rendezvous at the Dreamland Motel?"

Anson shook his head. "That's not her."

I catch Carl's eye, reading the disbelief on his face. "Are you sure?" I ask.

"Yes, absolutely. This girl was blonde, loud, pushy."

Carl sits, leans back, and rests his thumbs just inside the pockets of his jeans. "Did you ever drink with her?"

That surprised Anson. "Drink with her? Sure, we met a few times."

"A few times? How many times are a 'few'?"

"Three, maybe four times. She was a heavy drinker; I couldn't keep up."

"And you never met at the motel?" Carl asks, his eyes narrowing.

"No, never. We had drinks a few times, that's it."

I step back into the conversation. "How'd y'all meet?"

Anson, squirming again, refuses to look my way. "She approached me one night at a bar, said she's with the Vista News Service doing an investigative piece on money laundering involving politicians and interstate commerce. She wanted to know if I had any knowledge of it."

Smiling, I drag a second chair to the couch. "You schmuck. She already knew everything she needed to know! She just wanted you to corroborate what she knew. Damn, boy, you were fucked the moment she approached you."

Anson turns further away and almost has his back on me. He stares over the back of the couch toward the grime-streaked windows.

"Just one more thing, did I warn you off after you had a cozy little encounter at the Dreamland Motel with a black-haired beauty about," Carl holds his hand about five feet off the ground, "about this tall that involved pink handcuffs?"

Anson freezes, still facing the windows. He releases his breath in a long whistle, then shakes his head and turns back around. A resigned smile creases his face. "Ah, damn. I thought that little bitch looked familiar."

A cog drops into place and a realization forms. The dead woman on the loading dock was the woman Anson met at the hotel, not Claire. Somehow Milford's sister found someone to impersonate her. That's why she called to me in the video, that's why I have memories of her. It's my fault that she's dead, that somehow I dragged her into this. I'm silent long enough for Carl to notice.

"Something up, Jonesy? Another memory flash?"

"No, just ideas lining up in my head."

"Anything I need to know at this very moment?"

I shake my head. This is an internal memo for my thoughts only. And this wasn't the time to get into it. Carl was visibly seething from Anson's 'bitch' comment. I put my hand on Carl's chest to keep him from launching himself at the banker. "Just out of curiosity," I pause, redirecting the conversation. "How long did she leave you trussed up like that?"

"Goddamn woman left me like that until I broke the headboard and got out."

"That should have been fun, explaining to the ol' wifey-pooh why you have fuzzy pink handcuffs on your wrists."

Anson's face flushes crimson again, and his nostrils flare. "What do you want, Jonesy? I paid you off and said I wouldn't see her again."

"But you did!" I didn't know this for sure, but I feel it was a safe bet.

Anson is silent for a moment, then nods, almost too softly to notice. "We planned it, but we didn't meet. She called me and said she was going to give me one last chance to tell my side of the story before she went to press. She claimed she had enough information to rock everyone's world."

"That's putting it mildly," Carl interrupts. "Where were you two supposed to meet?"

"We didn't nail anything down; she said any place would be fine so long as it wasn't secluded."

"In other words," Carl says as his eyes drift across the room, "she didn't want to be alone with you? Wanted to make sure that there were witnesses."

"Witnesses? For what? She's the one that called me! I should have been the one worrying about witnesses."

"So, you were the one who recommended the Center Rack Pool Hall?" I ask.

"How in the hell do you know that!" Anson blurts out, sweat beading his brow.

"And you called Milford, didn't you?" Carl presses on.

"Are you insane?" Anson sputters and tries to stand before Carl pushes him back down. "We'd both be dead if he knew I met with that bitch!"

I lean forward. "You realize that the 'bitch' you're so fond of and Milford are brother and sister?"

Anson's face turns ashen, his mouth drops open, and he falls back against the couch. "No, I did not know."

"Anyone know you were meeting at the pool hall?"

"No one, I didn't tell a soul. I drove up, parked down the block, and waited for her. I was about to leave when I saw you show up." Anson points at me. "I figured it's a setup, that you wanted another five grand to keep your mouth shut."

Carl snaps his fingers to regain Anson's attention back on him. "What happened next?" He asks.

"Ask your pal! He was there."

Nodding my way and frowning, Carl queries, "You want to take this?"

I lean forward and lift the cap off my head. "See that spectacular bruise running from my left eye almost to my ear? Someone batted my head around with a brick or tossed me from a moving car. I can't remember jack since last Sunday except for fragments of memories. So, compadre, I can't help you."

"Is he serious?"

Carl sighs. "Unfortunate, but true. So, please continue."

Anson glances between us, skepticism written all over his face. "Like I said, I got there around noon and waited down the street. Twenty minutes later, your buddy comes flying up the road like a maniac and parks in the street. I wait another ten minutes, figure I'd catch Claire outside the building, and we'd have our talk elsewhere."

"And…," Carl prompts.

"And that's it. With your pal already in the building and Claire a no-show, I didn't see the need to hang around. I went back to work and didn't think about it again until you two show up this morning."

Carl leans back in his chair with his hands laced behind his head. He stares at the ceiling without speaking. I join him, trying to conjure up my own Zen moment.

"Did you see anyone hanging around the building, anyone at all?" Carl asks, breaking his reverie.

"No, not a soul. The place looked closed."

"You sure?"

"Of course I'm sure! They don't open to around twelve-thirty." Anson remains quiet for a moment, then says, "I think the bar staff was there, but that's it."

With his eyes still on the ceiling, Carl says, "Jonesy, tell him about your vision."

"Why?"

"Just humor me."

"Fine." I quit staring at the ceiling, my Zen moment a total bust, and return all four of my chair legs to the ground. I tell Anson about the gun, the bolt cutters, and the man in the leather jacket.

"That's horrendous," he gasps and shakes his head. "So, you saw it all go down?"

"I don't know. Could just result from having my head bashed. Why?"

Anson swallows hard as he plays with his tie. "The guy in the leather bomber jacket, I think he was there. As I drove off, I saw someone looking out the front windows. At first, I figured it was a bartender. But now I'm pretty sure I know who it was."

"Milford," Carl and I say in unison.

Chapter Thirty-Two

"So," Carl says. "We have you," he says, glancing at me, "and Milford at the same spot, same time. What we don't have is what in the hell you saw while you were there."

"Except for that one flash of memory, I don't even remember being there. I keep closing my eyes and trying to find the beginning of this nightmare, and there's just nothing there." I push from my chair and stretch. "At least his description of Millford matches what I see in my head. So the questions is, do we assume that the rest is correct? That Milford lopped off the blonde's finger and killed her?"

Carl shrugs. "Hell if I know. Maybe. Your vision of the bolt cutters, Anson seeing both of you at the pool hall, and the suspicion that Milford used the same tactic to torture his old man is pretty damn compelling."

"Even with Anson's testimony, Carl, it's not enough to bring this bastard down." I counter. "Let's hope the deputies are having better luck." I walk across the musty room, my brain hurting, my eyes burning, and my adrenaline spent. I feel deflated, as if all the air has been sucked from my body. The sun's glare off the front windows makes it hard to concentrate. Cupping my eyes, I stare through the glass where Carl has removed the planks and watch cars pass along the highway several hundred yards away. The dazzling light glinting off their windows is hypnotizing.

"Carl, have you heard from your men?" I ask and hear him walk across the room.

"No. I'll give them another thirty minutes, then ring them up. Why do you ask?"

"Just curious." I move down the row of plate-glass windows, peering through the gaps in the planks, watching the traffic fly by. "Don't wait. Call them now."

"What are you thinking?" Carl joins me at the windows. Using his sleeve, he clears a patch of grunge off the glass.

"I'm thinking we're not alone."

Carl doesn't question my statement. He pulls out his service weapon, checks the clip, then glances at me. "I jammed Anson's piece between the front seats of his car. Grab it, and I'll grab him."

Anson lumbers off the couch, and Carl snags him by the elbow, pushing him away from the door and deeper into the building.

"What's going on?" Anson asks.

Backing away from the window, I focus on the drive up to the motel. "Hopefully, nothing," I reply. "Maybe just a pair of kids looking for a place to get high."

"Boy, won't they be surprised to find the sheriff here." Anson says, barking out a quick laugh. The guffaw fades when neither Carl nor I join in.

I turn and hustle toward the door. "Could also be Milford's men." I pause and gaze out of the office. The parking lot is empty, with no movement from either end.

"How in the world did they find us?" Anson squeaks.

Carl shoves him deeper into the gloom. "Quit whining and move your ass. If it's kids, we'll know in a few minutes. If it's not, we need some place to hide."

Outside, I glance to the right, left, and then into the woods behind the motel. The only thing moving is the wind. It sighs through the pines and stirs the needles. Crouching, I stay low and dart over to the banker's big, shiny Lincoln. I open the driver's door and stretch across the seat. Anson's 9-millimeter is wedged between the seats and under the armrest, just as Carl said. Dropping the clip, I count the remaining ammo, snap it back in place, and chamber a round.

Raising my head high enough to see out the bottom of the tinted windows, I again check the parking lot and building. It is as vacant and silent as when I slid into the Lincoln.

I ease out of the car and drop to the ground, first crouching and sliding along the front fender, the gun nestled against my stomach. The entrance to the motel office is twenty feet away. Before bolting for the office, I pause again, listening to my heart hammer inside my chest as tires crunch on the gravel outside the fence. I see the nose of a late model Camaro edge up to the fence gate. It lingers there for an eternity before reversing and heading back down the gravel road.

"Fuck," I mutter. "Kids. Gonna give me a freakin' heart attack someday." Staying low, I wait until I hear the Camaro pull out onto the highway in a screech of rubber. Giving the motel one more glance, I pull myself up by the car's grill and dash back inside the office.

The door groans on its hinges as I ease it shut and wedge a chair against it. I keep out of view of the windows and stay in the dark, musty shadows. "Yo, Carl. It's cool. Just some kids," I say in a heavy whisper. I don't want to yell in case we aren't alone. And neither do I want to glide into the back room as silent as a ghost and have Carl turn me into one.

The motel lobby remains silent. Earlier, there had been a distinct ambiance in the building, caused by either the wind against the structure or vibrations from cars on the street. But now, nothing. I hug the wall and slide across the filthy carpet, my shoes barely making a faint hush on the floor—the hair on my neck tingles. The air, previously musty, is now uncomfortably dry.

I lick my lips, flex my fingers, and raise my weapon. My ears hurt from straining to hear anything but my breathing. Reaching the far wall, I shuffle along the mildewed paneling until I reach the manager's office. I rest my foot against the bottom of the door and add pressure. After a moment, the door swings inward, and the black gloom inside filters out. I wait until the door thumps softly on the wall behind it before stepping inside.

The room is almost pitch black. Its grime-covered windows allow scant light to seep in. I drop to a knee and wait for my vision to adjust. As the room focuses into view, a desk and chairs appear like ghost furniture. I survey the room from side to side before moving again. Using the same slight pressure with my foot, I nudge the door shut, stopping it just before the latch catches.

My eyes become more accustomed to the faint illumination. To my left and a dozen feet into the room, the wall juts out about six feet and then stretches forward another twenty feet. Training my weapon on the far corner, with my heart racing, I tread in a wide arc, providing as much of a line of sight into the recessed area as possible.

The weak illumination reflects off a tarnished doorknob. I put my ear against the door and waited. Nothing. "Shit, this only works in the movies," I mutter as I step to the side and pull the door open, training my gun on the widening gap. When the door swings wide, I step past the frame and see stairs ascending into the blackness. "Up it is," I whisper. Keeping the barrel of Anson's 9-millimeter pointing up the staircase, I take the first step.

The stairs darken as I ascend. With my hip touching the banister, and use it as a guide. After eighteen steps, I reach the top, my shoulder brushing against another door. Finding the knob, I turn it and push it open.

"Shhhh," Carl whispers. "We've definitely got company."

The darkness fades, replaced by gray light filtering through decaying curtains covering a row of dormer windows. Carl and Anson hide are hiding in an unfinished attic; old furniture and assorted crap fill the space. To my right, it runs the length of the building. To my left, it ends after a dozen feet. A rickety railing keeps careless visitors from stepping off the plywood flooring and falling through the ceiling to the floor below. I pick my way over cardboard boxes that collapse at my touch and ease the curtains away from a window overlooking the front of the motel. Parked at the base of the drive is a late model Ford Crown Victoria; its tinted windows prevent us from seeing the occupants.

"What's the chance that this is just a random broken-down car?" I ask.

Carl turns my way, and even in the diffused shadows and pale light, I can tell he is giving me a 'who-are-you-kidding?' smirk. "Dream on, Cowboy. Life's about to get interesting. Monitor that car and let me know if you see anyone." He then moves further down the attic to another set of dormers. Anson sits in a worn-out executive chair. Thirty feet across the attic, I see Carl's face illuminated by the green light of his phone.

The ghoulish light remains on for a few minutes before winking out. Keeping one eye on the window, I turn just enough to cast my hushed his way. "What's the word?"

"Nothing. Both of the deputy's phones go straight to voicemail."

"Maybe they can't talk."

"I hope so," Carl says, hooking his phone to his belt, "but I'm thinking there's a reason they can't talk."

"Man, you don't think something has happened to them, do you?"

"I don't know what to think," Carl snaps. His voice is still a harsh whisper, but it resembles a shout in the attic's quiet. "All I know is that Walters has an automatic, smart-ass reply when he sends a call to voicemail. If it's going straight there, then his phone's off. And I'll jump his ass over that."

The car at the end of the drive remains motionless, the windows up. "It's just too damn odd to be a coincidence," Carl mutters as I glance his way.

"Can't reach Railsteen either. Where in the hell could that fat bastard be?"

"What do you want with him?"

Carl stares at the road. "We need a new set of wheels. We'll never get the Ford out of the ditch and Anson's car has LowJack and who knows what else on it. Too easy to find and track."

"Speaking of the big lug, what do you want to do with him?" I glance into the dark, where Anson sits listlessly. "We could send him back to work. I don't think we're getting much more out of him. With what we know and what he's told us, he's not going to the law."

Carl's phone lights up and he answers immediately. "Where the hell are you?" he hisses into the phone. "What… slow down. What happened?"

The Sheriff is up and moving. He grabs me by the shoulder and pulls me away from the banker. "You got my cousin's number? Call him, tell him where you are," Carl says to the caller as he lets go of my shoulder and starts shaking his head frantically. "No, absolutely do not go to the hospital! Robbie can patch you up, then take you to someone we both know. Just keep your wits. Call me when he picks you up." Carl slaps the phone shut, leans against the wall, and stares through me.

"Carl, what's going on?"

Carl shakes his head, still not making eye contact. "I have no idea what's going on."

"Run that by me again?"

Carl smacks a fist into a palm. "Commissioner Drayton is dead. Deputy Eddie Walters shot him execution-style in his bedroom. He then turned his gun on Officer J.D. McClaren and put four rounds in his chest at point-blank range."

I stare at Carl, unable to say anything. "Why?" I blurt out after collecting my thoughts.

"Because Drayton could talk, and because Walters was told to," Carl growls.

"Your fat deputy is working with Milford?"

Carl nods. "Looks like it."

"Who called you?" I walk over to the door guarding the stairs and make sure I shut it. Unfortunately, it has no lock. Not that it would be necessary to kick in the door. All Milford's people had to do was set the building on fire. Then wait for us to rush out and pick us off one by one.

"That was J.D.. Sonofabitch never wears his vest, but he put in on today, thank God."

"He's okay?"

"For the most part, yeah. Probably has broken ribs and bruising, but he'll live. One round missed low and caught him in the side." Carl temples his fingers in front of his face. "That explains how in the hell they keep finding us. That bastard has tipped them off on our every move."

"I wonder why he didn't just shoot me when I recovered the box, or shoot us at the farm? He could have walked out of there with all our evidence."

Carl shakes his head, walks to a dormer, and cleans the dust off the glass. "Hell, if I know. He had all the time in the world." Carl holds his weapon out in front of him. "Pop, pop, pop… me, you, and J.D. bleeding out in the coop. The girls, Robbie and E-Lee, would be easy picking. There's enough debris out there he could have hidden our bodies, and nobody would have known for months, years, or ever."

"So why not take us out?" I ask, joining Carl at the window and staring at the distant highway.

The door to the stairs creaks open. We turn to the sound. "I'll tell you why, Jonesy," a voice says from the shadows. The drawl sends shivers down my spine. "Cause we needed to know what you guys know."

Carl and I reach for our weapons as the intruder fires twice at the banker. The muzzle flash and boom of the hand cannon startles me, leaving my ears ringing and spots dancing before my eyes.

"And now we know," the man says and fires twice more, striking Carl once in the chest and spinning him into me. We fall forward against the railings at the edge of the attic floor. The rails give way, sending us crashing down on the decaying ceiling joists. They snap, and we continue to fall.

I brace for the impact I know is coming. We land on a flat surface that collapses and drops us to the musty carpet; the floor covering doing little to soften the blow. I land on my stomach, and the air is forced from my lungs.

I gasp and writhe in pain. It takes several moments to catch my breath and gather my wits. The room is pitch black. I reach for Anson's weapon. It's gone. I must have dropped it when we fell. I sweep the surrounding ground with my hands, finding the remains of a table, crumbling sheetrock, and Carl. He's on his stomach, not moving. I find his neck and check for a pulse. It's weak, but at least he's alive.

Scrambling to my feet, I ignore the pain in my back and ribs and trip over more decaying cardboard boxes. Above me, footsteps are running across the attic. I hear the door to the stairs open, then hurried movement to the lower floor. The door at the bottom of the stairs opens on rusty hinges, then slams shut. Without a flashlight, phone, or matches, I do not know which way to move. I stagger forward and run face-first into a wall hard enough to knock me on my ass. Staying on all fours, I put my hand on the musty paneling and follow it. I find a door frame and climb to my feet. I brush the door with my fingertips. It's metal; I'm in a storage room. Finding the knob, I gradually add pressure, then try turning it. The doors locked. Paranoia strikes deep into my core as I realize we're trapped.

Chapter Thirty-Three

There's movement outside the door, someone shuffling around. The knob rattles in place, followed by a laugh. "Yeah, I'm good." The shooter says. He must be on his phone since I don't hear another voice. "Don't have to worry about the Sheriff or Mr. Goody Two-Shoes. I pumped a few rounds in both. They're either dead or soon will be." The man mutters under his breath. He must be getting an earful. "Yeah, yeah, hollow points. Trust me, they're both fucked."

More silence and the sound of pacing outside the door. The one-sided conversation continues. "No, didn't get a round in Jonesy. Lucky bastard fell through the ceiling when Carl collapsed against him. Yeah, both fell through the ceiling." Heavy laughter again. "No, I've got them contained. They're in a storage room at the far end of the building, locked behind a steel door." The knob rattles again. "No, he isn't going anywhere. The walls are concrete block; he'll stay put until you get here."

I hear a heavy sigh, followed again by more pacing. My eyes are becoming acclimated to the dark. A faint glow of light shines down from the attic, enough that I can tiptoe my way around the room and over to the fallen Sheriff. Carl is still on his stomach; he doesn't appear to have moved. I recheck his neck and listen to his breathing. The pulse is slow, and respiration is shallow. I hear his phone vibrate and find it in his coat pocket. The caller's number doesn't show a contact. After a half-dozen rings, it goes to voicemail. I play it back; it's J.D..

He reports Robbie drove him to a veterinarian friend who says he has bruised ribs but will survive. He also wants to know where to meet up. I text him back our situation. He responds with two words: "hold tight." I text one word back: "Hurry."

Holding the phone low and covering it with my hands to block the light from leaking upward, I check Carl. One slug nailed him dead center in his flak jacket. The other hit him on the right side, just below the protective vest. A steady stream of blood is pushing through the wound. I tear strips off my shirt and press them into the wound. I bind it as best I can. The cloth turns red almost immediately.

"Hang in there, man," I whisper to him, then roll him from side to side, searching for his weapon but coming up empty. I hold the phone face up, shining it at the broken ceiling. Scraps of wallboard and insulation hang from the gap four feet over my head. If we hadn't broken the table, I could have stacked chairs on it and climbed out. Now the table is no higher than the carpet.

Using the weak illumination from Carl's phone, I find stacks of musty boxes and a handful of cheap plastic chairs. There's nothing I can use to climb out. Hope spikes when I spot a four-drawer filing cabinet sitting in the corner of the room. Bingo. I give it a nudge. It's solid and feels as if it holds concrete files. I tug at the first drawer. Locked. Same with the other three. Trying to avoid giving myself a hernia, I muscle the cabinet up on a corner, then spin it toward the hole in the ceiling.

I position the cabinet beneath the hole. My arms tremble, and my back is wracked with spasms. Even if I find a weapon, there's no way I can shoot accurately.

Grabbing a set of stacked chairs, I quietly place them beside the cabinet. The chairs creak as I stand on them. Testing the stability of the filing cabinet with my hands, I take a breath and step up. My metal tower wobbles but says upright. I push through the gap in the ceiling. The rafters are at chest level. I pull Carl's phone from my pocket and shine the screen across the attic floor. A dozen feet away lies Carl's weapon.

I stretch as far as possible, grab the first unbroken rafter, and pull on it. It'll hold, but my arms are quivering from moving the concrete-lined filing cabinet. I bounce lightly on top of the cabinet to get a rhythm. It's go time. I spring up, and all goes according to plan until my push-off foot slips. Instead of going up, I go sideways. The filing cabinet teeters.

Can't stop now. I push straight up, ignoring the ribbons of fire in my shoulders. The filing cabinet falls over with a muffled clang, leaving me dangling in mid-air. I hear cursing and banging on the door.

"Jonesy, don't know what you got planned. Why don't you just chill a bit? We'll get this all settled, and you and the Sheriff can go on back to your simple lives."

I pull myself through the gap in the ceiling and balance on the wooden trusses. I don't want to move, fear the beam will crack and give my position away. But, It's time to get going. I ignore the pain pulsing from all parts of my body and struggle to my feet. Carl's weapon is lying in the middle of the attic floor.

The muted light in the attic makes it easier to pick my way across the rafters. As I cross the labyrinth of trusses, I hear the door to the steps open and someone rushing up.

Scrambling like a wounded monkey through the various roof supports, I leap for the attic floor the same instant the top door flies open. My foot catches on a nail, and I tumble to the decking, skinning my arms and driving the breath from my lungs. But I've kept my eyes on the weapon. With fire burning in my chest, I lunge for the gun.

The window above me explodes, raining glass down on me.

More cannon fire from the weapon blasts a string of holes in the wall ahead of me. I can see the world outside the attic through the gaping holes blasted in the wall. I freeze, waiting for the next slug to take me out.

"Don't do it, Jonesy-boy! This ain't personal, just business."

I remain frozen on all fours.

"Damn, son, you've fucked this all up." He kicks the weapon out of my reach. It slides off the plywood flooring and disappears down the hole in the ceiling. "Should have stayed on the sidelines, son."

The sound of a clip being readied tells me my time is up. This is my Flight 93 over Pennsylvania. Time to roll. I'm not in the best position to launch at this bastard, but I know my position could be horizontal and cooling in the next few seconds. I lunge for the man.

The shooter sidesteps me, and my vision flares white as pain bursts on top of my head. I crash back down on the floor, face first. I push up, and pain erupts in my gut. I fall over on my back, gasping, trying to catch my breath, and waiting for my vision to clear. The second I can see again; I focus on a boot coming down.

I can taste blood in my mouth, and it hurts to inhale. I'm lying on my right side; my face and ear are sticky. There are voices around me, ones I now recognize. My right eye is swollen shut, and my left eye is blurry. But I can tell that my tormenter has a friend. When I try to move, I discover my arms tied behind my back.

"Well, looky here! Jonesy-Boy is back with the living!" The shooter walks closer and crouches down beside me. "What say, Jonesy-Boy? Have a nice nap?"

"Danny Douche Bag, it's been a while," I say as a cog in my mind aligns itself with a memory. I cough and spit out a wad of bloody phlegm. Originally a star lineman in high school, he is now a twelve-pack-a-day loser. His shirt, once covering a six-pack of muscle, now stretches over a widening gut. The once shoulder-length blonde hair is mostly gray and cut short. His pig-snout face is still rather piggy.

"It's Dan Daniels, you prick!" He bends closer, his weapon pointing at my head.

"Cool it, Dan," the mystery person in the shadows orders. I see a match flare to life, and a cigarette cherry glows.

"Milford," I say. I still can't see much out of my right eye, but my left is clearing. He's wearing his patented leather jacket and polished, matching shoes. His hair is locked in place with liberal hairspray. "I'd stand and shake your hand, but I'm a little tied up at the moment."

Milford snorts. "Always the wise-ass, ain't you, Jonesy?" His southern-drawl was heavy.

"Always."

"Daniels, sit him up so we can talk."

Danny Douche leans over, grabs me by the collar, and yanks me upright. My face makes a sickening, smacking sound when I'm lifted from a pool of congealing blood. I lean against the wall to remain upright.

Milford crouches down, takes a big drag of his cigarette, then blows the smoke in my face. I stare through it, not giving him the enjoyment of watching me turn away or flinch. The smoke burns my good eye. Milford holds the cherry tip toward my face, waving it back and forth. He glances at Double-D but asks me the question. "Your memory? It's back?"

That caught me off guard. "My memory? It's…" Images coalesce like a movie running on a blank screen. My brain feels overloaded, as if a dozen people are trying to fill me in on the day's events. "Memories are still in a funk, but you two pieces of shit are too engrained to forget."

This time, Milford burns me, pressing the cherry from his cigarette against my face. I dodge just enough to avoid losing my good eye, only to feel the sizzle against my cheek. A flash of white pain envelops me again, and I scream and topple over. "You're a dead man, Millie. When I get free, I'm going to filet you!" I growl, waiting for the pain to subside.

"I don't think so, Jonesy. You'll not talk your way out of this one, boy. Your old man, he knew when to shut up and keep his ass out of things that didn't pertain to him. But you ain't your old man." Milford glances over his shoulder. "Set him up again."

"Right, boss," Double-D says. He grabs me by the shoulder, jerks me up, and slams me against the wall.

"What the hell do you want?"

"What the fuck do you think we want? My sister sent you a box. I want it."

"Box?" I hear the old Mexican peasant voice in my head again. *Box, senor? I know of no steekin' box.* I want to laugh but hold back. "Sorry, I don't know what you're talking about." Milford's hand trembles. Lightning flashes behind my eyes again. I didn't see Double-D pull his weapon and crack my skull; I just felt it, heard the laughter, and retched. Now I have blood and puke on my chest.

"Daniels, knock it off! If his brains are leaking out of his head, we won't get shit out of him. Pick him up again."

My vision has gone from watery to dark and blurry. I'm in pain, almost unable to breathe. The men are shifting shadows. I feel Double-D grab me and slam me against the wall. "Smart guy, you better answer his questions."

I try blinking to clear the fog. Blinking hurts, so I stop. "Oh, the box. Cardboard, about shoe-box size? I did, like you said, and left it in the locker. I guess whoever trashed the bus station took off with it."

"No, I can tell you for certain that the guys who trashed the building…."

"And killed the ticket agent?" I ask, stopping Milford in his tracks.

"… did not find the box."

"Damn vandals, stealing everyone's shit," I quip. That earns me another backhand from Double-D and more stars of pain shooting through my skull.

Milford pulls his weapon and chambers a round. "The box, Jonesy. Where is it?"

"Hey man, like I said, I have no idea."

Milford fires a round mere inches in front of my right knee. I feel the shockwave through the plywood.

"Wrong answer, son." He fires another shot into the decking beside my other knee. "Where's the box, Jonesy?"

"Like I said…." The next shot blows a hole in the wall beside my right ear. The round passes close enough for me to feel the heat.

"Jonesy, the box. Where is it?"

"Damn it, Milford, I don't…."

Milford puts the gun barrel against my skull, its heat blistering my skin. Pushing my head against the wall, he cocks the hammer. "Jonesy, where's the box?"

I can't help but laugh. "Nice theatrics, Millie! Shoot me, go ahead. Then you'll never find the box!"

"He's got a point there, boss." Double-D chimes in.

Milford's eyes flash at Double-D, and the big man cringes. When Millie turns to me and smiles, my blood runs cold. I've seen smiles like that on cold-blooded killers I have brought in for jumping bail. Most were smiling 'cause the police never found all the body parts they left to rot. I wish my memories had waited longer before bringing that image up.

Milford nods toward the street. "Go get the clippers."

Double-D laughs and offers Milford a high-five, which isn't returned. "Hell, yeah!" he cackles. "We'll toss him down the stairs in pieces, by God!"

Chapter Thirty-Four

Laughing like a loon, Double-D runs down the steps
and out of the building. I hear him whooping and
shouting outside the motel. Milford leans against a roof
truss with one leather-clad foot braced up behind him,
head tilted down like a poor imitation of the Marlboro
Man. He pulls out a small knife, extends the blade, and
cleans his fingernails. I work my hands behind my back,
fighting to loosen the ropes and untie my hands. Daniels
might be a psychopathic nut job, but that sonofabitch can
tie a knot.

"Where's the box, Jonesy?" Milford asks without
looking up.

"Up yours!" I snap.

"We'll start with your toes, move to your fingers,
then return to your feet," Milford says casually, still
working on his fingernails. "I don't think I've ever gotten
through both hands before they either crack or pass out.
I'm really hoping you hold out." The psycho continues to
clean his nails.

I hear a trunk slam shut.

"Did your father teach you this trick?" I ask.

Milford shakes his head and sighs. "No, father
enjoyed having his people beat the pulp out of folks, then
dump them in the swamp. I'm more hands on. Or hands
off, if you will." He winks and laughs.

"You first used this technique on him, didn't you?"

Milford takes a deep breath and rolls his head from side to side. "Come to think of it, I believe my old man was the first. I've refined the technique since then."

"Just between me, you and the roof joists, why'd you off your old man?"

The door behind us slams open, and Double-D comes dancing in, the bolt cutters dangling from his right hand. "Hey boss-man, after the main course, I got a dessert for you!"

Milford turns to him. "What are you talking about?"

"Paul Nowles got the box."

Milford ignores me as he speaks. "Say that again?"

"The box, we got it!"

Fuck. Either Railsteen ratted us out, or Milford's men ran him down. Either way, I feel he's not with the world anymore.

"I was right?" Milford queried, looking smug.

"Right as rain, boss-man. Good call on the car. We found the boy's truck, and what do you suppose we found inside? The box! Sitting pretty as a picture on the front seat for all to see. What dumb fucks these two are!" Double-D again raises his hand to give Milford a high-five. As before, the gesture is ignored.

"Did anyone open it?" Milford asks, taking the bolt cutters from Double-D.

"No sir, at least I don't think so. I told Paul to make sure no one opened it until you seen it."

"What about the kid? Was he there?"

"The kid, no, I don't think so." Double-D answers, shaking his head.

"What about Railsteen? Y'all round him up?"

Double-D twisted his mouth a bit, then chewed on his bottom lip. He shook his head a second time. "No boss-man, the place is empty. No sign of the fat man."

"Find him, now!" Milford orders, running his fingers through his hair.

"Yes, sir. I'll get right on it," Double-D says, now sweating at his crewcut temples.

I watch his hands shake when he pulls his phone out of his pocket and dials. He puts the phone to his ear and walks off into the gloom of the attic. A spark of hope dances in my brain. Did someone remove the box and replace it? I damn sure didn't leave it on the seat.

"Well, now that everyone has what they want, I guess you don't need me no more. If y'all untie me, I'll make myself disappear."

Milford closes the knife, then drops it into his right pocket. He straightens his coat, checks his fingernails once more, then glances at me with another sick grin. "Oh, you'll disappear all right."

The clippers sway in Milford's hand as if trying to hypnotize me, the silver cutters speckled with what looks like rust, but I know different. He catches me watching the cutters.

"Now, Jonesy, don't get all worked up." Moving the handles of his cutters, he opens and closes its beak. "It's only going to hurt a lot," Milford giggles; son of a bitch actually let loose with a round of titters. I push against the wall, planting my feet firmly on the floor.

Click-clack, click-clack, the beak snaps. Milford caresses the head of the bolt cutters and runs his hand down the neck. "Someone is getting hungwy!" he sings in a childish voice. "Vewy, Vewy hungwy!" He thrusts the beak at my face.

Double Douche reaches down, grabs me with both hands, and jerks me off the floor. The moment he does, I spring forward as hard as I can, driving my shoulder into his chest and the top of my head into his face. I feel knives digging into my skull and realize he has bitten my scalp. Danny stumbles back and falls toward the hole in the rafters. With my feet tied together, I don't have much lateral movement, but I can hop like a demented bunny. I spring forward again, head-butting his chin. His arms let go of me and pin-wheel as he tries to regain his balance. He loops an arm around my neck as I bounce him toward the maw in the attic. We teeter at the broken rafters.

Thunder roars, and lightning flashes out of the hole. I feel the impact as large-caliber rounds slam into Danny Douche's back. He shudders, gasps, and collapses through the opening, taking me with him. As I plunge into the darkness, I spot Milford rushing toward the gap, his eyes wide, the bolt cutters drop from his hand.

Knowing what waits below, I hug tight to the dying man and ride him to the concrete below. His head makes a wet, smacking noise when we hit the hard floor. I'm thrown clear but careen off the fallen file cabinet, hearing ribs crack from the impact. I land on my back; the breath driven from my lungs. Breathing is impossible as the world wavers, and the meager light fades.

The world forcibly returns in mono-chrome sharpness. I'm being slapped and hear shouting. I feel myself lifted, carried by my belt, shoulders, and feet, then lowered again onto a bed or couch. Someone pried my eyelids open under a blinding light.

Rolling my head to the right. I can just see blurry shapes huddled together, whispering. A figure moves closer, stepping out of the haze. I can't focus on the form before me, but feel a cool hand sweep over my face.

"You okay, Cowboy?"

The soft, female southern voice unlocks new cogs in my brain. My…. assistant? I see a flash of fiery red, shoulder-length hair, long legs…. a tough-as-nails former cop with a serious take-no-crap attitude. "Jane?" I whisper, the effort sapping my remaining strength.

"That's right, Cowboy." She brushes my forehead with a damp, cool cloth.

"How… where…" I ask, but the effort drains me.

"Shhhh," she cautions me. "Doc says you have a broken rib, maybe other internal injuries. From the looks of your head, we'll be surprised if you don't have a concussion."

"Carl?" I whisper.

"He's in bad shape. Took a slug through his left kidney, wrecked him up pretty bad inside. He's lost a bunch of blood. Doc's with him now."

"Where…?"

"J.D. brought you guys back to the clinic."

The 'clinic'… more cogs slip into place. A nondescript gray building outside of town, concrete block with fading animals painted on the outside wall. Doc is a vet, though once a people doctor. He decided he liked dogs better and changed his practice. J.D., he's not a deputy, he's—more cobwebs part—FBI… I am his confidential informant. God damn, Carl didn't know. Shit, he was working blind.

"Who was shooting?" I squeak.

Jane sits on the edge of the couch before answering and dabs my face with a towel. I can smell her perfume's subtle fragrance. I can't see well, but her face is close enough to see her soft smile. "Carl," she replies, "He heard some of the conversation between you and Milford. Said a gun fell on him, and he just aimed and fired when he saw Double-D back up to the gap."

"What about Milford?"

"He left before we got there."

"Double-D dead?"

"Yeah, but from the fall, not the rounds Carl fired. Doc says he broke his neck."

"Good, he was a cruel-ass bastard."

"Yes, he was," Jane agrees. "Doc says you need to rest. He'll be with you soon."

"What about the girls?" My voice is down to a whisper; I don't seem to have enough oxygen to manage anything stronger.

"Girls?" Jane asks, her face puzzled.

"Sheila, Permillia."

There is a hesitation.

"I don't know. I'll see what I can find out."

I want to get off the couch, but I feel like I have a thousand pounds on my chest. Jane's soft hand brushes my face again, and my world floats away.

Chapter Thirty-Five

Waking with a start, I instantly regret it. The discordant 'where in the hell am I?' feeling jars me. I try to sit up, but my back sizzles with pain. I want to take a deep breath, but my aching ribs prevent it. Giving up, I collapsed onto the pillow. At least my vision has cleared enough for me to see beyond two feet. My room is a paneled bedroom; the bed is an old, creaky antique. The room's furnishings are a decidedly cheap 1970s ensemble. Shit, I've gone to hell, and it's a mobile home.

The door to the room opens and Jane's redhead pushes through, followed by J.D.. Another cog slips into place…. they're husband and wife. And…. good friends of mine.

"So, Cowboy, you back with the living?" J.D. asks with a pronounced drawl as he lingers in the door, a lopsided grin on his face. Jane pushes through while dumping pills into her hand. She lifts a glass of water from the bedside table.

I try to sit up, but knives gut me from the inside. Surrendering to the pain, I lie flat again. "If this is living, sure wish I was dead." J.D. is leaning against the door, but there's flashes of pain in his eyes. "How are you?" I ask. "Heard you got some of the excitement."

"I'm good, sore as hell, but above the ground," he says. "Vest stopped all the rounds, but bruised me up pretty good. I'd show you how pretty I am if I could lift my hands high enough to remove my shirt."

"So…," I say, then take the pills Jane has been trying to hand me. I dry-swallow and attempt to wash them down with the water glass. I spill most of the water all over my face. "Where are we with Milford, the women, and everything?"

J.D. looks at Jane, then takes a deep breath and shakes his head. "Ol' Millie split as we drove up. We had a nice little shoot 'em up with some of his guys, but they all got away. As for Sheila, Permillia, and E-Lee," he shrugs. "We found their car, but no trace of them."

Shit.

"But we have Robbie, his mutt, and Railsteen in a safe house. I've got my best men with them."

Continuing to lean against the door frame, J.D. stares above me, not making eye contact. I think it odd, then I laugh, or I would have if it didn't hurt so much. "Hey, man, what you did at Permillia's house, we're cool. I know you couldn't break cover."

My friend—first time I've felt comfortable saying that in a long time, feels like forever — smiles and glances away.

"Aw man, I wasn't sure what in the hell was going on with you. I hear you're running with Milford's crew, then you vanish. Then I hear you're back looking and acting all weirded out. But I knew my friend was still in there somewhere, and I was hoping you hadn't flipped. Milford's done that to a lot of good men. I just had to play it out straight."

"Like Carl?"

He nods. "Especially like Carl. Man is a damn good Sheriff. Hated to watch it happen and not be able to intervene."

"How is he? Jane said he's in bad shape."

"He is. Doc had to drive him to the hospital. Too much damage for an old country doc. I've got a man stationed outside his room as well. He's in guarded condition but should pull through." J.D. pushes off the doorframe, walks into the room, grabs a simple chair, spins it around, and sits. "How about you? How's the noggin? Still fighting this amnesia thing?"

I raise my hand and rock it back and forth. "The last week I know. Prior memories are just now surfacing. Didn't recognize Jane at first. Her perfume flipped a few cogs in my brain. I just had to follow the memory-scent trail back to the source. Wasn't sure about you until a few minutes ago."

Jane shows mock outrage. "Really? For the last five years, I have been the brains of your business. I'm the one that helped you get your life straight after Claire dumped you!"

I try to laugh and again regret it. I didn't know what pills Jane handed me are until the first wave of yawns hit me. My muscles turn to mush, and I slump down in bed.

"Doc says to keep you sequestered and not let you roam." Jane pulls the covers over me like a mother tucking in her child. I want to blush, but I don't have the strength.

"One more question," I slur as the world around me fades. "What's going on with me and Sheila?"

Jane and J.D. stare at me, then shake their heads. "Cowboy, you aren't going to be awake long enough for us to delve into that!" J.D. says, laughing.

The room melts into darkness.

I awake slowly this time, not wanting to jar myself while I still have knives in my abdomen. I touch my chest and ribs. Streams of pain, like underground rivers, flow through every inch of my body. But, the hurt is dulling. I take a long tentative breath, then let it out. I'm getting better, that much I know. Pushing down on the mattress with my palms, I lift myself onto my pillow. My vision is also better, and the murkiness is dissipating. I can make out the windows, noticing how long shadows have squeezed through the curtains and invaded the room.

I guide myself into a sitting position, testing my pain tolerance. A few sharp bolts of pain flash through my gut, again taking my breath with them. But few stabs of pain return. With both feet planted on the old worn carpet, I wobble upright, take a step, then brace myself on the doorjamb. The door is ajar. I pull it open with little effort. Beyond the door is a hallway, weak nightlights casting an amber glow on the floor.

Keeping my left hand on the wall, I pad across the floor. The hall is about forty feet long, with closed doors to my right. Light spills under a door toward the end of the hallway. I can hear voices talking in soft tones. The door opens without making a sound, and I step into a room filled with men conversing on radios while computers whirl and flicker nearby.

For a moment, no one notices a bald, six-foot man standing in blue-striped pajamas. Then the talking and clicking stops. A dozen pairs of eyes fix on me over the top of monitors and coffee cups. Now I have everyone staring straight at me as if my fly is open and I am going commando.

"Hi," I say, feeling stupid. I gaze around the room, once a residential den. Dark paneling covers the walls; an old brick fireplace and hearth take up most of the wall to my right. Three rows of narrow desks—two-by-two — occupy the middle of the room. Straight ahead and just beyond the staring eyes of a dozen men and women is the front door. A single diamond-shaped window at its center. On both sides of the door are large windows with thick black plastic panels covering them.

"What's going on?" I ask, stepping into the room and moving past the fireplace hearth. Twelve heads swivel to follow me, hands frozen over keyboards. "Ya'll with the FBI like J.D.?"

A brunette with glasses large enough to fit a near-sighted moose nods.

"So, what are ya'll doing?"

Exaggerating her every movement, a graying, older woman slides her glasses from her face, folds the arms, and sets them beside her keyboard. "We have been reviewing the videos and notes from the box you found, then correlating them with known associates of Milford Parson and criminal acts we assume he is involved in. Then we're going to put together a profile on him, as well as a plan of action for his arrest, along with all known associates."

"Box?" I stammer. "You mean the one I found at the bus station?" The woman slips her glasses back on and turns her chair around to continue working. I grab the back of the chair and spin her around toward me. "How in the hell did you get hold of the box?"

Someone, definitely a female by the soft scent of perfume and velvety hands that cover my eyes from behind, speaks up.

"Because I brought it to them, Cowboy."

Memories explode in my head like nuclear skyrockets. Blonde female, shapely, blue eyes, red fingernails, a sly smile that could incite a dozen fistfights in a country bar.

Claire.

I pull the hands off my eyes, pivot, and hold her by the wrists. I count all her fingers—ten. A million questions attempt to force their way into my thoughts.

"You done good, Jonesy." Claire pulls her hands free and draws up tight between my arms. She takes my wrists and wraps my arms around her, snuggling against my chest. "Real good."

I involuntarily embrace the petite woman, her small frame feeling vulnerable against me. After a moment, the feeling shifts to awkwardness.

"Claire?" I disentangle myself from the vixen, take her by her elbows, and force her away from me. "Where in the hell have you been? And what do you mean, 'I did good'?" The room is stone quiet. The pressure of twenty-four eyes pushing against my back makes me uncomfortable. "What's going on?"

"What's going on, sweetheart, is that you busted up Milford's operation like a bull in a China shop." She tries to snuggle up against me again, but I restrain her. "Together, we are about to ruin one of the biggest sex-slave rings in the country. And I couldn't have done it without your help," she coos and again attempts to wiggle close. "Let's bring daddy's bastard child down." Her eyes flare with flashes of fire before returning to their seductive smokey blue.

I gently but firmly drive Claire back against a desk and force her to sit. She pushes a stack of folders out of the way; they fall to the floor, spilling their contents like a paper avalanche. Claire pats the space beside her, but I shake my head and back away.

She begins to talk, but I hold up a hand. "Where in the hell have you been?" I ask again.

"Around, here and there." Claire waves her hand in the air, her perfectly manicured fingers—once again, I count ten of them—flittering before me. "I was lying low, as they say." She winks, brushes her satin-blonde hair from her face, and leans back, tightening her dress against her breasts. "Why, did you miss me?"

"Did I miss you?" I want to say, 'last week, I didn't even know you existed. Instead,' I say, "Yeah, I guess. I've been running for my life for the past week and haven't had much time to miss anyone.

"What I want to know is…." I pause as the door to the room opens, and J.D. strolls in.

"Dang it all to hell, Claire! I thought I told you to stay put until we briefed Cowboy."

"Sorry," Claire purrs as she slowly crosses her legs. "But I haven't seen Cowboy in such a long time, I couldn't stay away." She blows me an air kiss.

I never thought a petite blonde woman with dangerous eyes and a body that could bring Lazarus back to life could be so—nauseating.

Chapter Thirty-Six

J.D. walks into the room, hands held high, palms out, already in a defensive posture. "Cowboy, I know what you're thinking."

"Boy, you ain't got a clue what I'm thinking!" And he didn't. Hell, I wasn't even sure what I was thinking. I wanted to leap the table in front of me and throttle him. If he had known that, he would have had his Taser ready.

Soft, velvety hands take me by the arm. "Cowboy…"

I round on Claire and jerk my arm free. "Damn it, stop calling me that!"

Now I have fourteen confused pairs of eyes staring at me.

"What?" I snap.

J.D., keeping his distance, pulls a business card from his pocket and tosses it. I catch it, flip it over and gape at the name: Jonesy 'Cowboy' Smith, PI. "Oh, goddamnit! Seriously? I call myself 'Cowboy'?"

Claire slides along the desk, pushing the FBI analyst out of the way. "As long as I've known you, sugar." She grabs me by the drawstrings on my pajama bottoms and pulls me her way. "You always said you wanted to be a rodeo rider, that you loved to ride bareback."

I snatch my strings from her hands.

Claire pouts her red, overly pursed lips. "Only ones that didn't call you that are the black waitress…."

"Permillia," I remind her.

"Yeah, her, and the sad-sack girl at the truck stop. What you see in her, I'll never know." Claire turns away, runs her fingers through her hair, and feigns looking bored.

J.D. approaches cautiously. "Cowboy… Jonesy," he corrects himself, "I wanted to tell you about Claire, just had to find the right time."

"Well, now sure as hell isn't it!" I can feel steam radiating from the top of my head, out of my ears. Every eye is on me, waiting to see what I'm going to do next. I was not sure what I wanted to do next. But standing in a pair of pajama bottoms saps some of the bravado out of me. I hold my business card by the corner, pinching it between my fingers. I'm about to sling it back to J.D. when I see the writing on the back. Block letters, written neatly. Just like the writing on a business card I found embedded in a stack of buttered toast.

"J.D., where did you get this card?"

He looks at me as if I've spoken gibberish. "From you, I guess. Why?"

"Because the note on the back of this card looks just like the writing on a blank card I found wedged in my breakfast at the diner. That card had the number of the locker at the bus station."

"Maybe you wrote it down," J.D. says as he scratches his head.

"Possibly," I mumble as I stare at the card. "But how would a card with my handwriting end up in my breakfast?" I glance around the room, and I'm met with a dozen shrugs.

Rounding on Claire, "I need some answers from you." She turns away, pulls a compact from her purse, and studies her face. My blood pressure spikes. I picture my head exploding, blood spurting out of my neck like an old-fashioned oil rig letting loose a black geyser. "How did my name end up on the box at the bus station?"

Claire powders her nose with infinite slowness, dabs her forehead, then closes the case so carefully it makes no sound. "Hm, Cowb… Jonesy, sorry." She smiles at me; the expression is damn near condescending. "You were asking about a box or something?"

"You know what the hell I'm talking about. The box you—or me, hell I don't know—put in the locker. The box you gave the FBI."

"Oh, that box." She yawns hard, showing off a mouth of perfectly straight white teeth. "I gave that to you weeks ago, told you to put it somewhere safe." She hops off the desk and walks past me, teasing her fingers across my chest. "I guess you were too drunk to remember where."

"That doesn't explain how you found it."

Claire walks along the fireplace, picks up a candle, and smells it. "Well, sugar, when y'all dropped off Goggle's truck at Railford's…."

"Goggles?"

Claire pantomimes Robbie cleaning his glasses and trying to see through the thick coke-bottle glasses. "You know, Carl's cousin?"

"I know who the hell you're talking about. How'd you know we were there?"

Claire grabs a laptop and spins it around on the desktop. A few keystrokes later, red dots flash on the screen. "Sweetie, I knew when you were at the chicken farm, the bank, Railfords…, that old abandoned motel."

The hairs on the back of my neck tingle. I circle the desk counterclockwise. Claire leaves the laptop on and circles across from me. "Why were you tracking us?"

I continue my circle around the desk. Claire mirrors me.

"Why, Claire? For what reason?"

"Sweetie, the best way for me to do my job is to know where all the players are at all times."

"So this is just a game to you, is that it?"

"No, it's not a game!" she snaps.

We continue to slide sideways. More hairs join the ones already at attention on my neck. Claire passes the laptop, pauses for a nano-second, and types with the speed of a striking rattlesnake. I glance over and see one, two, and then a third red dot appear over a grid of the city. All are drifting toward the city center.

"Claire, what's going on?"

The petite blonde smiles, then expands her orbit, nimbly jumping-sliding over a desk, moving closer to the front door. The FBI analysts stopped typing long ago and are now swiveling in their chairs and following us with their eyes.

"Who are the players?" I break loose of the desk-orbit I'm in, hit the jets, and try to close on Claire. She squeals like a twelve-year-old and kicks a rolling chair my way. I dodge it, but Claire has now put two desks between us.

"Now, Jonesy, let's have none of that!" When her phone rings, she answers it without breaking her sideways gait. "Dear brother, how nice of you to call!" she says while continuing to avoid me. From across the room, I can hear him screaming through the phone. Claire rolls her eyes and makes a yak-yak motion with her free hand.

"Now, Millie, this isn't the best time to talk." Claire winks at me. "I'm very busy bringing down your operation."

I can't understand what Milford is saying, but he's melting the earpiece. On the laptop, the red dots are closing on a central location. Claire holds the phone away from her head and rubs her right ear.

"Jeez, he's so hostile!" Claire ends the call and puts the phone in a pocket.

"Claire, what have you done?"

"I did what you wouldn't do!" she growls at me, then stops circling and stands with her hands on her hips.

Another twist in this damn rabbit hole. "What was I supposed to do, Claire?"

"You said if you got close enough to my brother and had the chance, you'd put him down."

"As in kill him? Are you insane?" I sit on the edge of a desk. "Claire, I'm not killing anyone."

A knowing, sick grin curls Claire's lips. "Thought you'd say that." She turns around and stalks past me, back to the laptop. She turns it around. "See that pretty little red dot? Guess whose car that is?"

I throw my hands up. "Surprise me."

"That, my inadequate former lover, is your little redneck sweetheart and the old waitress from the coffee shop." She taps another dot. "And this is my dear brother." Claire leans in close to the screen. "I don't know about you, but it appears they are getting closer to each other." The dots continue to flash, and the distance between them shrinks.

"The third dot, who's that?" I tap the screen. This tracker is further out but traveling toward the same location.

"Hm, I'm not sure." Claire stands over the computer, looking down. She bites her bottom lip, her feet crossed at the ankles.

"How many G.P.S. trackers have you put on cars?"

"I don't know, maybe a dozen?" She grabs the laptop, and a few keystrokes later, six more lights glow, but these are blue, not moving. She hovers the mouse over each one. Names appear Carl, Goggles, Anson, Railford, Becky P, and J.D..

I grab the computers and put the mouse over the red dots: Coffee Shop, Millie. The third comes back as unidentified.

"Claire, who's this?" I tap the screen.

She shakes her head. "I don't have any idea."

"You put trackers on these cars or had someone do it! Now who in the hell is this?"

"I don't know, all right?" She slams a hand down on the table.

"Where are they heading?" I try to figure it out by the small map projected on the display. As Claire remains mute, I run to the windows lining the front of the room and pull the plastic back. The street beyond the yard is empty. A couple of older homes line the road, separated by thick knots of trees. There is no traffic.

"Silly, you don't think Millie will come here to a house full of FBI agents, did you?" No, I think they're staying closer to town." Claire laughs. "I believe they are heading to your favorite watering hole." She joins me at the window and pulls the dark plastic back. "If you hurry, you just might stop my psychotic brother from torturing them too much.”

I turn to leave. Claire grabs my arm, stopping me in my tracks. “Oh, you might want to take a gun. I know Milford will.”

Snatching my arm free, I ignore the stabs in my abdomen and race across the room, down the hall, and into the bedroom where I’ve been sleeping. I open the closet, and there are the clothes I wore earlier. Dressing rapidly, I ignore the new bolts of pain in my side. The door opens before me, with J.D. blocking my path.

“Cowboy, whoa man, what’s going on? What did Claire tell you?”

“I don’t know how she did it, but I think she’s set up Milford. She’s using Sheila and Permillia as bait.” I put my hand on J.D.’s chest and push him back. “I need a gun. Now.”

“Cowboy, hang on a sec, let’s talk this out. Where in the hell are they meeting?”

“I think they’re meeting at the pool hall.” J.D. turns sideways and lets me pass.

“How do you know?” he asks, following me.

“Just do. Now, I need a piece, something big, along with additional magazines. I also need a set of wheels.”

“Fleet vehicle’s out front. I’ll meet you there.”

Grimacing, I jog back through the den, past the studious FBI agents who don’t know what’s going on, and out the front door. Sitting in the driveway is a nondescript Ford Crown Vic, already running. In the driver’s seat is the petite blonde. In her lap is a crumpled cardboard box. I yank the door open, grab Claire by the shoulder, and pull her out. She squeals, curses a blue streak at me and runs around the car to the passenger door with the box under her arm. I hit the lock button, but not in time. She jumps in and pulls the door shut.

"You're not getting rid of me that easily. I started this; I'm going to see it end." She buckles up and pulls a concealed small handgun from a thigh holster. Holding the gun straight out, she chambers a round, then hides the weapon under her skirt.

"How the hell did you get the box back, and what in the hell do you plan to do with it?"

Claire sits in the passenger side of the front seat, staring out the windshield, holding the box from the bus station against her chest. "Bargaining chip," she says without being asked.

Screw it! I don't have time to fight with this lunatic. I pull out of the drive as J.D. flashes across the yard—the man is incredibly fast—and stops in the middle of the road. He opens the driver-side rear door and jumps in. Dropping the car into drive again, I gun the engine and light up the rear tires, leaving a cloud of smoke trailing down the street.

J.D. leans forward and drops a blue-steel Glock on the armrest, followed by three loaded clips. "Will this work for you?"

Driving with my knees, I slap a clip into the grip, then chamber a round. I sight the weapon through the windshield.

"Yeah, this'll work."

We round a sharp corner, leaving the neighborhood, the rear end swinging wide as I stomp the gas to the floor. The Crown Vic engine howls as telephone poles pass by too fast to count. Claire hangs on to the armrest, not looking comfortable.

"So, what's your plan?" J.D. asks as I drive the two-ton tank like an Indy car, swerving through traffic and nearly running down a pack of spandex-wrapped bicyclists.

"Ain't got one. Just going to play it by ear."

"Better be careful, or Millford's boys will aerate the space between your ears."

"I'll take that under advisement."

J.D. braces himself in the rear seat as I rocket through a dozen intersections. Angry horn blare as we ignore red lights. "What more can you tell me?"

"Just that Claire has G.P.S. trackers on everyone's car—yours, Carl's, Robbie's, you name it."

J.D. leans forward, clinging to the headrests. "Didn't you tell Permillia to beat it, to head to the beach?"

I grit my teeth as I blast through a light that changed seconds before we reached the intersection. "I did and don't know how she got lured back to town." I throw a quick look at Claire. "You know anything about it?"

Claire, keeping a death-grip on the car door, shakes her head.

"You better not. If I find out you had something to do with this, I'm going to shove every one of those G.P.S. transmitters down your throat. We'll be tracking your shit for years."

I'm operating on auto-pilot, taking right and left turns as if I know where I'm heading. We break out onto Highway Nineteen. I turn to the left, heading toward the setting sun. The cracked, two-lane blacktop is empty of traffic. I push the needle past 90. A big Crown Vic with two shaven-head males and a bank of antennas on the trunk doesn't get a second look from a passing trooper. With an empty road, I turn the Q&A back on.

"J.D., when did Claire show up, and did she have the box?"

"She was waiting for us at the doc's clinic when we rolled in with you and Carl, had the box under her arm."

"Did it still have everything in it?"

"Looked like it. Why?"

"Because, while Millie and his friend were rearranging my facial features, someone called him and said they had the box, that they found it in Robbie's truck."

J.D. shakes his head. "No way. The box Claire had with her is the same box we opened at the chicken house. This box has the tape, discs, ledgers, everything. I don't know he found, but I bet he's pissed."

"Claire's behind that, I'm sure of it. No telling what she left for him to find. Right Claire?"

The woman remains mute.

I let up on the gas as we enter the town limits and take a wide route around the pool hall, parking a few blocks away near the alley. I throw the car in park and shut it down.

"You ready for this?"

J.D. looks at me and nods. He checks his clip, snaps it back in, and flips the safety off. "Let's do it."

I turn to Claire. "You remain here, stay down, and keep your ass out of trouble." She nods but doesn't make eye contact. I walk off, then turn and toss her the keys. "Don't leave unless it's absolutely necessary." She nods again and looks away.

I conceal my weapon against my thigh and jog toward the alley—for the third time. J.D. mirrors me. We reach the entrance and pause, listening for anything. The only sound in the breeze is the ambient buzz of traffic. When I look at J.D., he tilts his head to the right. I give him a 'thumbs up', and we dart into the alley, flattening against the cold brick walls. A utility pole provides minimal cover. J.D. sprints to the other side of the alley and hides behind a garbage bin.

My heart is pounding as we take turns running and jumping behind poles, walls, and garbage cans. Reaching the back door of the pool hall, we stop to catch our breath, and I cup my ear to the doors. J.D. holds his palms flat before him and gives me an 'anything?' question. I shake my head and put a hand on the door handle. The hasp drops easily, and the door opens without effort. Surprised that the door is unlocked, I turn to J.D. and mouth *trap?* He shrugs, then nods. I flash three fingers, then two, then one. We raise our weapons and step into the pool hall.

Chapter Thirty-Seven

The door opens into the kitchen. It's dark inside, but it won't remain that way for long. The pool hall will open soon, its patrons streaming in for a greasy burger or a brewski. I don't know how long it has been since I have been in a pool hall; somehow, I don't think it's been that long ago. It's alien and familiar at the same time. I find the smell of stale beer and cigarette smoke soothing, almost intoxicating.

We crouch low, pad silently past several stoves and refrigerators, their stainless-steel faces polished to a mirror finish. Fifty feet across the room are two swinging doors containing a small square window for the servers to see through. Remaining out of sight, we approach the doors, stopping just below the small windows, then carefully rising until the glass is at eye level. We now have a clear view of the pool tables lining the left side of the hall and the booths and TVs along the right side.

The pool tables are empty, the cues secured in racks, and the neon bar signs are quiet.

I recognize a private booth on the far-left side as the one the blond sat in, eating her nachos, and drinking beer. Nodding to the left, I let J.D. know where I was about to head. Holding my weapon at chest level, my finger teasing the edge of the trigger guard. I glide through the door. J.D. mirrors me once more and angles to the right. Keeping my left hand on the door, I arrest its swing, letting it close with a silent whoosh.

J.D.'s on the hunt, prowling through the dining tables.

Once again, I operate purely on instinct, my movements crisp, my eyesight sharp, as I sweep counterclockwise. I hear J.D. on the other side of the room, separated from me by an eight-foot-high lattice wall divider. Meeting at the far end of the building, we shake our heads and simultaneously engage the safety on our weapons before placing them on the small of our backs.

"I don't know," I say, answering J.D.'s unspoken question, *Where are they?*

"You don't think Claire led us on a wild goose chase, do you?"

"That crazy blond better not have." I slide over to a pool table and rest against it, my arms crossed over my chest. "The G.P.S. map showed all the cars heading this way."

"Maybe the bus station?" J.D. asks.

"Could be. But somehow I don't think so."

"You still think they're heading here?"

"I do. It's possible they stopped or got delayed." Pushing off the table, I walk around the room, inspecting the booth the dead woman sat in. I see nothing there, no blood, no stains. I motion toward the kitchen. "Everything seems to swirl around here. Think we should wait in the kitchen and see who shows up."

J.D. nods and turns to follow. I lean my shoulder into the first door, still thinking about where else the girls could be. Cold steel pressed against my back, interrupting my musings.

Before I can warn J.D., one of Milford's goons takes him out with a baseball bat to the head. The crack of wood-on-bone makes me shudder. J.D. drops like a bag of rocks, crumpling on the floor. Turning my gaze from J.D., I see Milford leaning against a stove, lighting a cigarette as if he didn't have a care in the world. A small, recessed storeroom door is just to the right of the metal doors leading to the loading dock. Milford has been here the entire time. I feel one of his goons remove the Glock from the small of my back.

Milford takes a big drag off his cigarette, then blows a cloud of gray smoke across the room. "Gotta give you credit, Jonesy. You did a fine job casing the building. Much smoother than your old man. He was more of a bull in a China shop."

"I'm glad you approve," I say, glancing down at J.D.. My friend hasn't moved since hitting the floor. Thankfully, his chest is rising and falling, but very slowly.

The goon relieves J.D. of his weapon, then uses J.D.'s cuffs to secure his wrists.

"Boy, how many more folks gotta die or get their brains bashed out before you learn?" Milford takes another hard drag, almost inhales the cigarette in one pull, then flicks it at J.D.. I want to break loose and smash Milford's against the stove, grinding him down with the burner on high.

"Learn what?"

"Learn that when you fuck with the bull, you get the horns."

My stomach explodes with pain, and my breath is driven out of my lungs. I grab the bat before the goon can cock back for another blow to my gut, and stagger across the room, taking the Louisville Slugger with me. I try to raise it but only get it hip high. The light in the room dims as I fight to refill my lungs.

Milford and his goon laugh. As it gets harder to breathe, the world wavers in and out. The bastard must have cracked more ribs. The bat slides from my hands and thumps to the floor. I stagger a couple of feet, trip over a mop bucket, and collapse into a metal chair by the loading dock door.

"You win, Milford." I cough up what feels like bone and see red speckles in my hands. "What the hell do you want to let the girls go?"

Fireballs of light still lace my vision, but I catch a quick flick of Milford's eyes. "You don't have them. Damn, should have known." I sag in the chair and feel more splinters of bone in my chest.

"What's he talking about?" the goon asks.

Milford shakes his head. "Not sure." He picks up the bat, and when he prods me in the gut, it feels like it penetrates my spine. "What'cha talking about, Jonesy?"

"Sheila, Permillia," I force through ragged gasps of pain. "Thought you had them." A wet chuckle escapes me, hurting like hell.

"She who…" Milford starts, then shakes his head and laughs. "Damn, should have known." He nods toward the alley. "Check it out, but be careful. She's as looney as a fucktard."

"Who is?" the goon asks.

"Claire, my ape-shit crazy sister. She'll pull the trigger, then ask you to freeze. If you run up on her, try to disarm her, then bring her to me."

"Right, boss."

"And Jerry, if she doesn't give you an option, take her out."

"Gotcha, boss."

I watch the man leave; the long-barreled gun resembles a toy in his massive fist. If he gets his meat hooks on Claire, he'll break her in half, snap her neck like a dry twig.

Milford shakes another smoke out of a gold-plated cigarette case, lights it, and draws in another lungful. He stares at the ceiling, releasing a column of gray smoke. The room is quiet, the silence only interrupted by the sound of the heat coming on and rattling the vents. He laughs.

"Damn bitch, she's good. I'll give her that."

I take the bait. "Good at what?"

"Working the angles. Dad nailed it, said she would have made a much better partner than opponent."

"You did pretty well for yourself. How many women did you kill, a dozen, maybe two?"

Milford's about to take another drag, but stops and flicks the cigarette across the room. "What did you say?"

"Oh, c'mon." I wheeze. "The FBI has everything they need to put you and your little crew away forever. Maybe crank up old sparky for you."

"What in the hell are you talking about?"

"The women beaten to death in the woods, way out in the swamp. You killed them; Carl found them. Those girls."

Milford stomps across the room and crouches in front of me. "Not me, buddy. I didn't have no part in that!"

"Maybe your hands are clean, but not your associates. They're dirty as hell."

He shakes his head vehemently. "We didn't kill no one!"

"What about the old timer at the motel?"

"Old man Cucose, that crusty pervert? That's on you, not me!" Milford argues.

"So, let me get this straight: you're just a garden variety extortionist blackmailing bankers, public officials; and whoever you can snare just to make a buck."

In a rare, almost human moment, Milford laughs. "Hell, when you put it in those words, it sounds terrible."

I can't help but laugh and instantly regret it as fire immolates my stomach. "So, all this racketeering is just good ol' American shenanigans?"

Milford sobers up. "Just business, Jonesy. Papa's business was toast. Nobody wanted that crap he peddled. Business was dead, but not his debts. Daddy-O lived large, mortgaged his world on his kid's backs. And we're not talking Wells Fargo, Citibank. We're talking the bank of Beau Lugiano. You probably don't know that name either."

Strangely, I did, or at least had a subconscious reaction to the name. A very dark man, a very scary man. Mafia wanna-be without the class and knowledge of fine wines. "Your old man was involved with Lugiano? That's not good."

"Yeah, no shit. They were puppet and puppet master. You don't have to be too bright to figure out who's the puppet master. Good old papa wasn't the one working the strings. From watching papa I realized that there was a lot more money to be made. I tapped into a darker market. Nothing that ain't been done before. Sex sells, son. I just took it to another level." Milford shakes out another smoke. He holds it in his left hand, his right hand still clutching a handgun.

We hear the front door open and the soft chime of metal bells on glass. "Jerry? That you?" Milford asks.

Silence. Milford motions with his weapon. "Get up."

Moving takes my breath away. I feel razors slicing through my stomach and across my ribs.

"C'mon, through the doors."

Milford pushes me with the barrel of his weapon. I hold my gut with my left hand and push through the swinging doors with my right. I feel the barrel of Milford's gun against the nape of my neck.

I glance to the left and see Sheila and Permillia on a bench. Their hands and feet are zip-tied. Both women are terrified. They glance to the right. Without moving my eyes, I turn just enough to see the fat deputy—Walter — standing just inside the door.

"Hey boss, look who I found getting gas."

"Walters, what's going on?" Milford asks, still prodding me in the back with his gun.

"Well, since they left us a box full of restaurant receipts, thought it might be nice to round up some insurance. I mean, after what your pal did to Double Deuce and everything. Thought they might come in handy."

Milford shoves me forward. "Move it, boy."

I take a few steps into the room. Walters bounces over to me, grabs my right hand, and slaps a handcuff on it. He snatches my other arm, yanks it around, and finishes cuffing me. "Now sit down." I'm forced forward, fall to my knees, then roll onto my back. "That'll work!" Walters laughs and claps his hands once. "So, what'cha wanna do now, boss?"

Milford glares at him. "First, shut up for a minute and quit calling me boss. You sound like some stupid TV show. Let me think."

Walters walks over to Milford and stands nose-to-nose with him. He's about half an inch taller, but fifty pounds heavier. His hand rests on the butt of his weapon. "Not talking to you," he sneers, looking past Milford. "Ain't that right, boss?"

I hear sharp heels clicking on the kitchen's hard tile floor. The doors to the pool room swing open, and Claire walks in. She glides over to Walters, places a finger on his shoulder, then slides around him, dragging the fingernail across his shoulders and teasing his ear. The fat deputy giggles.

Claire says, "That's right, sweetheart." She pulls a small semi-automatic weapon from behind her back and shoots Milford twice in the chest. The rounds blast Milford back toward the girls. For a moment he catches his balance, makes a swipe for Walter's sidearm, then crumples to the floor. His head rests at Permillia's feet.

Chapter Thirty-Eight

Sheila is screaming, and I mean letting loose with the vocal cords. Not that I can blame her. Having a man shot dead and land at your feet is traumatizing. Permilla has almost turned white. I'm too shocked to speak. I can't take my eyes off the well-coiffured man bleeding out not a dozen feet from me.

"Whew, that is intense!" Claire sings. "And completely liberating!" She clutches the weapon to her chest, the barrel under her chin, and lets a tremor run down her body. I wouldn't have been too upset if she'd pulled the trigger one more time. But that would ask too much of fate.

Walters glances at Claire, then at Milford's cooling body. "Uh, sweetie, was that necessary?"

"Honey, you know it was." Claire tosses the gun down by the body. "If I couldn't get Cowboy Jones to do it, guess I had to do it myself! Besides, that's his gun." She winks at me, and I recognize the weapon that J.D. provided me, and that Milford's goon relieved me of. Walters laughs and slaps his thigh. A real comedy team, these two.

"So, I guess you got Milford's man as well?"

Claire pulls a latex glove off her shooting hand. I hadn't noticed it before. "Of course I did, silly!"

"And he is…?"

"Same as his boss."

"You're a one-woman homicidal crime wave, you know that?" I rock myself to my knees, then struggle to my feet. "By chance, did you take out the desk clerk at the motel and grind one of Milford's men into hamburger?"

Claire looks toward the ceiling as if trying to remember. "Check and check."

Walters nudges Claire. "Uh, sweetheart, why are you telling him all this? Why don't we just clean up and go?"

Sighing, Claire nods. "Okay, you're right. Have you secured the doors?"

"Yes, ma'am."

"Set the timers?"

"Yes, ma'am."

Taking the fat man's face in her hands, Claire pulls up on her toes and kisses him lightly on the lips. "That's a good boy. Put the 'closed' sign on the front door, pull the shades, and open the valves. I'll see you in a few minutes."

"Claire, be careful. This place is going to fill with gas in no time flat." He glances at me, eyes narrowed. "He might be cuffed, but I don't trust him, not one bit."

"I can take care of myself, now shoo!"

Walters walks the perimeter of the building, pulling the blinds, the room darkening. He then enters the kitchen, and I hear a hiss. He returns to the poolroom with an electric kitchen timer hooked to an automatic lighting element for a grill.

"It's all set. Doors are locked. I'm going out through the alley."

"I'll be along; give me a moment with my ex."

"Hurry Claire. Don't fuck around. This building is going up in just a few minutes."

Claire's eyes focus hard on the deputy. "I said I'm coming. Now get."

Walters holds his hands up, palms out. "I'm getting, I'm getting. Timer's set to go in five minutes, but the building will be loaded with gas before then. I'd hate to have an appliance cycle create a spark and blow you and your ex to smithereens before you're ready."

When the deputy pushes through the swinging doors, the smell of gas is already building in the kitchen. The fat man is right. With fumes heavily concentrated, a freezer cycling on could ignite the gas. The crazy bitch in front of me might have a death wish, but I don't. The entire time she'd been talking, I'd been working the cuffs with a key I had in my back pocket, one I found on the Crown Vic. Claire sashays over as I work the lock. She hooks a finger inside my shirt collar and pulls me in close.

"Jonesy, I sure wish this could have worked out for us." She kisses me hard on the lips, and I drop the key. She glances down as the key bounces across the floor. "Jonesy, what are you doing?" she asks, looking back up.

"Not a damn thing," I say, smiling.

Claire cocks her head. "Really?"

I nod.

She stoops to pick up the key, and I punch her hard in the head when she stands. She drops fast, unconscious, before she hits the ground. I take a deep breath and dart into the kitchen to find the gas valves, but it doesn't do any good. Walters has broken the controls; there's no way to stop the gas. I grab J.D. by the back of his shirt and drag him into the billiard room. He starts to gasp and retch.

"Hang on, buddy." Thankfully, he has his tactical knife on his hip. I remove it, snap out the blade, and slice the zip ties holding the woman to the bench. Sheila and Permilla jump free and wrap me in a massive hug.

"Time for all that later! Y'all grab Claire; I'll grab J.D.." Together, they wrestle Claire off the ground, not caring about inflicting additional pain. As J.D. comes around, I recover my handcuff key, take of the manacles on his wrists, and help him stumble to the door. When I push on the door, it barely moves. Through the glass, I can see chains wrapped around the outside handles.

"Step back!" I pull my weapon and aim mid-door to blow out the bottom panes.

"No!" J.D. croaks. "You'll ignite the gas."

"Good call. Stay here." I run a quick circuit of the pool hall, looking for something to shatter the thick glass but find nothing. The air is getting thick with fumes; the timers must be close to going off. Cupping my face with my hands, I run back through the kitchen to try the rear door. It's also locked or wedged shut. The fat bastard apparently gave up on his gal pal. I spin around, trying to find a battering ram. Above the stove is a medium-sized fire extinguisher. I rip it from the wall and dash back through the swinging doors.

"Get back," I yell, running full speed at the door. The canister, thrown like a javelin, hits dead-center above the push bar. The tank ricochets back, coming close to decapitating me. I scramble after it, feeling that time is running out. Milford suddenly grabs my foot. I damn near scream and trip, thought the cruel bastard was dead.

"Don't leave me behind!" he whispers.

Shit. "Hang on a bit longer." I retrieve the extinguisher and again launch it at the door. This time the nose of the cylinder hits the door, exploding the glass into the parking lot. Turning around, I grab Milford by his coat and drag him toward the entrance. My ribs, which were an inferno of pain earlier, have now gone full nuclear. The girls are already through the glass and running while J.D. drags Claire by the arms. When he pulls her legs across the threshold, the glass shards at the bottom of the door slice the back of her calves, leaving a nice winding trail of blood up the sidewalk.

I reach the glass door and realize there is no way I can drag this bastard through it. "Milford, you're gonna have to crawl out. I don't have the strength to help."

Milford's lips move, but his words are inaudible. I glance back toward the pool tables and see an immense red slick of blood on the floor. Sonofabitch is bleeding profusely. "Sorry, man. Nothing personal, just business."

I drop to all fours, crawl through the broken glass, and stumble down the sidewalk a couple dozen feet. Soft hands lift me by the arms and guide me to the parking lot. My vision is swimming, but I still see a pair of black boots go sprinting by.

"J.D., don't…." I try to pull free of the women, but I'm no match for their terrified strength. They practically run me across the car park and down the road. A flash of light followed by a wave of heat and a thunderous roar knocks us flat. I hear the girls scream in fear. Car alarms blare as the crackling of flames increases in volume. I roll over to watch a column of fire merge with a mushroom cloud of smoke. Sheila is on her feet first, running back toward the fire. I shout for her to stop as she disappears into the smoke. Moments later, I see her dragging J.D. onto the road, his shirt and hair smoking. He drops beside me and lies on his back, gasping.

"I almost had him," he gasps.

Using the last of my strength, I pat him on the shoulder. "Forget about him; he was an evil piece of shit."

"Still…," J.D. whispers before going silent. The world is quieting down, the light dimming. In the distance, I hear the faint warble of sirens, lots and lots of sirens.

Chapter Thirty-Nine

Pale light spills through the curtains at the end of my bed. The window treatments are open just enough for me to tell that it is dark outside. Wherever I am, the room is silent, with a strong antiseptic odor. I glance around the room, searching for a clock. I notice an IV in my arm. To my left, I see an array of medical devices with blinking lights and numbers. A hospital. Figures. I reach along the side of the bed and find the short, fat remote control. It only has one button on it. I press it several times, then sink back against the pillows. Not long after, the lights in the room brighten, and a nurse in pale green scrubs pushes through the door. She's about forty, her dark hair pulled back in a loose ponytail; a stethoscope is draped around her neck.

"Good evening. I'm nurse Lauren, how are you feeling?" she asks with a warm but tired smile. The nurse steps beside the bed and studies the monitors and IV solution. She makes a few adjustments, then turns back to me.

"How long have I been here?" I ask.

The nurse walks around the room, removes a blood pressure cuff off the wall, and wraps it around my arm. "Oh, not that long, several days." She pumps the bulb on the cuff, the band growing tight on my arm. She takes my wrist and studies her watch. Releasing the pressure, the nurse turns around, smiling. "We have kept you heavily sedated," she says. "You were busted up pretty good. Your friends told us we'd have to either strap you down or knock you out to keep you in bed. We thought medication would be more humane."

"Is there a phone nearby? I need to check on some friends."

The nurse laughs. "You don't need a phone. Most of them have been camped out here since you arrived."

I sit up gingerly, expecting the pain in my ribs to feel like serrated knives. But they are just a dull ache now. "They're here?"

"Uh huh," she says as she updates my chart. "Especially a couple of women. Hope they aren't girlfriends, or they just might put you back in the ICU." Lauren winks and pats me on the arm. "I'll let them know you're awake."

"Thanks."

She dims the lights, opens the door, and nods to someone in the hall. Sheila practically runs over the nurse getting into the room. Rushing to the end of the bed, she pulls up short. Her eyes are red, her hair stringy. I can tell she's been here for days, sitting just outside the door, twisting her hair.

Permillia follows Sheila into the room, sporting a smile that could illuminate an operating theater. Carl trails behind. He's moving haltingly, leaning hard on a crutch. He offers a quick nod, then a smile. Robbie, wearing blackout shades, follows with a blind man's cane and Orvy dressed as a service dog. I just about burst out laughing, but don't want to give his act away.

Nurse Lauren leans back in the door. "Technically, guys, visiting hours are over. But since y'all are family," she air quotes 'family.' "I can let you stay an hour. But at ten o'clock, you folks are going to have to skedaddle. Especially the blind guy and his not-seeing-eye dog."

I wave and thank her for the extra time, fluff my pillows and sit up straight. They all look at me for a moment, and then at the machines I'm hooked to, then at me again. No one speaks. "Hey," I say to break the ice. "What are you guys doing out this late?"

Orville breaks loose and vaults onto the bed, attacking my face with his big, wet tongue. "Orville, get down!" Robbie shouts, trying to pull his mutt off the bed. The big lab spreads out wide and rolls over.

"He's good; just don't let the nurse see him." I reach over and pat the fat belly of the massive lab. He moans and licks my arm. Permillia takes my free hand in her cool, brown palms. "Son, we thought we were going to lose you and J.D.. Y'all gave us a big scare!"

Sheila's hands cover her face, showing only her eyes. She's crying again. "Damn it Jonesy, I've been praying for days!" Her fingers muffled the words.

"I'm fine, ladies. Just got myself a little banged up."

Carl raises his eyebrows. "Broken ribs, lacerated liver, internal bleeding, collapsed lung… just another day in the park for you, huh, Jonesy?"

I took me a moment to realize Carl isn't being sarcastic but is actually trying to make light of the situation. "Yeah, what I call a boo-boo." Carl laughs briefly, and Permillia playfully swats my face.

"Well, your boo-boos had you in the ICU, touch-and-go for a few days," Sheila says, forcing a weak smile.

Grinning, I look from Permillia to Carl. "How's J.D.?"

"He's fine, got released yesterday. Lucky that boy has a very hard head. Milford's man cracked his skull, damn near killing him. FBI is debriefing him."

"Speaking of our esteemed cookie salesman, what's his status?"

"He was DRT."

"D-R-T?"

"Dead Right There," Carl says. "If J.D. had been a couple of seconds faster, they'd both be dead. The explosion leveled the pool hall. Milford was burned beyond recognition. Wouldn't have mattered if you had gotten him out or not. His little sister blew him apart inside. He was dead when he hit the floor, just hadn't realized it." The sheriff leans hard on his crutch.

"What of his little sister?"

Carl snorts. "You're not going to believe this, but no one, and I mean no one, knows where she is. Sometime between the building blowing up and emergency services showing up, she vanished. Poof. Gone."

"She was unconscious!" I almost shout. "How in the hell did she get away?"

"Best guess is that Walters circled back and spirited her out of there. They found her shoes behind the building."

"What was her game in all this? What did she hope to accomplish?"

Carl shakes his head. "Those answers will have to keep until we find her."

"What about our little treasure trove of evidence? Do we still have it?"

Carl stares at me, then shakes his head.

"What? You've gotta be kidding me!"

"As I understand it, while all the attention was on the exploding and burning pool hall, someone looted the FBI safe house, then torched it with enough accelerants to burn it to the foundation. Nothing, and I mean nothing, survived. We believe Walters has the originals."

I sigh and slump against the pillows. Ovry whimpers, crawls up on my pillow, and licks my face. Damn sure gonna get a dog—once I figure out where I live, that is. "Can you get a search order for the Milford estate?"

"Funny you should ask. Went to a judge for just that after the FBI house was torched. And you'll never guess what happened."

"A giant house-eating tornado appeared out of the west and sucked it up to never-never land?"

Carl laughs. "Close, but no cigar. During a heavy rainstorm, and I mean of biblical proportions, 'lightning' apparently struck the house, reduced it to rubble."

"Damn."

"Lightning has been quite bad lately." Carl grows serious. "Jonesy, I don't know what in the hell we had by the tail, but it made a tiger resemble a pussy cat. Every place we went is gone, all burned to the ground."

"Everywhere?"

Permillia leans forward. "On the bright-side, I hated my carpet."

"Your house?" I ask, startled.

Permillia nods as a tear slips from her eye.

"Robbie's cabin, the bus stop, Dream Land motel, Railford's place, the farm… everywhere you went or touched." Carl says. "Damnedest thing I've ever seen. As you can guess, the investigation is over."

"Only thing not burned is us." Robbie almost
whispers

"Thanks for the reminder, buddy," I reply, trying to
joke but failing miserably. "Let's keep it that way."

The room lapses into quiet again. Orville's now
sleeping on his back beside me. Nurses make their way up
and down the hallway. The ten o'clock hour is
approaching, and my friends will leave soon. I stand as far
as the wires I'm attached to will allow. We exchange brief
hugs—Carl will only go as far as a warm handshake—and
they leave. I catch my appearance in a small mirror in the
bathroom. I still don't recognize the face or the eyes.
Brief flashes of a prior life flicker just beyond the mental
veil. The only life I have knowledge of only extends back
a couple of weeks.

The moment I get out of here, I'm going to recreate
my life and find a new starting point. I've got about a
dozen loose ends I need to tidy up. The first item was to
find out who was the woman on the loading dock. After
what I've discovered, it's imperative that her murder must
be solved. Once that is done, I will track that blond nut
job. I'll find her; I feel confident that I will. Then I'll run
down her bosses and deliver her bosses' heads to Carl.
Afterward, I'll dump their bodies in the swamp,
somewhere the alligators can make good use of their
rotten souls.

About the Author:

Jay is a proud resident of Chapin, South Carolina (Go Gamecocks!) and is the author of six novels ranging from Mystery/Detective, to Sci-Fi, to NASCAR-based racing to Thrillers. He's been married to his beautiful wife Sherry since 1986 and is the proud father of two amazing kids, Dakota and JJ. Completing the family members is Walter, a 13 year old cocker spaniel, and Pip and Patches, two overly spoiled and highly-opinionated guinea pigs.

When not writing Jay can be found driving his beloved Pontiac Aztek, riding his Suzuki Bandit 'Sir Blurr' or sailing on Lake Murray.

www.ingramcontent.com/pod-product-compliance
Lightning Source LLC
Chambersburg PA
CBHW071238300726

48975CB00002B/474